Slashing Through the Snow

Also available by Jacqueline Frost

Christmas Tree Farm Mysteries
'Twas the Knife Before Christmas
Twelve Slays of Christmas

Kitty Couture Mysteries
(writing as Julie Chase)
Cat Got Your Secrets
Cat Got Your Cash
Cat Got Your Diamonds

Slashing Through the Snow

A CHRISTMAS TREE FARM MYSTERY

Jacqueline Frost

CROOKED
LANE

NEW YORK

Published in the United States by Crooked Lane Books, an imprint of The Quick Brown Fox & Company LLC.

Crooked Lane Books and its logo are trademarks of The Quick Brown Fox & Company LLC.

Library of Congress Catalog-in-Publication data available upon request.

ISBN (paperback): 978-1-63910-444-4
ISBN (hardcover): 978-1-64385-776-3
ISBN (ebook): 978-1-64385-777-0

Cover illustration by Rich Grote

Printed in the United States.

www.crookedlanebooks.com

Crooked Lane Books
34 West 27th St., 10th Floor
New York, NY 10001

Trade Paperback Edition: August 2023
First Edition: October 2021

10 9 8 7 6 5 4 3 2 1

To Darlene Lindsey, with love

Chapter One

"I'm not sure there's enough gift wrap left in Mistletoe to cover all these toys," I said, setting another heaping bag of donations onto a precarious pile in my office. The amount of toys collected already outnumbered our town's population, and folks were apparently attempting to double that. "On second thought," I said, stepping cautiously away, "there might not be enough wrapping paper in the entire state of Maine." With only eleven days until Christmas, I wasn't sure I *could* get them all wrapped, even with enough supplies.

Cookie, my dearest and literally oldest friend, lifted two more bags of teddy bears. "Where do you want these?"

"I'm keeping plushies and soft things over there." I pointed to a stack of animal-shaped pillows and stuffed creatures of every kind.

She hurried to the growing mound beneath my bay window, her keen blue eyes going bright with excitement. "There are going to be a whole lot of happy children on Christmas morning!" Cookie balanced the bags carefully, then spun back to me with a grin. "Now, before the doorbell rings again, I have some-thing I want to give you. Don't go anywhere."

She darted away, and I waited. She'd volunteered to answer the door each time someone arrived with another delivery, and the job had kept her busy. Cookie never divulged her age, but it was somewhere between sixty-five and eighty, as best I could tell. My guess varied severely, depending on the story she was tell-ing. Regardless, she was as spry as anyone half her age and had at least twice as much sass. I often had trouble keeping up with her, and I was only twenty-eight. Cookie had lived a full and adventurous life, making her by far the most interesting person I knew, and her heart was good to the core. I couldn't imagine life without her. Though she was, admittedly, delightfully odd at times, and I was a smidge concerned by her announcement of a surprise.

Cookie could easily return with a plate of warm cookies or a reindeer in a Santa suit—it was really anyone's guess.

I fidgeted as I waited, staring through open French doors into the foyer. The inn had been built only a year ago but was modeled after the sprawling Victorian homes of the past, and dressed eternally for Christmas. Red carpet runners spanned the hardwood floors, holly or pine greens rested on every table, windowsill, and stand. Images of Santa, elves, and snow-covered villages were on display in every work of art. A decked-out tree stood tall in every room. And scents of cranberries, vanilla, and cinnamon hung perpetually in the air.

The inn was my parents' newest addition to Reindeer Games, our family-owned Christmas Tree Farm in Mistletoe, Maine. The farm was a town attraction people flocked from all around the country to see, especially this time of year. Visitors could do so much more than pick their perfect tree. They could grab something warm at the café, shop at the craft store, enjoy a horse-drawn sleigh ride, or even participate in holiday-themed events, our own unique set of Reindeer Games, during the twelve days leading up to Christmas.

My new office was situated to the right, just inside the front door. A parlor sat opposite me, adorned in shades of rose and cream, with a fire crackling in the hearth. A sweeping staircase rose from the back of the foyer, carrying visitors to six well-appointed guest rooms upstairs. The first floor had a number of areas available for relaxing and entertaining, including a formal dining room, a massive eat-in kitchen with breakfast nook and walk-in pantry, a laundry room, a mud room, a gathering space, and a library. My personal suite was also on the ground floor, just beyond the kitchen, and equipped with a master bedroom and bath, plus a sitting area with a couch, television, and Christmas tree.

The bag of teddy bears shifted on its perch and I dashed to the rescue, narrowly avoiding it turning into an avalanche. My new role as innkeeper required me to wear many hats, and gift wrapping a million toys wasn't technically one of them, which was why I'd convinced my friends to join me for a wrapping party after dinner. "This outpouring is bananas," I marveled. "Incredibly generous, but definitely nuts."

"Did someone say nuts?" Cookie asked, pulling my attention back to her. "Merry Christmas, Holly." She held out a rectangular box wrapped in cheery red paper and topped with a pristine white bow.

I set the bag of bears on the floor and accepted her gift. "Thank you. You shouldn't have."

"You haven't seen what it is yet," she argued. "Maybe I should have."

I laughed. "True." I pumped it up and down a few times, listening for sounds inside. "It's heavy."

"Yep." Cookie rocked back on her orthopedic boots, practically vibrating with urgency. "You're going to love it. Open it!"

A flutter of voices rose above the soft holiday music in the foyer, and the grandfather clock began to chime. Inn guests were making their way down from their rooms, rested after a late afternoon break and ready for another delectable meal.

"Dinnertime." I nodded to the bustling mini-crowd, and Cookie huffed, clearly put out by the interruption.

Twice a day inn guests made their way to the Hearth, Reindeer Games' adorable, candy-themed café and hot chocolate shop. They were on their own for lunches, but I kept a buffet of snacks on hand in the kitchen in case someone preferred not to go out. But no one ever stayed behind when the Hearth was an option. My mom was the cook, chef, and baker, and anything forged in her kitchen was not to be missed.

Couples donned coats, hats, and gloves for the trek across the snowy property, chatting merrily in anticipation.

My dad did his best to manage the snow on our roads and walkways, but during December in Maine, there weren't always enough shovels for the job.

"Open it!" Cookie demanded, small hands wringing. "If you love nuts, you're going to love this."

"Sorry." I tugged the satin bow and slid a finger beneath the transparent tape on top. "I don't have your gift yet," I told her. "I haven't had time to shop."

"Open it," she repeated, giddy and refusing to be distracted. Cookie's trademark enthusiasm was contagious and part of her charm. It was one of the many reasons I'd been so drawn to her as a child and why I adored her so completely today.

I peeled the paper off a green cardboard box embossed with an unfamiliar logo. I set the box on my desk and lifted the lid.

Inside, a metal nutcracker stared up at me, the overhead light gleaming off his shiny body and sword.

Cookie clapped her hands, then shoved them both into the pockets of her silver cardigan. "He really works! Watch." She opened her fingers, revealing a variety of shelled nuts.

I held out my palms in acceptance while she righted the nutcracker and tossed the box aside. I stuffed a walnut in his mouth, then Cookie used a lever on his back to crush the shell in one easy move. "Nice."

"Yep," she said, gathering the broken pieces and tossing them into the trash bin under my desk. She worked the nut free from the shell with nimble fingers and popped it between her lips before pitching the shell. "You love it, right? I thought you could keep it in your office for festive snacking. Maybe put him out with the finger foods for your guests once in a while."

"He's perfect," I told her, pulling her into my arms. At five foot eight, I easily towered over her, and I rested my chin on top of her puffy white hair.

"Told ya," she said, and I squeezed a little tighter.

Behind Cookie, a middle-aged woman named Meg Mason glared across the foyer. She had a teddy bear tucked under one arm and seemed a little miffed.

I released Cookie and went to see if I could help. I waved as I approached, putting on my most inviting smile.

She turned with a start, and I realized she'd been staring at another guest.

Karen Moody, *New England Magazine*'s most infamous travel journalist and hospitality critique, chatted quietly on her phone, oblivious to Meg's intense scowl. Karen was in town to review the inn, and I couldn't afford to let anyone ruin her experience.

"Hi, Meg, anything I can help you with? Maybe I can take that teddy," I offered. "It's so generous of you to contribute."

Meg wheeled back, clutching the bear tighter and looking as if I'd offended her somehow. "Don't touch me."

I flipped both palms up, confused and horrified as Karen took notice of the exchange. "I'm so sorry, Meg. I didn't mean to upset you. I'd assumed the teddy was for the toy drive." I motioned to my office so she wouldn't think I'd planned to steal her bear.

She pressed her lips tight, then shook her head. "It's for . . . someone else."

"Oh," I returned brightly, seeing my way out of the awkward moment. "I didn't realize you knew anyone in town. Are you meeting them for dinner?" She was, after all, coming from her room at dinnertime and heading out the door.

"No," she said flatly, hoisting her chin into the air.

Before I could think of a response, she turned on her heel and left.

A puff of cold air and snow swirled into the foyer as she yanked the door shut behind her.

I forced a tight smile and looked to Karen. "Everything okay?"

"Everything is not okay," she said, tossing thick salt and pepper hair away from her puckered face. "I have to walk halfway across creation to get my meals. Twice a day. There's a chill coming through the fireplace in my room, and it took ten minutes for my turndown service last night. How can you call this a full-service inn?"

I opened and shut my mouth like a fish out of water. Explanations and apologies raced through my mind, but words failed to form.

Cookie patted my back and cleared her throat, urging me to speak.

"I understand completely," I said, my stunned senses returning. "Why don't I request a horse and sleigh to take you to and from your meals? And I was unaware of the chill in your room, but now that I know, I'll look into it. Perhaps we can keep a fire going through the night, until I can speak to our handyman."

Karen pulled her chin back, expression blank.

"I apologize, again, for the delay in your turndown service last night," I said, biting the insides of my cheeks to keep me from saying what I wanted to.

Karen had called me out of bed at half past midnight to fold her comforter and sheet back. I'd assumed she wouldn't want to see me in my pajamas and blue moisturizing mask, so it'd taken an extra few minutes for me to dress and wash my face before running up to her room. "If you'd like, I can turn down your bed while you're at dinner. Then your room will be ready when you return."

"I'm not going to bed at six o'clock for heaven's sake," she snapped. "And if I have to wait for you to call a horse and sleigh now, my meal will be cold, if it isn't already." She flung a thick wool scarf around her neck and huffed. "Now, if you'll excuse me, I'd better start hiking."

"I don't like her," Cookie said, the moment Karen Moody was gone. "There's a lot in a name, you know?"

I did. My parents had named me Holly White, a nod to their Christmas obsession and eternal holiday spirit. Cookie's real name was Delores Cutter, but she'd gotten her adorable nickname from her late husband, Theodore, because she loved to bake. With a name like Cookie Cutter, what wasn't to love?

I stepped back into my office and Cookie joined me, pulling the doors shut behind us. "She's difficult," I said, "but I really need her to have a good experience. A positive review for the inn in *New England Magazine* would make the perfect Christmas gift for my parents—not to mention an excellent way to keep this place making money."

"Hogwash," Cookie replied, reaching for the nutcracker and cracking a few more nuts. "This inn's been full since it opened, and there's a waiting list some weekends. You are a delight, and Karen is a bully."

Cookie smashed another walnut in the nutcracker's jaw, then scooped the shell into the trash. "I guess every Christmas has a Grinch," she said.

"But look at all the elves," I said, surveying all the donations around us. "You're coming back here after dinner for the wrapping party, right?"

Cookie tossed the nuts into her mouth. "As long as Karen's not coming. She's a real bummer, and I don't need it."

I grabbed the shapeless down ski coat off the back of my chair and threaded my arms into the sleeves.

Cookie tugged a knit cap over her head, then hefted the nutcracker off my desk with a mischievous smile. "Maybe we should bring this guy along. In case anyone needs to shell some nuts or maybe knock Ms. Moody over the head with a little Christmas spirit." She tapped the figure against an open palm like a weapon.

I swung the office doors open with a grin, then froze as Meg's open-mouthed face came into view.

Cookie yipped, then swung the nutcracker behind her back.

"I forgot my phone," Meg said, brows knitted and gaze locked on Cookie. She shook her head as she marched back into the snow.

"Oops," Cookie said, putting the nutcracker down and bundling into her coat.

"It's okay," I told her. "I'll talk to Meg later." Meanwhile I'd cross my fingers and hope she hadn't overheard too much.

We stepped onto the porch with a simultaneous shiver.

Cindy Lou Who, my calico rescue cat, meowed from the porch railing.

"Goodness!" I grabbed her before she could run or claw me, then set her on the rug inside the door. "No more sneaking out,"

I scolded, but she was already on her way to the kitchen, probably to overturn her food bowl.

I pulled the zipper on my parka up to my nose and burrowed inside. "She's getting out all the time since we moved to the inn. Guests come and go, and she just goes right along with them. The lunatic is going to freeze out here. Why on earth would she keep running off in snow up to her shoulders?"

Cookie sighed as she tied the belt on her coat a little tighter. "Freedom is nature's call to all of us."

"I like nature as much as anyone," I argued, "but I wouldn't want to be out here for more than a few minutes without a coat, boots, and shelter." I stopped mid-rant to groan at the giant gift-shaped donation receptacle on my porch. "When did these get here? You *just* emptied this."

"Leave it," Cookie said. "All those nuts made me hungry. I want dinner."

"Okay." I followed her down the steps to the walkway.

"When did Christopher say he's picking up the toys?" Cookie asked, her breath coming in tiny white puffs.

"Christmas Eve."

Christopher was the contractor who'd built the inn for my dad and refinished the Hearth's kitchen for my mom. He was gray-haired and a little portly, with a nice white beard and a hearty laugh. He had a crew of men about Cookie's size, and they'd finished both jobs in the blink of an eye. My best friend and Cookie's business partner, Caroline, thought Christopher might be Santa Claus, but I tried not to think about that too much.

Cookie's step gained a little bounce. "I'm coming over that day so I can run into him," she informed me. "He's a real looker.

You know I'm a sucker for a nice beard, and I can't resist a man who works with his hands." She went a little doe-eyed, then added, "I'd better wear my new lipstick."

I nudged her with my elbow and laughed as we trudged through the snow. "Maybe he'll let you make a Christmas wish."

Cookie worked her brows. "What would you wish for?" she asked, her tone light but serious.

"I don't know," I admitted. "My life is pretty great right now."

"Mine too," she said, linking her arm with mine.

Chapter Two

I held the door for Cookie as we shuffled into the Hearth, one of my favorite spots on the tree farm. With its chocolate-bar tabletops on hand-carved black-licorice legs, and gumdrop chandeliers overhead, the café's interior looked like the inside of a life-sized gingerbread house. White eyelet lace hung in the windows, and brightly colored lollipops posed as barstools along a broad caramel-colored counter. I'd brought all my biggest cares here as a child. Lost pets. Traitorous friends. Crushes unrequited. None of it had ever been too big for a hot chocolate cure.

Libby, the Hearth's newest waitress and the town sheriff's younger sister, rushed to meet us, a wide smile blooming on her beautiful face. "There you are! Come in! I saved you both a little of everything. Your mom made pot roast with mashed potatoes and homemade gravy. There's also warm biscuits and corn. A vegan soup and veggie bake for those opposed to pot roast."

"Sounds yummy!" Cookie stripped off her coat, hat, gloves, and scarf, then headed to her favorite booth in the corner. "I'll try it all!"

"Thanks, Libby," I said, following Cookie across the floor.

My mom loved to cook, but until the inn opened, the Hearth had only served her sweets and hot drinks. Now, breakfast and dinner were provided specifically for those staying with us, making them the envy of everyone else in the room.

I waved at locals, friends, and neighbors as I hummed along to the "Jingle Bell Rock" melody, piping cheerfully from speakers dressed as chocolate kisses. The inn's guests were gathered at a long reserved table in the room's center. Their plates were nearly empty.

Libby returned to our booth a moment later with a half-dozen bowls and dishes. "Pot roast, potatoes, and gravy for you," she told Cookie, setting the dishes on a red and green plaid placemat before her. She added to the table's center a big bowl of rolls swaddled in a linen cloth, then smiled.

Cookie's blue eyes widened. Her lips parted in anticipation as she unwound the paper napkin from her fork. "Thanks!"

"And for you," Libby said, delivering my plates next.

"Thank you," I said, my stomach gurgling happy sounds in anticipation.

She cast us each a bright smile, red curls spilling over her narrow shoulders and framing her ivory cheeks. "What can I get you to drink?"

"I've got everything I need right here," Cookie answered, stuffing a generous bite of pot roast into her mouth. "I brought my special tea." She patted the large, quilted bag at her side.

Cookie's "special tea" was one part Earl Grey and ten parts peppermint schnapps. I'd learned from experience not to let the sweet flavor fool me. The concoction had enough alcohol to kill germs, clear sinuses, and start campfires.

Libby nodded, her pale green eyes twinkling with good humor. "So, your special tea now, and lots of black coffee later."

Cookie winked.

"Coffee for me too," I said. "I have a feeling we're all going to need it. You should see the pile of toys in my office. I'm going to need to host nightly wrapping events until Christmas Eve if the donations keep coming."

"Well, count me in," Libby said. "I love to wrap presents. I could spend hours just browsing ribbons and wrapping paper. I even made a few tags from recycled paper this week. You should use them on your holiday jewelry orders," she added.

"I'd love to." I wasn't crafty on the whole, but I'd made a small business out of melting old glass bottles into tiny, colorful replicas of holiday candies. My bracelets, necklaces, and earrings were sold online as well as at a few local venues, including the Holiday Mouse, the Reindeer Games craft shop. Adding Libby's handmade tags was a lovely idea and completely on brand. "You should bring some with you tonight."

"Okay," she said, grinning. "I just have to make a quick pit stop at my place on the way."

Libby's new place was my old place, aka the tree farm's guesthouse. I'd moved out to run the inn only weeks after Libby had moved to Mistletoe from Boston. She'd been staying with her brother, Sheriff Evan Gray, and had planned on returning to the city, but life had a way of changing even the best-laid plans.

I was thankful Libby had stayed, and I wasn't alone in that. Her presence made a lot of people happy. I liked having another friend nearby and knowing my mom had enough help at the

Hearth. Evan was slightly less stressed with Libby in town, knowing his sister was safe from the goons who'd chased her out of Boston was an enormous weight off his shoulders. And these days, my buddy Ray was thrilled to call Libby his girlfriend. All in all, she'd been an unexpected holiday gift to everyone last year.

"Evan will be glad to see you," I told her. Aside from being her big brother and the town sheriff, Evan was currently acing his role as my boyfriend. "He missed you the last few times he was here."

She nodded. "Yeah. I've been at Ray's a lot. His mom's wedding is so close that she's starting to get a little . . ." Libby circled a finger around one ear to indicate Ray's mom was going crazy. "It's a lot of pressure this close to the big day."

I frowned. I knew more than I liked about those last days of chaos before a wedding, when all the plans made throughout the engagement had to fall seamlessly into place. I'd been engaged to a real dud a few years back. We were supposed to marry on Christmas Eve, but he'd run off with his yoga instructor instead. I never saw it coming, and I'd crawled back to Mistletoe in search of healing and refuge. I'd found both—and a lot more. As it turned out, calling off my wedding was the best thing that had happened in my adult life so far, but I was definitely a little crazy before it happened, so I could relate.

A few of the inn guests headed out into the snow, leaving a cuddly couple, Jim and Kate, at the long table. I sighed in relief to be rid of Karen's prying gaze. She'd seemed to watch me from the moment she'd checked in, and I hated feeling as if I was under a microscope. There was too much pressure to be perfect.

"So, when is my big brother planning to make an appearance tonight?" Libby asked, cocking one hip and curling freshly manicured fingers over it.

I took a bite of pot roast and smiled. Libby's time in Mistletoe had done nothing to diminish her Boston accent, which reminded me of the man in question. The small-town sheriff who'd once accused my dad, and later my best friend, of murder, had then quickly, ironically stolen my heart.

"He'll be here any minute," I said. "He's finishing up a few things, then stopping by the pie shop."

"Sugar to fuel the night," she said. "I like how he thinks."

"Me too." I actually liked a lot of things about Evan, but everyone knew that already.

"What about Ray?" I asked, changing the subject slightly. "Will he be wrapping tonight? Or is he helping his mom with wedding details?"

"Not tonight," an airy tenor cut through the air, and Ray appeared a few feet away. "I wouldn't miss this." He unfurled a scarf from his neck before planting a kiss on Libby's head. "How are you?"

"Better now," she said, cheeks pinking at his kiss.

I patted the cushion beside me, then scooted against the wall, making room for Ray to join us. "How do you feel about pot roast?"

His smart blue eyes went soft, and I could practically see a bit of drool forming at the corner of his mouth.

Libby laughed. "I'll be right back."

Ray slid onto the seat and folded his hands. A mop of dark hair fell across his forehead, and he flung it back with a toss of his head. The hair returned to its place a second later. "I've been on wedding planning duty for so long, I feel like I should be a bridesmaid. Please bring me up to date on reality. Stat."

Cookie's phone buzzed as she filled him in. She glanced at the screen when she finished, then dropped the device into her purse. "I've got to run." She wiped her mouth on a napkin, then slid out of the booth, the food on her plate nearly gone.

"Where are you going?" I asked, ripping a warm roll in half with my fingers, then pressing it into the gravy on my plate.

"Home. Theodore's got another eye infection, and he can't apply the ointment himself. I'll have to meet you at the inn. Good thing I set the reminder on my phone."

Theodore was Cookie's pygmy goat. She'd named him after her dead husband because she thought they looked alike. According to her, both Theodores had keen brown eyes, would eat anything put in front of them, and kept a nice black and white beard. She treated the goat like family, and so did half the town.

"I'm sorry to hear Theodore isn't feeling well," I said. "Give him my best."

"I will, but you know he hates when folks make a fuss." She pulled her coat on and stuffed the knit cap back over her head.

"Do you need any help?" Ray asked.

"No. He'll be fine, and I won't be long." She popped her collar, tied her belt, then rushed off.

Ray snagged a roll from the basket, then stole my knife to butter it. "I don't know where she puts all that food. She can't weigh a hundred pounds."

"I think it's that tea," I said. "It burns calories."

"And your throat," he said with a wicked grin.

Libby returned with my coffee and Ray's meal. She lifted a palm, and her perfectly sculpted brows, to the vacant seat across from us.

"Theodore has an eye infection," I said.

Libby frowned. "How's the pot roast?"

I opened my mouth to ask what I was missing, but the door to the Hearth swung open before I could speak.

A woman I recognized from the Gumdrop Shop, a local store selling nothing but gourmet gumdrops, stormed inside. Her short brown hair was wedged behind both ears, and a smart black beret sat atop her head. The rest of her was wrapped in a holiday sweater and pencil skirt.

Ray leaned forward, forearms pressed to the tabletop. "This ought to be good. Bonnie's on fire about something, and she's not one to be trifled with."

I cast him a sideways glance. Ray worked for the local newspaper and liked to cover community interest stories. He also played photographer from time to time and had broken one or two investigative stories as well. He had a nose for news, or so the saying went.

I was just thankful Karen wasn't around to overhear anything.

"I wonder what's gotten into her?" Libby asked, angling her hip against the table for a better view of the newcomer.

Bonnie scanned the crowded seats, then made a beeline to a table with three women and a basket of cookies. "What did I tell you?" she seethed loudly. "That nuisance never has anything nice to say, and it makes me crazy."

Her friends pushed the basket of cookies in Bonnie's direction. "Just ignore her. She's a critic. It's her job to be a horse's patoot."

"I can't ignore her. This isn't high school," Bonnie grouched. "This is my business. My reputation and livelihood are at stake." She snatched a snickerdoodle from the basket and rammed it into her mouth.

I leaned closer to Ray. "I think they're talking about Karen, the critic writing a piece on my inn."

"Is she reviewing the Gumdrop Shop too?" Ray asked.

"I didn't think so." But clearly she'd upset Bonnie. I couldn't help wondering exactly why.

"She started badgering me about how my gumdrops are made and where I got my recipes, all in front of a crowd at the shop this afternoon," Bonnie said, as if answering my question. "Then she left a similar set of inquiries in a comment online! I tried to take it down, but I can't. Everyone can see it! This is last year all over again."

I cringed at that. I wasn't sure what she'd meant by "last year all over again," but it reminded me of the body that had turned up on the town square last Christmas, and the danger I'd wound up in when I'd tried to find out who'd been responsible. It had been a series of unfortunate events I hoped to never repeat.

"You just missed her," the woman wearing a red blouse and pearls told Bonnie. "She was here for dinner and left. So, at least there's that."

Bonnie looked to the door, then finished her cookie.

Libby pushed away from our table. "I'd better get her something to drink and a couple more cookies. Sounds like she had a rough day."

I finished my dinner while Ray filled me in on the details to his mom's upcoming wedding. The ceremony and reception would be held at Reindeer Games two days before Christmas.

Cookie returned a few minutes before closing time, appearing a little flushed and frenzied—but it might've been the tea.

We helped Libby clean the dining area, then I kissed Mom's cheek and said goodbye. I looked like my mother. Brown hair. Brown eyes. Narrow chin, short nose. We were separated by twenty-some years, and it showed in her well-earned laugh lines and crow's feet. Mom was always smiling. I was four inches taller, but she was thirty pounds heavier and gave better hugs than anyone I knew. I'd gotten my height from Dad, a lumberjack in size, trade, and upbringing.

"Your dad and I will be there just as soon as my kitchen's clean," she promised. "And we'll come bearing leftovers." Mom winked, and I knew they'd likely arrive with enough food and sweets to sponsor a massive late-night feast.

Evan's cruiser pulled into the small lot outside the Hearth as we headed back to the inn.

"Hey," he said, waving as he crossed the snowy pavement to my side. "Sorry I'm late. How was dinner?"

"Good," I said. "Do you want me to grab something for you?" I motioned toward the dark dining area behind us. "Mom and Dad are still working in the kitchen."

"No. I'm good. Thank you." He eyeballed Ray's arm around Libby's shoulders, then sighed, the way he always did. He liked and trusted Ray, but apparently there was something about seeing a man touch his little sister that put him on edge anyway.

Cookie called it an instinct leftover from the caveman days, also known as the mid-twentieth century.

I tipped my head back slightly, admiring the abundance of stars twinkling overhead. The night was still and quiet after a long day of crowds and activity.

"It's a pretty night," Cookie said, blowing a warm breath into her cupped hands. "A little dark, but I always enjoy the new moon. Feels like a good omen despite the lack of light. A fresh start on the horizon. Who doesn't like one of those?"

"Here, here," Libby agreed, leaning more heavily against Ray as they walked.

"What happened to your gloves?" I asked.

Cookie frowned. "I left them in my car. I have a pair of backups in my pocket, but Theodore chewed a hole in one last fall."

"Do you want one of mine?" I asked. "We can share a pair."

She put her hands in her pockets. "I'm okay. The walk isn't long, and I have nuts to snack on. I sure hope Caroline brings cupcakes tonight. I had to rush off without dessert." She cast a look in Evan's direction as we all fell into step along the road to the inn.

I looked his way too. "Weren't you supposed to be bringing pies?"

"I ran out of time," he said, his eyes flickering quickly to Cookie, then back. "I didn't want to be any later than I already was."

She pursed her lips, eyes narrowed and fixed forward. "Look at that," she said, hurrying ahead several paces before crouching to plunge a hand into the snow. "Your new nutcracker!" She

21

straightened with a humph and a frown. "Now, who would do something like that?" she asked as we caught up with her. She passed the soldier hand to hand as she fished her spare gloves from her pockets and pushed her fingers inside. "It's all wet now. Tossing it out was just mean. I bet it was that eavesdropper."

I curved an arm around her shoulders as we began to walk once more. "Well, I'm going to look at this as a blessing. I'm doubly lucky tonight. First, you gave me a lovely and thoughtful gift, then you found it when it was lost. Thank you."

Her tension loosened under my touch as I led her up the front walk. "All right," she said. "I'll give you that."

The inn's porchlight was off, and the toy collection receptacle was full again, with the lid on the ground. A large velvet bag, like the ones given to each participating shop in town, hung over the edge of the container.

I scoffed. "The idea is to put the toys *inside* the bag."

Christopher had provided matching bags and collection receptacles for every shop that participated in the toy drive. He'd also hired a service to make daily collections in town, but folks visiting the farm often made their own drop-offs. Regardless, the pretty crimson cinch sack was a bag, not a blanket.

I lifted the lid off the porch and debated the merits of covering and ignoring this round of toys versus dragging the contents inside and adding them to the piles already in my office.

"Is that leaking?" Libby asked, pointing to the floorboards. "People know that's not some kind of over-the-top holiday trash bin, right?"

A light flashed on, and Evan swept the beam of his phone's flashlight app over a dark spot on my porch.

"Is that . . . ?" Libby asked, leaning forward as Ray tugged her back.

"Oh no." I released Cookie, then jumped around Evan to open the inn's front door. I slipped a hand inside and flipped on the porch light, certain it had been on when I'd left.

Evan pocketed his phone as light flooded the porch. "Can everyone take a step back, please?"

We easily obeyed, and he peeled the large velvet bag back by one corner.

Karen Moody's unseeing eyes stared at us from below a patch of blood-soaked hair.

Evan scrubbed a heavy hand over his mouth. "Blunt force trauma. This is officially a crime scene."

Cookie shook her head, expression grim. "Someone really did hit her over the head," she whispered, looking unequivocally guilty for her earlier comment. Then she seemed to follow our collective gaze to the nutcracker in her grip. Her spare mittens lightly marred with blood. "Ah, nuts."

Chapter Three

R ed and blue lights sliced through the winter sky, casting an ominous and heartbreaking glow across the land outside the inn, as first responder vehicles lined the narrow road at the end of the flagstone walkway. Men and women in various uniforms crawled over the inn's porch, interior, and immediate surroundings, searching for clues about Karen's final moments and her killer.

I sat on the sofa in the parlor, holding Cookie's thin hand.

The only clue so far was my new nutcracker, and Cookie's fingerprints were all over it. *Only* Cookie's prints. I hadn't touched it after removing the lid from the box. She'd set the nutcracker on my desk and powered his jaws. She'd lifted him from the snow, and it was her gloves that were now marked with what we could only assume was Karen's blood.

I hated that once again something so violent and ugly was happening here, in a town filled with community spirit and love. At an inn on a Christmas tree farm that looked like it had been pulled from a snow globe or storybook, no less.

I scanned the pretty room around me, with its boughs of evergreens lining the mantle and a large red canvas with white stenciled letters, encouraging onlookers to "BELIEVE," hanging above. A row of festive stockings bore the embroidered name of each current guest, a little extra touch my mother had dreamed up for Christmas. Everyone would leave with an orange for good luck and a box of her whoopie pies for fun. Everyone except Karen.

I bit my lip to stave off an emotional outburst and concentrated instead on the soaring spruce before me. Dad and his farm hands had hauled it inside last week when the previous tree had run its course. Mom and I had wrapped it in a thousand chasing lights and hung more bulbs and ornaments than I had dared to count, then topped it all with a star. The quilted satin skirt beneath had been handstitched by my great-grandmother nearly sixty years ago and loaded with gifts by me this week.

Evan's deputies had sequestered inn guests to their rooms as they'd returned for the night. Each would be questioned and briefed on the evening's events. Surely someone other than the killer had seen Karen after she'd left the Hearth but before her death. The group had been served dinner together, then all but Jim and Kate had left. Where had they all gone? And what had they done?

"They think I'm a killer," Cookie whispered, her voice creaking with disbelief.

I patted her back with my free hand. "No one thinks that," I said.

"I made that mean remark about hitting her over the head." Cookie gripped my fingers tight. "It's not a literal expression. But it sounds awful, and now my prints are on the murder weapon."

"I know," I said, "but Evan knows you wouldn't do this. He's going to figure everything out. Don't worry."

Her bottom lip trembled, and she batted wide, tear-filled eyes. "Okay."

Evan strode into the room as if on cue. He dragged a chair in front of us and took a seat, adjusting the fat velvet throw pillow behind him. "How are you guys holding up?"

"About as good as expected," I said. "What have you learned?"

He slid to the edge of his seat, resting both forearms along his thighs. "Not a lot," he said, "but we're just getting started. The coroner agrees the cause of death was likely blunt force trauma."

"So anyone could have done it," I said.

Evan's cautious gaze swept to Cookie. "Anyone could have, yes. Some fragments stuck to the wound seem to confirm the metal nutcracker was the murder weapon."

Cookie's shoulders slumped impossibly further.

"Any chance she was hit with something else?" I asked, hoping against the odds.

Evan pursed his lips. "Forensics will have confirmation in a day or two. Until then, Cookie, I have to ask that you don't leave town and that you talk to an attorney."

"The killer really lucked out tonight," she said glumly. "A clueless old lady was dumb enough to pick up a murder weapon and carry it back to the scene of the crime."

He released a small sigh. "Talk to Ray's mom. Her fiancé is a partner at a law firm. He'll get you in touch with someone who can protect your rights. Meanwhile, don't say a word about tonight to anyone. You don't want to put something out there that can be twisted and used against you."

"What about my guests?" I asked. "Should I try to find them alternative lodging?"

Evan shook his head. "The crime scene is out front, and you have back and side doors that can be used for exit and entry. I'd like a look in Karen's room, and we need to talk to all the guests, but they might be able to stay. Your parents are preparing hot chocolate and warm cookies in the kitchen and are willing to reopen the Hearth if the guests feel like getting out of here for a bit. We're advising them of the refreshments after they answer our questions. Now, do either of you have any questions for me?"

"Actually," I said, easing into the thing that had been circling my mind since I'd set eyes on Karen's body. "Karen was a critic," I said, softly. "She was respected, but could be pretty tough."

Evan nodded. "I've heard."

"She probably has enemies with perceived reasons to do her harm, unlike Cookie," I added, feeling awful for speaking ill of a recently murdered woman.

"Holly," he warned, eyes stern and jaw set. "Don't."

"I'm just saying," I pressed. "You can't keep Cookie as a suspect. She doesn't make any sense as Karen's killer."

"I'm going to follow procedure," he said. "You know that. No matter how uncomfortable it makes me, the woman holding the murder weapon, and whose prints are all over it, will remain a suspect until proven otherwise." His gaze slid to Cookie. "Will I find any reason to keep you on as a suspect once I investigate?"

Cookie shook her head.

27

"There," he said, moving his gaze back to me. "Once she's absolved, I'll move on. You have no reason to get mixed up in this case."

My jaw sank open, and I had to force it shut. He'd just told me the woman who was like a second mother to me was a murder suspect. The victim was a woman reviewing my family's new inn. Her body was found on the inn's porch. I was the innkeeper. I had a whole parade of ponies in this show, and I wasn't one to sit in the audience.

Evan raised a finger at me. "I can see your wheels turning. Stop."

I raised my brows.

"No," he said. "You will not interfere in this investigation. You have your hands full with this inn, the toy drive, your shaken friend, and a total public relations nightmare. Concentrate on those things, and you'll be safer and happier in the end."

"*You'll* be happier in the end," I challenged, hating when he got bossy.

"Yes," he said. "I will be. Because you'll be safe."

Cookie slumped beside me. "We were so close when it happened, but no one was here to help her."

Tension flashed in Evan's eyes, and he glanced away.

My intuition spiked, and my mouth opened with a new question. "You never told me why you were late," I said. "Was there another crime in town? Maybe it was related to this somehow."

He shook his head while I spoke, as if he knew where I was going and planned to cut me off before I finished. "I wasn't working on anything. Nothing is going on in town."

"Okay," I said, dragging the word into several long beats. "Then why were you late? I thought you said you were working." Whatever he'd been doing earlier, he was acting undeniably squirrely at the moment.

His attention darted from me to Cookie, then back.

I waited. People often gave up more than they intended when faced with silence to fill.

"I was speaking with McDoogle about his holiday lights," Evan said. "No crime. I just lost track of time."

"Oh." Well, that wasn't useful to the case. I sank back against the sofa. "I love his lights." Mr. McDoogle had the best holiday light display in town. It ran the length of Old Trail Road for nearly two miles and illuminated the historic covered bridge. He added new displays every year, set the chasing bulbs to music, and sometimes dressed as Santa to hand out candy canes to all who dropped by.

"I know," Evan said. "I told him."

"Excuse me?" A woman I recognized as Mary Hathy, a retired teacher from Idaho and current inn guest, stepped into the parlor with a remorseful look on her wide face.

"Mary," I said, pushing swiftly to my feet. "I'm so sorry you're experiencing this. Is there anything I can get you?"

She shook her head, a cup and saucer already in hand. "I've helped myself to the tea in the dining room. Thank you," she said quietly.

I'd already forgotten I'd set a kettle and tray of shortbreads out before Evan had steered me into the parlor to wait with Cookie.

"I have the room beside Karen's," Mary said, her voice low and cautious. "I don't know who she was talking to, or if this even matters, but I overheard her arguing with someone on the phone before dinner. I didn't catch a lot of the words, but they were loud and angry in tone and cadence. She was abrupt and tense at dinner too."

A deputy moved into view behind her.

"Ms. Hathy?" He waved her toward him. "I'd be happy to take your complete statement now, if you're ready."

Evan blew out a long sigh, then stood. "I'm going to take a look at Ms. Moody's room. I'd appreciate it if you'd both stay here until one of my deputies is able to speak with you on the record." He walked away without awaiting a response.

Cookie uncorked her thermos and took a swig of tea.

"I'll be right back," I told her, hurrying after him.

I smiled politely as I cut through the crowd of officials, then raced toward the curving staircase where two massive wooden nutcrackers stood sentinel on either side. The thick white handrail was wrapped in more greens and twinkle lights. A red carpet runner centered the white wooden stairs.

I'd put Karen up in our grandest room, a sprawling master with a tiled walk-in shower and personal balcony overlooking the rear patio and ice rink. The room gave me shivers when I entered. A memory I refused to entertain pressed its way into mind, and I shoved it back.

Maybe the room was cursed, or maybe it was me.

Evan stepped out of the en suite bath and scrutinized my face. "I assumed you wouldn't listen when I asked you to stay in the parlor, but I'm not sure what that expression you're wearing means. If you know something else about what happened tonight, you need to tell me. I can't help Cookie if you don't."

I gave the closed balcony doors a long careful look, then took a purposeful step further away. "Three murders in the three years since I returned to Mistletoe," I said, emotion brewing in my chest. "And someone I love is accused of the crime every time. This is the second body found on my family's property. I swear I'm not trying to make this about me, but I can't help feeling as if I'm a harbinger. Maybe I should've moved to a deserted island."

Evan offered a small, sad smile. He moved in close and gripped my hands in his. "You aren't bad luck. And I think I speak on behalf of the town when I say I'm glad you're right here where you belong."

I tried to smile back but couldn't. My heart was heavy with grief and despair. "Everyone will realize I'm the common denominator in all these violent deaths. My parents' beautiful Victorian inn will become a stop on the Haunted Mistletoe Tour. A Cursed Christmas Castle. A Bed, Breakfast, and Bedlam."

Evan snorted. "Don't be silly. There isn't a Haunted Mistletoe Tour."

I smiled.

"Your family and this tree farm are beloved here, and I hate to break it to you, White, but bad stuff happens everywhere and to everyone. In a town as small as Mistletoe, you're practically guaranteed to know the victim or the accused, or both, and that makes it feel personal. It doesn't help that you consider everyone a dear friend. You see where I'm going with this?"

I pulled my lips to the side. "I do."

Evan's expression suddenly flattened, and he released my hands. "So . . ." He stepped back, stuffing his fingers into his pockets. "I need you to take care of that stellar reputation. Focus on the inn and your family's legacy. Let me handle the investigation. I need you to listen to me this time." He dropped his chin and peered up at me with pleading green eyes.

My heart thrummed in response. "I make no promises," I said, knowing I couldn't leave this alone. Evan had been in Mistletoe for three years, but I'd grown up here. I had deep and binding ties to the community. I could help if he would let me.

"I have a surprise for you this year," he said. "And I'd like you to be around to receive it, preferably not via livestream from a hospital bed."

My tapdancing heart began to bounce with glee. "A surprise?" I loved surprises. And I hated them. They were my Achilles heel. I wanted to know everything, but I also craved the zing of exhilaration when things were sprung on me. "What is it?" I asked.

Evan grinned.

"Give me a hint."

"Sheriff?" The deputy who'd escorted Mary away earlier stood outside the bedroom door, hat in hand. "I've got something you might want to hear downstairs."

We followed the deputy into the kitchen, where Meg waited.

Cookie came into view, bustling around behind her, clearly no more capable of sitting still in the parlor than I'd been. She'd refilled the tray of shortbreads and added another kettle for tea in the dining room.

"She wasn't with the group when this happened," Meg said, jabbing a finger in Cookie's direction.

Cookie stilled, and Meg cocked a dark brow.

"She left the Hearth before any of us," Meg said. "And she left alone. I saw her."

Evan's eyes snapped from Meg to Cookie. "Is that true?"

Cookie's skin paled. She crossed her arms, then let them hang loosely at her sides. "I had to go home," she said. "Theodore needed his ointment."

"So, you have no alibi for the time of the murder?" Meg asked.

"I do!" She gasped. "I was with Theodore."

I groaned inwardly while attempting to maintain a confident front. "She was with Theodore," I said slowly, hoping to pass a message to Evan with my eyes.

Cookie wasn't a killer.

Meg was apparently a troublemaker.

And most importantly, she had no idea Theodore was a goat.

Meg's gaze flicked from me to Evan. "Well, when you talk to Theodore, you should ask him if she told him she threatened Karen before dinner."

Evan's eyes darkened and his body went eerily still. "Cookie?"

"I was talking to Holly," Cookie explained, embarrassment reddening her cheeks. "This woman was eavesdropping." She gaped at Meg, horrified.

Meg wrinkled her nose in distaste. "You said you wanted to hit her over the head, and you were holding that silver nutcracker when you said it."

I fought the urge to cover my face and peek between my fingers at the train wreck before my eyes.

Cookie made a choking sound, then turned to me, panic-stricken.

Evan looked at me too. Both awaiting my response.

"It wasn't like that," I said lamely.

"Christmas spirit," Cookie spluttered. "I thought she could use a blow of holiday cheer."

Evan stepped forward, motioning Cookie in my direction. "Why don't you and Holly wait for me in the kitchen?" he asked, though his expression made it clear his words weren't really a request. "I'd like to speak with Ms. Mason alone, and I'm sure Mr. and Mrs. White can use your help with the other guests."

I narrowed my eyes at him, then bit my tongue. I didn't like all the orders he was doling out tonight any more than I liked the reason for them, but I understood, so I sucked it up. But I wasn't making any promises that he wouldn't hear about it later. "Fine. Cookie?"

I waited while she made her way to my side, and then we headed to our exile in the kitchen.

"This is just like last year," she said, taking a swig on her thermos as we climbed onto seats at the island. "It's like some kind of gruesome new Christmas tradition."

My stomach churned at her words, and I knew she wasn't wrong.

"I just hope I don't wind up in jail. That'd be a terrible way to spend the holidays. I don't think Theodore would understand."

I wrapped a protective arm around her shoulders and pulled her close as my parents piled sweets in front of us.

When Cookie passed me the thermos, this time I accepted.

Chapter Four

Cindy Lou Who and I put the last remaining guest on a horse-drawn sleigh and shipped her off to the Hearth for breakfast, then grabbed the morning paper from the mailbox and hustled back inside.

Cindy stood beside her partially full food bowl and looked at me.

"Don't give me that," I told her. "We've got problems. Cookie's being investigated as a murderer, and every shady reporter in town is probably clamoring to get the inside scoop on how one cuckoo finally flew over the nest. You know why that's no good, right?"

Cindy gave a long, uninterested blink, then turned away.

"If we don't find real answers, people are going to draw their own conclusions, and right now, all the available evidence points to Cookie."

Evan and a pair of men from the crime scene team had stayed late into the night, processing Karen's room, the front porch, and everything in between, but they hadn't found anything to point them in a new direction. Thankfully, they'd allowed the other guests to return to their rooms, and the deputies had been considerably quiet as they finished their work.

I still hadn't slept, and I wasn't the only one. When I'd entered the kitchen to put on the coffee just before dawn, I'd found a note from Meg. She'd checked herself out and wanted a refund for the remaining nights of her stay. Given the situation, I couldn't blame her.

Cindy knocked her head into the stay-fresh plastic container where I kept her food, then gave me another look. Her notched ear turned like a satellite. When that didn't work, she rubbed her face against the lid while I chewed my nails.

"There's food in your bowl," I told her, flopping the newspaper open on the countertop as she glared.

The headline confirmed my fears.

Hospitality Critic Dead. Mistletoe Local Found Holding the Murder Weapon

A collage of snapshots underscored the words. A professional headshot of Karen. Candids of Cookie. Photos of the inn. "Uh-oh."

Cindy put her paws on the container and dug wildly at the side.

I huffed, then scooped a few pieces of kibble into her bowl. She walked away.

"I'm leaving," I called after her. "I'll be back, but we'll probably have the place to ourselves soon." Maybe forever.

The remaining guests were likely firming up their exit strategies over cinnamon roll pancakes and cocoa at the Hearth.

I grabbed my coat and keys, then headed for my truck.

I needed to see a woman about a gumdrop.

* * *

A few minutes later, I climbed behind the wheel of my red Reindeer Games pickup truck. The tree farm's logo was stenciled on both sides. Stuffed brown antlers protruded upward from the driver and passenger side windows, and a fat red ball was tied front and center on the shiny silver grill.

I gunned the engine to life and cranked up the heater, then pointed the vents at my face, which was half frozen from the short walk in frigid wind. I had a little holiday shopping left on my list, and a trip to town would fix that problem. While I was there, I could keep my ears open and see what folks were saying about the morning headline. And if Bonnie happened to be at the Gumdrop Shop when I arrived, maybe I could find a way to ask her some questions about what I'd overheard her saying at the Hearth last night. Evan had said there weren't any crimes in town before he arrived last night, but maybe something else that was significant to Karen's murder had gone down quietly, and Bonnie had the details.

I cranked up the local radio station, playing nothing but holiday classics until New Year's Day, and got lost in the melodies as the winding road carried me toward town. Rolling hills and snow-laden forests lined the route for several miles, until it gave way to crystalized fields and valleys. Slowly, homes popped onto the horizon, adding to the view with their smoking chimneys and cheery holiday gear.

The view was so enchanting, so delightful and wholesome, I wondered again how a killer could live here. And I hated that they weren't the first.

Several minutes later, my truck rumbled to a stop beneath the twisty, wrought-iron "Welcome to Mistletoe" sign, hindered by tour buses dropping riders at the square. Public benches were painted a bright Santa red, and pine green wrapped every lamp-post. Traditional mistletoes hung from Main Street lanterns, where hundreds of people stood each year for selfies. With only ten days left until Christmas, it seemed half the state had turned up to shop.

Evan's cruiser came into view outside the pie shop, and I briefly considered stopping. He and I had started dating, officially, on New Year's Eve, and after nearly a year, I was as happy as ever. Maybe happier. Life was better with Evan. He made things fun, and he comforted and challenged me in ways I'd never known I needed. We'd gotten serious pretty quickly, but it all felt right. And while I wasn't sure what the next year might bring us, I was ready for it. At the moment, however, keeping Cookie out of jail for Christmas was my biggest priority.

I trundled onward to Bonnie's Gumdrop Shop, then crammed my oversized work truck into a spot vacated by a sedan and congratulated myself on a job well done.

My breath rose in little white clouds as I hopped over the icy puddle outside my door and hustled onto the sidewalk, where crowds of shoppers hurried in and out of adorable boutiques, their arms heavy with packages.

"Merry Christmas," I called to familiar faces as I ducked and weaved through the throngs toward my sugary destination.

Classical holiday tunes carried through the frigid air around us, piped from carefully concealed speakers on telephone poles. I bobbed my head in time, enjoying the peppy selections. The air smelled of kettle corn, candied nuts, and a dozen other wonderful things sold by vendors in little booths along my way. I bought a bag of candied pecans for later and tucked them into my pocket.

The Gumdrop Shop had a new window display, and folks had gathered around to admire it. Bonnie's displays were the stuff children's dreams were made of, and I was still a child at heart. I hurried inside for a closer look at today's masterpiece.

A winter carnival had been created from gumdrops of every size, shape, and color. The paths between gingerbread houses, candy rides, and licorice coasters were lined in shimmering sugar crystals. Tiny gumdrop people waited at ticket booths, food vendors, and games. An unseen motor carried gumdrop cars along hilly coaster tracks and cranked a Ferris wheel in small, jerky motions.

Bonnie's gumdrops were homemade and gourmet. They came in a million variations and flavors, drawing the attention of the candy world all year round. Her elaborate and edible works of art had graced the covers of multiple magazines over the years and the pages of many more.

"Can I help you?" Bonnie's voice turned me around with a jolt.

She smiled from only a foot away, a clipboard in hand and half-glasses seated on the end of her nose.

I laughed at the start, pressing a palm to my chest. "Sorry. I get so caught up in your displays. One look, and I'm ten years old all over again."

"Well, that's the goal," she said, evidently pleased. "We're all much too serious once we hit thirty, it seems."

I frowned, not having yet reached that particular age, and suddenly wondering if I needed a better skin care routine. "Right."

"Are you looking for a gift?" she asked.

I shook my twenty-eight-year-old head, bringing myself back to the task at hand. "I'm actually here to see you," I said. "I'm Holly White. We've met once or twice, but it's been years." I smoothed my hair with a hand. "My family owns Reindeer Games." *The tree farm where Karen Moody was murdered approximately twelve hours ago. Around the time you came in ranting about her.*

"Of course," Bonnie said, her smile flattening slightly. "I read about what happened at your inn. Quite a shame."

"It is," I agreed.

"Your family just opened that inn, and already it's getting tanked in the media. That's the way it goes sometimes, but don't worry. Bad press always blows over." Her pinched expression wasn't very convincing, and I wondered if she was still talking to me or if the encouragement could be directed at herself.

My frown deepened. A woman had been murdered and stuffed into a toy-drive box, but Bonnie saw the problem as negative attention for the inn? "I'm not worried about that," I said. "I'm concerned about Karen Moody's death."

Bonnie's lips pressed into a thin white line, and she hugged the clipboard to her chest, possibly to shield herself from whatever was making her uncomfortable—in other words, me. Or, if I was reading the heat in her eyes and cheeks correctly, it was because she didn't trust her hands to be free. As if she might want to lash out at someone or something. Hopefully not me.

"Did you know her?" I asked, watching her expression as she chose her words in reply. If I was right about her temper, I thought she'd keep it under control inside her busy shop.

"Unfortunately, yes." Bonnie glanced over her shoulder, then back to me, clearly unhappy with the topic at hand.

"Then you must be shocked by what happened to her," I prodded, carefully evaluating her response.

"In my opinion, it seems fitting that she would go out in a way that ruins someone's business since that's how she lived her life as well," she said, her tone harsh and bitter. She raised an eyebrow in challenge.

"I don't think this is going to ruin our business," I said. "Whoever did this has no affiliation with Reindeer Games or my family. I'm confident Sheriff Gray will prove that."

The shop had gone still around us, conversations dimmed as curious ears turned our way.

Bonnie shook her head, a tired smile tugging her over-glossed lips. "It sounds as if the sheriff already knows who killed Karen, and if I'm not mistaken, Delores Cutter is tied so tightly to your family, half the town thinks she's part of it."

"She is part of it," I returned, a little more hotly than intended. Cookie might not have been a blood relative, but she was one hundred percent family, and I would fight for her. "She didn't do this. Regardless of what the paper says."

Bonnie dropped her clipboard to her side and sighed, temper melting into pity. "Well, then local authorities have their work cut out for them. There's an endless supply of suspects. Just try reading Karen's column. She practically shredded hardworking business owners and entrepreneurs for sport." She turned on her heel and walked away, leaving me to stare after her.

Not exactly the conversation I'd had in mind, but quite telling nonetheless.

Shoppers who'd stopped browsing to watch our exchange broke into whispers while I blinked myself out of my shocked stupor.

A woman was dead, and Bonnie, who'd been irate with the victim last night, seemed just as angry today. I couldn't help wondering if whatever had her so upset was enough to drive her to murder. I considered going after her and asking for details but decided not to press my luck.

I saw myself out and resolved to do a little shopping as planned. The last thing I needed was any attention while I drummed up some viable suspects for Evan to pursue. Evan wouldn't approve, but the sooner folks stopped looking at Cookie as the culprit, the sooner I could stop fearing she'd wind up in jail for Christmas.

Chapter Five

Two hours and a half-dozen stores later, I hustled across Main Street with a mob of shoppers in the crosswalk, then beetled my way onto the next block in search of a pick-me-up. I'd made short work of the pecans and had begun to lose steam several stores back, but I'd persevered by promising myself one of my favorite rewards at the end of a job well done.

Caroline's Cupcakes came into view a few paces later, complete with a line of customers streaming out the door and onto the sidewalk. Outside, the shop was pale pink and lined in twinkle lights. Its front door had been whitewashed to match the reclaimed wooden sign in the little patch of snow-covered grass by the front stoop, a preview of things to come. Caroline's was possibly the busiest shop in town. People traveled far and wide to take home a dozen or two of her light-as-air creations, and she often sold out hours before closing time. I indulged at least twice a week. Sometimes more.

I wedged my way into the cramped space, bypassing a line of guests waiting to select their cupcakes for carryout, then snagged the last empty chair in the room. My little table was just wide enough for two friends to share a quick bite, but the family beside me had borrowed the second chair, leaving me the only seat I needed.

I waved to Caroline behind the register and inhaled the sweet scents of spun sugar and vanilla as I unwound from a full morning of shopping. Caroline and Cookie had gone into business together two years back, when Caroline's uptight, political family had refused to support her dream of baking for commoners. Cookie, having money to burn after a large lottery win, offered to partner up in exchange for free cupcakes, and the town had never been the same. Or at least the townspeople would never again be the same pant size. No one had the wherewithal to pass up a Caroline's Cupcake. And most folks couldn't stop at one or two. Myself included. I was working on a personal record for the most eaten in one sitting—seven.

"Hey!" Caroline appeared beside my table, having left her employees to handle the lines. "I hoped I'd see you today," she said, setting a silver tray of cupcakes and a bottle of water before me. Her long platinum locks had been pulled back in a low ponytail, and her brilliant blue eyes sparkled with delight.

Caroline and I had gone to high school together, but we hadn't been friends until two years ago, when I returned home after too many years away. In high school, our paths had rarely crossed. She'd spent her time in the spotlight as our mayor's daughter, and I'd spent my time studying art and reading books. As adults, we'd bonded over a mutual love of our town. These days I couldn't imagine my life without her.

"What's this?" I asked, already peeling a pale blue and white striped paper away from the base of a cream-colored cake with petal pink frosting and red sugar sprinkles.

"Vanilla cake. Hint of cherry icing." Her glossy pink lips curved into a smile. "What do you think?"

My eyelids fluttered, and I moaned unintentionally as the blessed goodness melted over my tongue.

"Excellent. Now try another," she said. "I brought a fork." She pulled the utensil from her apron and presented it to me.

I frowned, licking crumbs from my lips. "I haven't finished this one."

"These are for sampling," she said dryly, as I polished off the treat in hand. Her perfectly sculpted eyebrows rose. "I want you to try them all."

"That's the plan," I said, eyeballing the other choices.

"You can't eat six cupcakes!"

"Wrong," I sang, stripping selection number two of its paper. A chocolate confection so moist and decadent the cake was almost black. The perfect peak of fudgy frosting had been rolled in chocolate jimmies. "Is this an early Christmas gift? Or do I owe you thirty dollars?" I asked, fully prepared to pay for the indulgence.

"I just need your honest opinion," she said. "Rate them for me from most favorite to least."

I bit into the dessert and a dribble of thick syrup ran over my fingertips and chin. "Is this even real?" I asked, lost to the heavenly wave of pleasure.

Caroline snorted delicately and shook her head. "I'm glad you like them."

I reached for a third sample while I chewed the second. "I don't like them. I want to marry them."

A goofy, prideful smile returned to her pretty face. "Stop it. Which do you like better so far? Be serious."

"Both," I said honestly. "I could live on nothing but your cupcakes forever."

"You have to pick," she insisted, pulling the tray away before I made a third selection.

"Hey!"

"Pick," she repeated. "Vanilla with a hint of cherry or triple chocolate?"

"Mean." I stared at the empty wrappers, unable to decide. "What's this all about anyway?" I asked, buying time to make my choice. "These aren't new flavors you're trying out. Why do you need my opinions so badly? Not that I'm trying to look a free cupcake in the . . . wrapper."

Caroline stared at me, nibbling her bottom lip. "They're for Fay and Pierce's wedding reception," she said finally, nodding as she spoke. The cadence of her speech was off, as if she was reciting a line from a play instead of answering a question.

I wrinkled my nose. "I didn't know you were catering desserts."

"Mm-hmm," she said, still nodding.

"Oh." That made sense. "Are you taking a date?"

"Nope," she said, pride gleaming in her eyes. "I've decided to go stag."

I smiled.

Attending formal events without a date would have pushed her over the edge not long ago, but opening the shop and pulling away from her parents' grip had made her stronger and more confident in new and awesome ways.

"Good for you," I said. "I'm kind of hoping Evan will ask me." I tapped a finger against the table. "I have no idea what to get him for Christmas, by the way, and I've been in half the shops on Main Street today."

"You'll figure it out," she said. "And he'll ask you to be his date to the wedding as soon as he thinks of it. I'm sure he's just been busy with Christmas, and now the murder." Her eyes sprung wide. "Oh my gosh. I didn't even ask you about that. I'm so sorry. How are you doing? How are your parents?"

I waved her off. "We're fine. I'm a little worried about Cookie, but other than that, I'll be okay. Have you seen her today?"

"No. She called to say she wouldn't be in for a while. She didn't want her presence to hurt sales." Caroline shook her head. "I offered to stop by and check on her, but she said she had things to do and that I shouldn't fuss."

"She was pretty shaken last night," I said. "Maybe she's putting on a brave face. I've been shopping all morning, and there's a mixed bag on public opinion." I lifted a peach-colored cupcake with white icing off the tray before Caroline could stop me. "Folks are definitely talking about what happened, and the paper practically announced Cookie as the killer. They used her picture for heaven's sake. Folks are . . . confused."

"What are they saying?" Caroline asked, checking for eavesdroppers before leaning in closer.

I wrinkled my nose. "Some think she might've finally cracked. She's getting older, and she marches a goat around town like he's human." I shrugged. "Some think there's a fine line between eccentric and good old-fashioned bonkers."

Caroline straightened with a snap. "Who's saying that?" She reached for her apron as if she might strip it off and go hunting.

"People," I said, setting my hand on hers before she got her strings untied, literally and figuratively. "They aren't being mean. They're just trying to make sense of it. Which isn't easy to do. I've been setting people straight store by store, but I don't know if my opinion will hold water long, since she's such a close friend." I finished the cupcake, formulating my next words carefully. "I think it would be best if there were other suspects to present to the people. Don't you?"

"You're not investigating this," Caroline said. "Because doing that would be the absolute opposite of a Christmas gift for Evan."

"But," I countered, "clearing Cookie's name so she can put this behind her would be an excellent gift for Cookie."

Caroline frowned. "Holly."

I lifted a shoulder. "I'm not investigating. I'm looking for other names to throw into the hat. Then, maybe I can get Ray to leak those to the paper." I couldn't actually ask him to write the article or Evan would know immediately where he'd gotten his information.

Caroline studied me.

I dragged the cupcake tray closer with one finger.

"Every time you get involved in something like this, you get hurt," she insisted. "I don't want you to get hurt."

"I hear what you're saying," I said, nibbling on the peaches and cream selection. "But this is different because I'm pretty sure Karen's killer was someone who'd received a terrible review from her, then lashed out. Whoever it is probably followed her to Mistletoe, did the deed, then vanished to establish an alibi. I'm only looking for names to turn attention away from Cookie. It's win–win because while everyone is looking at other suspects, the real killer might come to light."

"Karen's reviews could be unnecessarily harsh," Caroline admitted. "She called the new chef at that Gordon Ramsey restaurant in Bangor a cabbagehead."

I wiped my sticky lips with a napkin. "I didn't realize she was so tough," I admitted. "Once I saw the magazine she worked for, I got excited about the potential positive exposure. Then I pinned my hopes on impressing her, and I let my parents do the same."

"People love her column," Caroline said. "She seemed to be snarky but fair, if not especially warm or fuzzy. Those who got her praise usually thrived after the review was printed."

I nodded, a little disappointed in Karen's readership. "I'm getting a feeling the snark was the part readers liked most."

Caroline sighed. "People can be the worst."

"Yeah, or the best," I said, arranging the empty cupcake papers in a row, favorite to least favorite.

Two cupcakes later, Caroline thanked me for voting on the flavors, then brought me a box with a dozen assorted mini cupcakes for the road.

"I'll swing by Cookie's before I head home," I told her. "Your cupcakes always do the trick."

"Thank you," she said, then hugged me goodbye. "Let me know how she seems after you see her."

"Will do," I promised.

I looked at my icing-speckled hands, then at the mostly empty shop around me. The crowd had thinned as folks made their ways to cafés and restaurants for lunch.

"Care if I leave this here a sec?" I asked, rising with my purse and phone, but leaving my coat and cupcakes. I pointed to the ladies' room in explanation.

"Go for it." Caroline smiled, wiping tables and cleaning up after the midmorning rush.

My stomach ached with fullness when I stood. I fought the urge to unfasten the top button on my jeans before it popped.

I scrutinized my face in the mirror and considered texting Evan to fill him in on the gossip I'd overheard while shopping. I hated that so many people were willing to believe Cookie had finally gone around the bend and that locals were looking at the evidence instead of into their hearts.

I washed up, then shut the water off and pulled a handful of paper towels from the dispenser. Hopefully Evan had gathered new evidence. Maybe even found a substantial lead to turn the attention from Cookie, or better yet, uncovered something that would exonerate her.

I wasn't sure what that would be. The only obvious clue was the nutcracker. Though there was sure to be DNA on the velvet toy-drive bag used to cover Karen. I gaped at my reflection as a new thought occurred. I didn't have a way to check the bag for DNA, especially now that it was in evidence at the police station, but I might be able to figure out who the bag belonged to.

Christopher had provided identical red bags at every designated collection site.

All I had to do was find out who was missing their bag.

I sent a quick text to Evan, floating the bag idea for his review. Someone had covered Karen's body with a toy collection sack. It seemed reasonable to assume the bag belonged to the killer.

Then I sent a text to Cookie, letting her know she had a cupcake and hug delivery on the way.

Cookie responded immediately.

Cookie: Rain check? I'm full of whoopie pies.

I puzzled at the statement. Had Dad made a dessert delivery today too? Then, I remembered Caroline saying Cookie had things to do today, and I sent another text.

Me: Where are you?
Cookie: Reindeer Games. Theodore has a photo op.

I laughed. I'd imagined her holed up at home and horrified at the murder accusations, but I suppose I should've known better. She'd raised a lot of money last Christmas with a calendar she'd called A Goat For All Seasons, and she'd told me more than once she wanted to make a sequel. With only ten days left until Christmas, it was probably time to get started.

Me: Fun! On my way.

I checked to see if I'd missed a text from Evan, before tucking the phone into my pocket.

I hadn't.

"Holly Jolly Christmas" burst from the little speaker, and I pulled the device back into view to silence the reminder. I'd promised Mom weeks ago that I'd judge the first Reindeer Game of the season this afternoon, and in all the commotion, I'd completely forgotten.

Reindeer games were a tree farm tradition that invited visitors to partake in everything from cookie decorating to bingo. Every event had a holiday theme and a delicious Hearth-baked prize.

I hurried back to my table, eager to check on Cookie before the games began.

Once I'd fulfilled my duties at the farm and inn, I'd see about a master list of all the designated toy-drive locations. Then I could investigate without talking to anyone. I'd just pop by each shop to see if their bag was missing. I'd report my findings to Evan, and voilà!

Stealthy.

Helpful.

"Pardon me. Merry Christmas," I said, sidestepping a woman and little girl on their way to the ladies' room. Then I smiled at the fresh line of customers. Caroline and her employees spun like tops behind the counter, waiting on the mass of tourists freshly delivered by a tour bus, now double-parked just outside the door.

I stopped short as my table came into view.

Someone had opened my box of miniature cupcakes, and a pink plastic knife had been jammed into the strawberries and cream selection, nearly cutting the treat completely in half. Thick red filling spilled out and pooled around the slaughtered cupcake's base.

I didn't want to overreact, but it sure seemed like a threat.

Chapter Six

I raised my camera and swept the scene, then snapped a few photos of the mess on my table. I'd send both to Evan later. Maybe someone in the room would turn up in his investigation, and I could prove they'd been here now.

A little hopeful voice in my head suggested someone might've just been upset that I'd hogged a table and left the area, but it seemed more likely that person would simply have moved my things to the counter or chucked them onto the floor.

I instantly regretted how openly I'd spoken to people this morning about Cookie's innocence.

This was how my previous nightmares had begun.

And I didn't want to walk that line again. I wanted to be wiser and better prepared. I needed the last two years of close calls and near-death experience to have taught me something. Like how to get answers more safely.

One thing I knew for certain was that if I didn't tell Evan immediately, he would lose his mind when he eventually found out.

And he always found out.

I took a quick video of the busy sidewalks outside. I recognized many of the faces, but I couldn't be sure the one who'd made the mess wasn't long gone by now.

"Oh my goodness!" Caroline squeaked as I put my phone away. "What happened?"

I did my best to explain while I helped her clean up, then I said my goodbyes again and hurried out the door.

I rushed along the sidewalk, trying not to think about the awful things I'd been through in the last two years. My hands shook, and my breath came more quickly as I moved away from the scene of the cupcake disaster.

I unlocked my truck with the fob, then paused at the sight of Evan's cruiser still outside the pie shop.

Had he been there all this time, drinking coffee and extracting gossip from locals all hopped up on caffeine and sugar?

The pie shop was every Mistletoe teen's nightmare—it was where all the moms went to talk. On the flip side, it had proven to be the new sheriff's favorite resource. Hot coffee, fresh pie, and an endless flow of information fourteen hours a day. It couldn't be beat for convenience or efficiency.

I deposited my bags onto the truck's passenger seat, then locked up and made a dash for the pie shop.

The hostess met me with a wave and a smile, her retro chic uniform complete with ruffled apron, bobby socks, and ponytail. "Merry Christmas, Holly! Sheriff Gray is right over here."

"Thanks, Emmie," I said, thrilled by the fact she'd so easily identified me as Evan's friend.

My smile widened as she gathered a menu and a set of silverware from the hostess stand and led me to the sheriff's booth.

I'd known Emerson Cline for most of her life. She'd been in preschool when I was in high school, and she was just as bright-eyed and cheerful then as she was now.

"You picked a good day to stop by," she said. "We're celebrating the Twelve Pies of Christmas, and today's pie is peanut butter cream. We also have holiday apple, lemon-lovers, chocolate supreme, pecan paradise, and coconut."

I scooted into the booth across from Evan, not able to even think about pie after I'd just eaten a half-dozen cupcakes. "I'll just take coffee for now."

"Coming right up!" Emmie slid my placemat and silverware onto the table, then zipped away.

Evan raised his brows. "How's your investigation going?"

My jaw dropped in faux offense. "I have no idea what you're talking about, Sheriff. I've been shopping for the perfect gifts all morning. Unlike you, who's been here so long you must've sampled everything in the house by now."

"You got me," he said, sipping his mug of steaming black coffee. "Any chance you overheard or spoke to anyone about anything related to Ms. Moody's murder during your shopping expedition?"

I shifted on the seat. "Maybe, but I only intervened when I heard someone repeating the ugly notion Cookie could be a killer. And I'm here to talk to you about all of it."

Emmie returned with my coffee.

"Are you going to tell me it seems as if Karen Moody was here to review more than just your family's inn?" Evan asked, looking slightly bored and more than a little smug.

"Maybe," I hedged, working his question over in my head. I hadn't planned to say that at all, so why had he assumed I would? "How do you know?" I asked.

"Probably the same way you do," he said. "I did a little online research. Read her column and the comments, skimmed her blog, and contacted her editor. I gave my actual name and credentials when I called, but I suppose you posed as a town liaison. My personal assistant or a reporter of some sort."

I raised my cup to my mouth and worked to hold my tongue. I'd learned from experience that Evan didn't share information often, so I shouldn't interrupt him when he did.

"It didn't take long to figure out she wasn't exactly known for her glowing reviews and that she didn't hold any punches when she wasn't satisfied with a product or service. And her readership seems to love it."

I deflated a bit, shoulders slumping. "It stinks because I went above and beyond for her. Whatever she wanted, asked for, or even hinted at, I was on it, and always with a smile. Even when she got me out of bed to turn down her comforter after midnight, I never complained. I only apologized that it took me so long to get there."

Evan pressed his lips into a regretful frown. "There wasn't anything you could've done. That was her schtick. And I don't mind telling you, based on the notes found in her room, she didn't just come here to slam the inn. She came here for you and a chance to rip the whole town into pieces. She thought other reviews about Mistletoe and it's shops were too good to be true, so she"—he raised his fingers to form air quotes—"'came to pull the veil back and reveal all the lies.'"

I scoffed. "That's insane. Mistletoe is wonderful."

"I agree," he said, "but for people on the outside looking in, it seems a little too good to be true. And there were some documents with her things that suggested she might be looking to transition from critic to something more serious, like investigative reporting. Her stay here could've been a great opportunity. A few specific, tersely worded reviews, then a shocking look at the real Mistletoe." His voice deepened dramatically at the end.

"She thought our entire town was a scam?" I asked, having a hard time making sense of the concept.

Sure, we were a tourist destination, which tied our town's commerce and financial health to outsiders' willingness to visit, but would a whole town really put together some kind of nefarious scheme to get people here? How would that even work? It seemed like the plot of a *Twilight Zone* episode more than a plausible reality.

"Do you remember my sister's first impression? She thought the water supply might be drugged," he said with a grin. "I don't know how you've missed it, but people in general aren't quite so . . . jolly."

I bristled, nonsensically, at the comment. "Well, I have another reason to feel terrible for Karen Moody now. She was pursuing a story with no foundation. No merit. No teeth."

Evan cradled his mug in his hands, watching me with his signature compelling look.

"Did you say she came here for *me?*" My mind raced back over everything he'd said.

He dipped his chin infinitesimally. "The amateur sleuth townsfolk adore and criminals fear. People love you, and she'd planned to expose you as a fraud."

I guffawed. "Surely you're wrong."

"She had extensive notes in her room. She'd been following you and the cases you've mixed yourself into for two years. She suspected you, like the town, were hiding a more sinister side."

"Well, that's just bananas," I retorted. "And I suppose whoever eventually gets her notes will run with the story anyway, trying to cast shadows over Mistletoe to make themselves feel better about their own subpar town."

"I guess we'll see." He shrugged. "Are you heading back to the farm anytime soon?"

I puffed air into my overgrown bangs, frustrated and admittedly on a clock. "Yes. I have to judge a Reindeer Game this afternoon, and I want to catch up with Cookie. She and Theodore are there taking pictures for a new calendar."

Evan released the mug, sliding his hands into his lap instead. "I plan to head up that way later today. I'd like to take another look at the inn and perimeter by light of day. My men are there now, but I like to see things in person."

I nodded, completely familiar. "Right."

Evan was a good sheriff, and from what I'd read, he'd been an excellent detective in Boston before moving here a few years back. He'd worked homicide cases in the city, but the work had taken a toll. He'd told me once that it was an endless, thankless, grinding job that would've burnt him out by the time he was thirty if he hadn't made a change. He was thirty-three now, and I was glad he'd found his way to my town.

"Sounds good," I said, sipping my nearly forgotten coffee. "I like seeing you around."

A strange expression flickered in his cool green eyes, there and gone too quickly for me to name. I wondered again about the surprise he'd promised.

"What?" he asked, a small grin forming on his handsome face. "What are you thinking about? You got this dreamy-eyed look out of nowhere."

Heat spread across my cheeks, and I glanced away to center myself. "I was just thinking it's been a good year, and I'm happy," I hedged. All true, though not precisely what I'd been thinking. "I'm also wondering about the surprise you teased me with."

His brows furrowed. "What surprise?"

I gaped, and he laughed before I could stammer out a response.

"I'm kidding," he said, the Boston accent coming thick in his humor. "It's a surprise, so by definition, I can't tell you, but I've had a good year too," he said. "My best so far."

I squashed a massive smile as the pleasure of knowing I was a big part of his best year washed over me. "At least give me a hint."

"Nope."

"How am I supposed to find a gift of the same caliber for you if I don't have any idea what you've gotten me?"

Evan smiled.

"You aren't playing fair."

His smile widened.

"Fine." I sipped my now-tepid coffee, unsure what else there was to say. I couldn't make him talk, but maybe I could convince

Libby to point me in the right direction. Surely he'd told his sister what he was up to.

His eyes twinkled as I stewed.

My phone erupted with another round of "Holly Jolly Christmas," and I jerked back to the moment. "I have to go," I said. I fished enough bills from my wallet to cover the coffee and a tip, then set them on the table beside my cup. "Hey," I said, purse in my lap and inching toward the edge of my seat. "Something odd happened while I was at Caroline's Cupcakes earlier." I filled him in on the purposefully stabbed cupcake, then waved goodbye as I scurried away like the coward that I was.

I'd already admitted to talking about the case, and it was an easy jump to assume the ruined dessert was a threat. It was a jump I'd already made, and I didn't need to hear him say it.

Mostly because I was afraid I was right.

Chapter Seven

I parked in the narrow lot alongside the inn, attention fixed on the flimsy yellow crime scene tape marking off the porch and a portion of the front walk. A collection of tree farm guests stood a few feet away, cell phones raised to snap a picture. They scattered, red-faced, when I opened my door and climbed down.

"Merry Christmas," I said sharply as they hurried away, stealing peeks at me in their retreat. *Busted, gawking at the site of a woman's recent murder.*

I gathered my shopping bags and trudged to the inn's rear door, stopping to stomp snow from my boots before entering. I toed off the wet footwear, then scooted on socked feet over the kitchen floor and down a short hallway to my private quarters.

I hadn't noticed Cookie and Theodore on my way in, so I sent a quick text to see where she was. If guests had been ogling the crime scene, it seemed a good assumption that Cookie would've drawn at least a little unwanted attention today too, courtesy of the dumb newspaper.

I brushed my hair and reapplied lip balm while I waited for her response. When that didn't waste enough time, I viewed the short videos I'd taken at Caroline's Cupcakes. I recognized several locals, people I could ask whether they remembered anyone behaving suspiciously near my vacant table.

Wendy, a barista from the Busy Bean coffee shop was at the edge of the frame, cutting through the dining area and carrying a white pastry bag. Millie, a co-owner at Oh! Fudge, bustled up the sidewalk outside the window, delivery boxes stacked in her hands. I recognized a teacher from my elementary school days, a few regulars at the Hearth, Debra Jo from the bookstore, and . . . I rewound the video taken inside the dining area, then played it back in slow motion. A woman with her back turned toward me edged sideways through the crowd. Her face was hidden, but I recognized the canvas tote bag hooked over her shoulder and the teddy bear poking out of the top. *Meg.*

Mistletoe was a small town, but was it so small that the woman staying three doors down from Karen at the inn, whom I'd caught glaring at her two hours before her death, was also inside Caroline's shop when my cupcake was attacked?

I sent the videos to Evan, a task I'd meant to complete before our little chat.

Another full minute later, Cookie still hadn't responded to my text.

I locked the door to my private living space, then headed back through the kitchen. Two bedroom door keys, with their corresponding crimson ribbons and black room numbers, lay on the island beside a copy of the morning paper.

I moved closer, already knowing what the keys' appearance meant. A note on inn stationery lay beneath one. Mary Hathy had scribbled an apology. She simply wouldn't be able to stay in light of last night's tragedy. A business card with another guest's contact information sat beside the second key. Both guests had been scheduled to stay several additional nights.

I sighed, then stuffed my feet back into waiting boots. I had a game to judge. I'd have to deal with the inn's mass exodus afterward.

* * *

The Hearth was busy, but not packed, when I arrived, hoping to find Cookie before the game began. I took a seat on a lollipop at the counter and smiled at Mom as she rang the service bell. Another basket of cookies ready to go.

"Hey, sweetie!" She pushed through the swinging door in the next heartbeat, coming at me, arms wide and eager for a hug. "How are you? I missed you at breakfast. I'd hoped to tell you how sorry I am that you're going through this again. Your dad and I are so concerned." She squeezed and released me, then cupped my face in her cool palms and stared into my eyes.

"I'm okay," I told her. "But I'm worried about Cookie."

She released my cheeks. "I know," she whispered. "I hate what's happened."

I scanned the room around me, half expecting to find Cookie among the masses. "I thought she might be here."

Mom shook her head. "I haven't seen her, but I've been busy all day. I could've missed her."

"Busy is good," I said. At least the Hearth hadn't been affected by the previous night's tragedy. Unlike the inn, where I was losing guests so fast I'd likely have an empty house before

63

dinner. I rose to kiss Mom's cheek, then smiled. "I'd better go start the game. I'll be back in a few minutes."

Outside, a group of guests had gathered by a collapsible lunch table covered in a bright red Reindeer Games cloth. The sign on the easel behind it announced "Reindeer Rescue Today at Two."

I turned the dial on my childhood karaoke machine, lifted the microphone, and waved.

"Welcome!" I infused the word with as much pep and joy as I could muster, knowing that enthusiasm, like most other emotions, was contagious. This was my opportunity to get and keep folks excited about our farm. If I did it right, I might even be able to distract them from the recent tragedy a hundred yards away. "It's time for today's Reindeer Game! All players are guaranteed to receive an excellent time, lots of laughs, and a free hot chocolate for participation. Just let the Hearth waitress know you played. We trust in the honor system." I winked, then realized how much I wished that was true in other circumstances of life. Like Cookie's predicament as a murder suspect, for example. I sighed inwardly with the need to hear from her and know she was okay.

The crowd shifted, looking to one another when I went suddenly quiet.

I cleared my throat and refreshed my smile. "Today's challenge is Reindeer Rescue! So, pick a partner, then choose a lane." I motioned to the wide flat plot of land in front of me. Dad and the farm hands had spray-painted blue lines across the snow with diluted sidewalk chalk, marking ten narrow lanes. A pile of snow, three feet tall and as many feet wide, stood at one end of each lane. Candy-cane-striped flags on the other sides declared, "North Pole."

"It seems an avalanche has trapped all eight of Santa's reindeer inside the piles of snow," I said. "Without them, no toys can be delivered!"

A hush rolled through the crowd as the contestants hurried to select their lanes and snow piles.

"The first team to find all eight of their buried reindeer and carry them down the lane to their North Pole in time for Christmas gets a dozen freshly baked, beautifully boxed cookies from the Hearth, in addition to the complimentary cocoa, plus bragging rights until next year and a picture in the monthly newsletter featuring our Reindeer Games champions."

The crowd hooted, and the teammates turned to one another, strategizing. The air beat with energy.

"One catch," I said, my wry smile growing. "The path to the North Pole was watered last night and appears to be fully frozen today." I set the microphone on the table, then moved to the nearest lane. I grinned as I slid my boot over the frozen ground.

The crowd gasped, then broke into roaring applause and laughter. Players chatted loudly, rethinking their plans.

"Also," I said, reclaiming my microphone, "Christmas begins in three minutes, so you'd better hurry. All the children of the world are counting on you!" I blew an air horn without further ado, and the players burst into action.

Team members fell to their knees, thrusting their hands into the snow, digging and hunting for toy reindeer. Some pairs split up, with one digging and the other attempting to race a few rescued reindeer to the finish line. Other teams worked together, tearing their little avalanches apart, seeking all the reindeer first, then making one effort across the ice. All of the runners went down within a few feet, spinning and sliding on the ice, plastic reindeer ejecting from their grips.

A surprisingly spry older woman in a rainbow-striped knit cap and glasses loaded all eight reindeer into the pockets of her ski coat, then launched herself headfirst down the lane, as if she was riding on a slip and slide. She and her partner screeched with laughter as snow and fog collected on her glasses. Other teams stopped to watch her fly past. She collided with the North pole sign, then unloaded the reindeer between bouts of breathless laughter.

"Christmas is saved," I announced. "And in record time! Great effort, everyone. Fantastic enthusiasm. How about whoopie pies all around?" I suggested.

A cheer went up, and I led the crowd into the Hearth.

Libby was waiting to take their orders.

I returned to the counter and waited for Libby. "Hey," I said, smiling when she arrived, filling mugs with cocoa from the dispensers. "Have you seen Cookie?"

She shook her head. "Not today. Why? Everything okay?"

"She said she'd be here with Theodore, but I haven't seen her, and neither has Mom." I reached over the counter and tapped a dispenser, filling a large white mug with white chocolate cocoa. I plucked a peppermint stick from the display to stir with.

"Be right back." Libby piled baskets of whoopie pies and cookies on a tray with a bunch of cocoas, then bustled off to make deliveries.

Mom popped through the swinging kitchen door as I sipped my cocoa. "Oh good. You're back," she said. "Will you sample these cookies?" She set the tray before me. "The white frosted are vanilla, and the pale blue have a touch of lemon."

I stared at the cookies. Normally Mom made traditional holiday shapes, like stockings and snowmen, or birds decorated to look like cardinals for luck. These cookies were all circles. "Misplace your cookie cutters?" I asked, biting into a white circle, then a blue. "These are both terrific," I said after sampling each flavor. "What are they for?"

Mom's cheeks were rosy with delight, and I noted a distinct twinkling in her eyes. "Fay and Pierce's wedding reception."

I narrowed my eyes. "I thought Caroline was making cupcakes for that?"

"A party can never have enough desserts," Mom said, her smile going dopey, not unlike the smile Caroline had worn while feeding me cupcakes.

"Are you okay?" I asked, sipping the hot chocolate and wondering if everyone I loved had a hole in their marble bag, through which the contents were slowly falling out.

Mom nodded.

Libby made a second trip with cookies and drinks before collapsing onto the lollipop at my side. "What did I miss?"

"Mom's getting weird and misty-eyed over cookies," I said.

Libby frowned. "Well, there's no reason for that."

Mom nodded quickly, then sniffed and patted my hand. "Tell us about your morning," she said.

And I did.

She and Libby looked appropriately horrified by the cupcake attack, which felt more menacing each time I recalled it.

"Let me try Cookie again," I said. "This is the sort of thing she hates to miss. Girl talk and cocoa."

Libby muttered something about what did and didn't qualify as girl talk while I sent the text.

A wolf whistle spun us around on our stools a moment later.

Ray strode in our direction, then lifted Libby in a bear hug when she climbed off her stool to greet him. He set her down and smiled at Mom and me. "It's no wonder I come here so often. All my favorite people are here."

"Except Cookie," I said, appreciating the compliment but beginning to worry. "Have you seen her? I can't reach her."

Ray gave a sad smile. "Yeah. She took Theodore home about half an hour ago."

"Why?" I asked, tension creeping into my neck and shoulders. "Did something happen? I thought she was taking photos for the calendar."

He sank onto the seat beside Libby, then leaned forward, peeking around her as he answered. "I helped her set up for photos near the Holiday Mouse this morning. She thought it would be fun to get pictures of Theodore with kids visiting Reindeer Games. She dressed Theodore as Santa and invited children to join him. She told the adults all about her Goat for All Seasons calendars and how she raised money for charity, but the parents wouldn't give permission. I heard a few of them mention the morning paper. They recognized her from today's headline and hurried their kids away."

"Mean," I said. "Cookie's probably crushed."

Ray clasped his hands on the countertop. "I tried to cheer her up, but she's really bummed. She said Theodore was tired so she took him home."

My phone rang and Cookie's face appeared.

"Maybe we can all go see her later." Libby and Ray nodded as I answered my cell. "Hey, Cookie. We were just talking about you. Libby, Ray, and I were thinking of swinging by your place in a bit. What do you think? I bet Caroline will bring cupcakes."

"I'm not home," she whispered. "I'm at the police station, and I need you to spring me."

I froze. "What do you mean you're at the police station?"

Mom, Libby, and Ray made matching pop-eye expressions.

"A deputy came and got me," she said. "I don't even have my car. But I sent the deputy after some tea so I could call you for help."

"Are you under arrest?" I asked, imagining all the ways I would tell Evan what I thought about this. "Are they questioning you? If so, don't say anything without an attorney present."

"I don't know what they want," she said. "But Theodore was very upset when I had to leave so abruptly, and I don't know how long I have to stay." Her voice quivered, and my heart broke.

"We'll look after Theodore," I promised. "What did the deputy say when he picked you up?"

"He said the lab confirmed my prints were the only ones on the nutcracker, that the nutcracker is without a doubt the murder weapon, and it was Karen's blood on my mittens."

I gripped my forehead.

Ray fished his phone from his pocket. "Tell her I'm calling my mom. She'll get Pierce over there."

Ray's mom was about to marry Pierce Lakemore, one of the town's most powerful attorneys. He'd see that Cookie's rights were protected.

I passed on the news for Ray, and Cookie sighed.

"I'm heading back to the inn soon," I promised. "If there's a deputy at the crime scene, I'll ask him what he knows. Evan said he was coming up later, so I can ask him too. I'll take a close look around before then. Maybe I'll see something that's been missed."

"Thanks," she said, sounding a little relieved. "I knew you would help. If they lock me up, take care of my book club tonight, okay? Uh-oh! Gotta go." She disconnected.

"Yikes," I said. "This isn't good." And I'd completely forgotten Cookie's book club was coming to the inn for their holiday meeting.

Mom squeezed my hand again. "Everything will be okay."

Libby's thumbs danced over her phone screen while Ray spoke to his mom. "Evan says he'll look after Cookie until Pierce can get there," she said, apparently texting with her brother.

"Mom and Pierce are on their way," Ray said. "They're out shopping, and only five minutes from the station."

Mom set a mug of cocoa and pair of cookies in front of him. "Thank you."

He smiled. "No problem." He eyeballed the circles. "Did you lose your cookie cutters?" he asked, nearly echoing my question exactly.

I laughed.

Mom pressed her lips together, fighting a smile. "These are for your mother's reception."

"You're kidding." He frowned. "My aunts are making cakes, tarts, and brownies. I hope there's going to be some kind of food at this party too."

"Don't hold your breath," I said on a laugh. "I just sampled six of Caroline's cupcakes for the same event."

Libby tipped a cookie to her lips and smiled at me. "Do you think you'd ever consider marriage again?"

"Maybe," I said.

Libby knew all about my ex-fiancé dumping me a couple of weeks before our fully planned Christmas Eve wedding two years ago. The betrayal and lost trust had haunted me for a while, but sitting here, surrounded with true friends and dating the best man I'd ever known, I could see myself saying "I do" someday. "Yeah," I revised. "I think I would."

Mom turned and fluttered into the kitchen.

Libby nudged Ray with an elbow, and I couldn't help wondering if there was a point to her question. Could Libby and Ray be planning an engagement? The notion made me fizzy with excitement. Maybe all his mom's wedding planning had planted the seed in him. Would Libby say yes?

What would Evan think of his little sister as a married woman?

I hoped I could be a bridesmaid.

I watched her a moment, then recalled an extremely important question about her brother. "Do you have any idea what Evan has up his sleeve for me?" I asked. "He said it's a surprise, so I don't need complete details. Just a hint. Unless you want to give complete details—then I'm definitely game. And please know that if you have information but refuse to share, I might actually die without it."

She tented her brows, then pretended to lock her lips with a little key and toss it. "I know nothing."

"Lies," I accused. "And you can't talk after you use the key. That's not how it works."

Libby slid off her stool with a grin. "I'd better get back to work. And don't bother badgering Ray. I've told him nothing."

Ray shrugged, already finishing his second cookie.

I made a sour face as Libby walked away. Now I had two mysteries to solve.

Challenge accepted.

Chapter Eight

I took my time walking back to the inn, replaying the same trip I'd taken with friends the night before, attempting to recall everything about the moments leading up to our discovery of Karen's body.

The place where the nutcracker had been found was bare. A hole had been dug through the snow, down to the grass, and a little orange flag had been planted. It was hard to believe how drastically my thoughts about Karen had changed in the last two days. Before her death, I'd known she was standoffish, not nearly as friendly as everyone else who came to the farm, but I'd accepted her disposition as a side effect of the job. Being a critic had to be tough. Making friends with the people she reviewed would only cause hurt feelings later if she gave a poor review, or be perceived as preference if she gave a good one. I'd had no idea she was essentially a sensationalized snark columnist and that her attitude reflected her work, or that people loved her for her scathing reviews.

Not everyone *had loved her,* I reminded myself. Someone had disliked her enough to kill her.

I released a long intentional breath into the wind, watching a small white cloud form and dissipate before me. I should've looked into Karen more closely before her arrival. Instead, I'd spent all my time preparing to awe and woo her in hopes of a great review. *New England Magazine* was a respected regional resource. I'd never dreamed anyone on staff would be intentionally rude. My fault again. I was too trusting.

I stopped on the porch steps, the space before me still roped off. I recalled the feeling of my arm around Cookie's shoulders, seeing the donation box lid on the floor, and the velvet toy collection sack across the top. And the darkness.

Someone had turned out the porch light. Had they done that before or after dumping Karen's body into the bin? And why? To make the body less visible? Or had the darkness been part of an ambush when Karen returned to the inn?

I stared at the now-empty porch, willing the floorboards to speak to me.

Instead, the sensation of being watched tickled the back of my neck, and I raised my shoulders instinctively against it. I turned, slowly scanning the world around me. Reindeer Games was busy, the bright white snow polka-dotted with footprints and people in brightly colored cold-weather gear. No one appeared to be looking my way.

I went around back and let myself into the kitchen, kicking off my boots once more.

Another key lay on the island with a note. I read slowly, suspecting once again what it would say and finding I was right. The Wilsons had had a lovely stay, but in light of the recent tragedy, they no longer felt as if they could continue to enjoy their vacation at this location.

I sighed.

As long as someone had been murdered on the inn's front porch, presumably by a close friend of my family, no one would want to stay here. And even with the massive discount Christopher had given us when he built the place, my family couldn't afford to make the mortgage payments without guests.

This was another Christmas nightmare. *Just like last year,* I thought sullenly. *Just like my friends said. Just like* Bonnie *said,* I remembered. I'd overheard her tell her friends at the Hearth before we found Karen's body. What had the words meant to Bonnie? What was happening to her now that had also happened last year?

Someone knocked on the back door, and I straightened. A woman I vaguely recognized from town waved, and I invited her inside.

"Holly White?" she asked. "I'm Jenny Owens, a reporter for the *Mistletoe Gazette*. I'm writing a follow-up article about the critic who was murdered here last night."

I groaned. I wanted to demand Cookie's innocence and rant about the insanity of the accusations from today's paper, but talking to reporters rarely had the effect interviewees wanted. "I don't have any comment," I said instead. "And I'm not at liberty to discuss the details. There's an open and ongoing investigation. You should speak to Sheriff Gray or one of his deputies."

She nodded in understanding. "I know. I just wanted to give you a chance to speak your truth, to state your position. To defend Delores Cutter. I understand she's a dear friend of your family's, and you've gained a bit of a reputation for chasing the annual Christmas Killer."

My jaw dropped. "Please don't say that anymore. 'Christmas' should never be followed with the word 'killer.'"

"But you don't deny your annual involvement or your family's connection to the accused. A woman known to talk to a goat she named after her dead husband . . ."

I let my head drop forward dramatically. Inhaled. Exhaled. Then straightened, a polite smile in place. "I have no comment," I repeated.

I reached around her and opened the door. "I hope you'll enjoy the remainder of your time at Reindeer Games. Have some cocoa, a sleigh ride, or walk among the trees, but please refrain from questioning anyone else about last night's events, or I'll have someone escort you from the property. And Jenny, Cookie is more than connected to my family. Cookie *is* family."

I politely shoved her out the door, then texted Dad to warn him of her presence. I added a picture of her retreating form for good measure, and he responded quickly, assuring me that his staff would keep their eyes out and hopefully reduce her chance of ruining our other guests' good times. Meanwhile, it was time to prepare for book club.

* * *

Cookie arrived three hours later, rosy cheeked and with a hint of victory in her eyes. "That Pierce Lakemore is a looker," she said in lieu of a greeting. She unwound the scarf from her neck and hung it on a hook in the kitchen, then put her knit cap on top. "Ray's mom is one lucky lady. Pierce is smart too. I was released in a jiffy after he showed up." She unfastened the buttons on her wool coat, then shucked it off with a little effort, leaving tufts of snow all around her on the floor. "I'm glad I didn't have to miss book club. I've been looking forward to this all month. I even brought presents!"

She set a pile of small gift boxes on the dining room table. "These are for all the ladies who brave the weather tonight. Temperatures are really dropping."

"What did you get them?" I asked.

"I ordered book-shaped cookies decorated to look exactly like last year's December read, *'Twas the Knife Before Christmas.*"

"You mean 'the *night* before,'" I said, carefully opening a box for a peek inside.

"No. The knife," she said, kicking off her boots and lining them up on the mat beside the door. "It was a holiday mystery. Completely adorable. You'd love the sheriff."

I rolled my eyes.

The chatter of voices rose outside, and Cookie opened the back door.

A pair of ladies with books smiled when they saw us, or maybe when they saw Cookie.

She wrapped them each in a hug as they made their way inside.

Three additional women followed.

"Welcome," I said. "I'm glad you all made it safely. I hope the roads weren't too bad."

Debra Jo, the local bookstore owner, passed me a velvet toy-collection bag, then a book with a bow. "The roads are clear. It's cold, but a beautiful night. I brought some donations for the drive." She nodded to the bag. "*The Count of Monte Cristo* is for you. Cookie told me it's your favorite. I knew you needed this one the minute I saw it in a catalogue."

"Thank you!" I hugged the book briefly, treasuring it. I'd been an avid reader since my dad had introduced me to the Anne of Green Gables books as a child. *The Count* had become my favorite in college, when the idea of self-reinvention had really taken hold. The book was possibly even more special to me now, after learning on the night I'd met Evan that he too read it every Christmas. His father had been a literature professor before he'd died, and the love of literary classics was passed naturally to him. We'd had some of our best talks and debates on the subject.

Debra Jo had short sandy hair, lobbed at her chin and tucked behind one ear. She was shorter than me but taller than Cookie, and her bright blue eyes twinkled behind rectangular, dark-framed glasses. I envied her easy grace. I was never quite sure what to buy anyone, and I always got a little awkward when delivering a gift.

"It's beautiful," I told her, trailing my fingertips over the gold-embossed title. "I love it."

She smiled warmly.

Jean and Millie, the co-owners of Oh! Fudge, the town's most popular confectionary shop, drew me into a group hug. "It was really gracious of you to open the inn like this for our Christmas meeting."

"Anytime," I said, meaning it to my core.

"Normally, we gather in my stockroom," Debra said. "Eating fudge and drinking cheap wine."

I laughed, then waved for them to follow me into the formal dining room. "I have some top-notch wine for you tonight, courtesy of Wine Around, and a selection of finger foods and desserts, courtesy of my mother. So please, help yourselves." I stopped at the open pocket doors and let them pass.

The table sat twelve, but the group only needed half the seats.

The ladies set their things down and helped themselves to small plates and snacks.

I slipped away, then came back with a carafe of coffee and a pot of tea. "Is this everyone?"

Cookie nibbled her way around a snickerdoodle, crumbs sticking to her lips. "Everyone who RSVP'd," she said. "It's hard to get a lot of confirmations this close to Christmas when everyone's already got a full calendar. The six of us must be the hardcore readers."

The other women raised their cups and glasses in agreement.

Debra Jo posed a hot cup of tea near her face like a treasure, letting the sweet steam curl around her nose and chin. "Jon and I have been in Mistletoe three years now, but I don't think I'll ever get used to all this snow. Some days I don't think the flurries will stop until we're all buried."

Becky, a local physical therapist, faked intense shock. "What?" Her blond hair danced against her shoulders as she laughed. "You didn't get four feet of snow every Christmas in New Orleans?"

"No, ma'am," Debra Jo answered, intentionally slowing her natural drawl.

"Well, we're all glad you're here." I said. "What does Jon think of the snow?"

"He likes it," Debra Jo said. "It was a great justification for buying a big truck. And he really likes the snow plow on our lawn tractor."

Becky let her head fall back with a whoop of laughter.

The woman across from her, Brooke, gave an audible groan. "I didn't shovel after work today. If I don't stay up late enough to get it done tonight, my little sedan might not make it out until spring."

"I'll send Jon and his tractor," Debra Jo joked. "He can transport it in his big ole truck."

I took a step back, slipping away so the book discussion could begin. "Let me know if you need anything else," I said. "And thank you again for my beautiful book." I smiled at Debra Jo, making a mental note to take some of Mom's whoopie pies to her bookstore. I wanted to formally thank her for the gift and get lost in the aisles a while.

Cookie pulled a worn paperback of *The Count of Monte Cristo* from her bag. "You can stay and discuss it if you'd like."

"Tempting," I admitted, but I had other work to do, and I feared someone wouldn't love the story as much as I did. Then I'd be disappointed. Or offended. I took another step back. "Go on. Enjoy."

"I'll try," Cookie said, "but I prefer mystery stories, if I'm being honest."

Brooke leaned on her forearms across the table, eyebrows pinched in concern. "This town has a new mystery every year lately."

Cookie smiled at me. "And those cases always get solved, thanks to Young Sherlock over there."

I blanched. "I am no Sherlock Holmes. I'm barely a member of the Babysitter's Club. And I think Arthur Conan Doyle just rolled over in his grave at the suggestion."

She patted my arm. "Sometimes things don't go completely wrong when you're investigating."

I slid my eyes in her direction. "Back to *The Count of Monte Cristo*," I said, reaching to close the pocket doors, then slipping into the hall.

I checked in on them every fifteen or twenty minutes, between bouts of gift wrapping in my office. Ninety minutes later, the group had put their books away and opened a third bottle of wine.

"Holly," Brooke called as I peeped in to see if they needed anything else. "We're just chatting now. Join us."

The group beckoned, so I obliged.

"Good meeting?" I asked, smiling at their empty plates and joyful expressions.

"Yes." Cookie patted the seat next to her. "Sit. Tell us everything you know about what happened here last night. Maybe seven armchair detectives are exactly what this case needs."

I *really* doubted that, but I liked the idea of bouncing some ideas around.

I scanned their eager faces as I considered how much I could or should say. "The murder weapon was a metal nutcracker. Cookie had just given it to me a couple hours before we found it in the snow. Cookie's fingerprints were the only ones on it." That much had been in the paper, so I was safe to repeat it without angering Evan.

"Why throw the weapon into the snow?" Brooke wondered.

"Yeah," Becky said. "Why not take it far away instead? Dispose of it properly?"

"Does the sheriff have any real suspects?" Debra asked, covering Cookie's hand with hers briefly and offering a supportive squeeze.

"No," I said, answering the last question first. "And I suppose it was a crime of passion. The killer might've shocked him- or herself with the physical outburst and the deadly outcome. It's possible that person fled the scene in a panic and without thinking. Maybe they even dropped the nutcracker during the escape."

Jean frowned. "Well, that doesn't make any sense. This couldn't have been an accident if there weren't any other prints on the weapon. The killer must've worn gloves."

"Or took the time to wipe their prints," Millie said.

"It's winter in Maine," Becky said. "Everyone's wearing gloves."

"What else?" Brooke asked.

The ladies collective stare returned to me.

"We found her in the toy donation box," I said.

The women grimaced.

"She was covered with one of the red toy collection bags. Like the one Debra brought with her tonight. Did any of you notice yours was missing?"

Millie shook her head. "The bag was at Oh! Fudge when we locked up for the day. We checked it."

Jean nodded. "We'd planned to bring any new donations with us tonight."

"I'll check for the bag outside the clinic tomorrow," Becky said.

I nodded. "Thanks. Right now, the only real theory I have is that the person whose bag is missing might be the one who left it here last night."

The group exchanged looks, and I feared I'd created a mob of well-meaning amateur sleuths. Evan would die. Then he'd return from the grave to kill me.

I reached for the coffee carafe. "I'll be right back."

I needed a good excuse to leave the room, and I could use the coffee. I was surely in for another long night of overthinking.

I carried the pot to the kitchen, then set my machine to brew. I pulled the kitchen curtains shut when my skin began to crawl. It was hard to tell if the feeling of being watched was real or imagined. My nerves were too on edge to differentiate.

I thought of Evan and his investigation. He'd hate the fact I couldn't let this go. But if the local paper was determined to create a stir around Cookie as the culprit, odds were Cookie would be dragged back to the station soon, maybe in handcuffs. There was only so much Pierce Lakemore could do in light of all the evidence pointing directly at her. And that was a thought I couldn't bear.

I paced a loop around my island, hating that Evan had found notes in Karen's room suggesting she'd come to declare Mistletoe a large-scale fraud. I loved my town and everyone in it. We weren't frauds. We were a warm and welcoming community of holiday-loving souls. Real people with real problems who knew they could lean on and count on one another without question. What was wrong with that?

And why had Karen singled us out?

A shadow appeared at the back door, and I nearly swallowed my tongue when the doorknob turned.

"Hello?" I called, reaching for my marble rolling pin and positioning myself on the opposite side of the kitchen island, for protection if necessary.

"Hello," Evan said, stepping inside.

Cindy darted past his legs, snow clinging to her fur. She dug into the kibble in her bowl, as if she didn't know she'd done anything wrong.

I groaned. "How did she get out again? She's going to freeze to death one day, and I will never stop blaming myself."

Evan shook his head. "I doubt that. She was an alley cat. She's resourceful, and she knows where the food is." His brow furrowed, and his gaze fixated on the rolling pin. "Baking?"

"You scared me," I said. "I didn't know who might be coming through the door."

Evan peeled off his heavy gloves and tucked them into his coat pockets. "Hopefully not your inn guests. They might find the rolling pin concerning."

"Funny," I said. "As if I have any inn guests."

His lips quirked. "You still have two. My deputies and I are keeping track." His thick black sheriff's jacket and matching ball cap were dusted with snow.

"You're staking out the inn?"

He grinned. "I was. Now I'm here."

"Okay." I folded my arms. "So, what's up?"

"I got the videos you sent me," he said. "I sent them over to tech. We'll see what they can find. Why'd you run off after telling me about the knifed cupcake when we spoke at the pie shop?"

"I was in a hurry to get back," I said. "I had to help Mom with a Reindeer Game."

He watched me closely, likely seeing straight through my attempt at bravado. "I'm glad you did, but I've got to ask. How many people did you talk to about Karen Moody before the cupcake was punished?"

"A few?"

He nodded slowly. "Any idea who could've followed you to Caroline's and left that message?"

I bit my lip, feeling the sting of panic in my eyes. "No. Which is why I took the videos," I said. "Cookie didn't do this."

Evan sighed. "I know how much you care about her, Holly. I know how much you care about everyone, but I need you to stop playing defender. Just let folks talk, and trust me to figure this out and set things straight."

"One of your deputies took her in for questioning today," I accused. "Why didn't you tell me that was going to happen? I could have warned her or offered to go with her so she wouldn't have been alone and afraid."

"We're doing our jobs," he said gently. "No one's trying to upset or offend you."

"Is that why you're here now?" I asked, chin jutting upward. "To tell me to stop being a good friend?"

"That's not fair," he said, his voice going hard and flat. He rounded the island to my side and pried the rolling pin from my grip. "Your passion is one of the things I like most about you. You'd go to bat for anyone, and everyone knows it. Your friends are the luckiest people I know."

I tried to maintain the frown for good measure, but he was softening me up.

He opened his arms and I tipped forward, falling into them. The icy fabric of his coat warmed quickly beneath my cheek.

"I'm here because I worry about you," he said softly. "And I worry because I care."

My heart thudded, and I tightened my hold on him in response.

A round of laughter from the dining room broke the moment, and I pulled reluctantly away. "Cookie's book club is here for their holiday meeting," I explained. "I just made a fresh pot of coffee."

Evan searched my face with keen green eyes. "I'm going to have another look at Karen's room. Maybe you and I can catch up afterward, when we're both off the clock for the night?"

I smiled. "I'd like that."

His lips twitched, fighting a small smile. "It's a date."

Chapter Nine

I stopped by the Hearth the next afternoon to help Mom set up for Holiday Bingo. The dining area was nearly empty thanks to a number of events happening throughout the farm. I set bingo cards on each table, one for every seat. Then I placed a small bucket of red and white striped mints, one per table, for players to use as markers. Little tags on the mint pails announced, "Nine days until Christmas!" My stomach tightened at the thought. I only had a little over a week to sort out Cookie's mess, or she could find herself in jail for Christmas.

"Looks good," Mom said, smiling at me from behind the counter.

"Thanks."

"Are you staying to play?" she asked.

I hesitated. It was hard to say no, but I had more gifts to wrap, and I wanted to make another trip into town. "Can't," I said. "Will you have enough help without me? Until Libby gets here?"

Mom bent forward at the waist, leaning her forearms on the counter. "I'll be just fine. Libby's got the afternoon off, but your dad has already volunteered to help out."

There was a strange inflection in her voice as she mentioned Libby, but it was gone before I made heads or tails of it.

"Did you get any sleep last night?" she asked, one hand on a hip, and looking a little concerned. "I know you worry about things. You've got a big heart, and it keeps you up at night."

I went to the counter, drawn by her natural peace and kind soul. "Last night was good. Cookie and her book club met at the inn for their holiday party and discussion. She was in great spirits, and Evan dropped by near the end. He stayed and we watched old movies while wrapping donated toys until after midnight. I tried to catch up on my jewelry orders after he left, but I conked out around two."

Mom came around the counter and pulled me near, resting her head against my shoulder. "I wish you'd gotten to bed sooner, but I like knowing that you're spending time doing normal things. Holiday things. And with people who care so much about you."

My cheeks heated nonsensically at her inclusion of Evan in that statement.

"No investigating then?" she asked, utterly failing at nonchalance.

"Only a little," I said, not wanting to alarm her. "I looked for Karen on the usual social media channels this morning. That was interesting."

"Oh, hon," she cooed, playing absently with the ends of my hair. "Your dad and I really wish you wouldn't."

I shrugged, hoping to seem less invested than I was, never intending to upset or hurt my parents. "I was just a little curious." An admitted understatement. Like saying Mistletoe was "a little Christmassy."

I'd read dozens of blog posts and online articles by Karen. I'd checked out her personal and professional profiles. Read her reviews and about a million responding comments. I'd fallen headfirst down a digital rabbit hole and had had a rough time climbing out before coming over to set up for bingo.

"Well, there's no danger in reading the internet," Mom said.

I nearly laughed, but she wasn't joking.

"How's everything else?" she asked. "Are you happy?"

"I'm worried," I said. "About Cookie and the inn. The newspaper didn't point a finger at her today, but Evan says he hasn't found anything that can exonerate her. Her prints were on the nutcracker. She was unaccounted for at the time of Karen's death, and another guest overheard Cookie make a crack about hitting Karen over the head with Christmas spirit. It's bad, Mom. And you know how Evan is about protocols. It doesn't matter if he knows she didn't do it. He won't ignore the evidence. And right now, it's all stacked against her."

Mom squeezed my hand. "Everything will be all right," she said. It was becoming her unofficial catch phrase. "All you have to do is let Evan work his magic. And stay out of his way." She added the last part with a slide of her eyes.

"It's not that easy," I complained. "Even if you're not afraid Cookie will wind up in jail for murder, what about your new inn? Someone left a body in a donation box on the porch. If that's not completely horrible enough, rumors are spreading that a good friend of our family is a homicidal lunatic."

"I didn't read anything like that," Mom said. "Only a few articles with a hodgepodge of facts and speculation. Nothing direct or incredibly pointed."

I made my best "get real" face. "We're down to our last occupied room at the inn," I said. "And this morning, I had a cancellation by phone for New Year's Eve. The timing can't be a coincidence. How many more cancellations are on the way?"

"Ray's mother and her wedding party will fill the available rooms soon," Mom said. "They won't cancel, and before you know it there will be wedding photos galore. We can use those to replace the crime scene photos being spread around right now."

I sighed. Maybe she was right. If the media left Cookie alone long enough, maybe the good wedding-related publicity could dilute the bad murder vibes.

I stuffed my thumb into my mouth and bit the skin along the edge of my nail.

Mom stared at me until I looked her way again. "Please don't look into this," she said. "Your insatiable curiosity has given your father and I two very terrifying Christmases, and we don't want another. I'm not sure my heart can take it. And I know I'd never survive losing you."

"You aren't going to lose me," I said. "I promise."

Her eyes misted. "You can't know that. Not unless you're going to stay away from this mess. Because once you start down that path, the killers always find you. Give your father and me this one gift for Christmas."

I groaned inwardly, torn and frustrated. "I have to go," I said. "I have some last-minute shopping to do. Maybe I'll run into Libby. Do you need anything while I'm in town?"

Mom lifted her palms. "Just think about my request and come back safely." She reached under the counter, then produced a stack of white bakery boxes. "Drop these off at the Holiday Mouse before you leave the farm? Christopher's remodel streamlined everything in this kitchen. I'm making more cookies than I can sell here every day, so I started boxing them for sale at the store."

I grinned, thinking again of Caroline's belief that Christopher was Santa Claus. "Glad to help."

I carried the boxes into the frigid wind, then up the heavily salted path toward the Holiday Mouse, our little craft shop and souvenir store.

A line of guests had formed alongside the small log building, and a giant sign with the words "Meet Theodore, A Goat for All Seasons" stood on an easel near the front.

I changed trajectory, curiosity piqued. Just yesterday Cookie had abandoned photographing Theodore after being treated like the plague by farm guests. What had changed the narrative today?

A small man in an elf costume stood beside Theodore, who was once again dressed as Santa. A family of tourists posed around the goat, offering a bucket of treats.

"That's perfect," the little elf said in a scratchy voice and terrible British accent.

I gaped as I made my way to the front of the line, then stepped aside so no one thought I was cutting in.

Cookie noticed, then winked at me as she snapped the family's photograph with a camera on a tripod.

The family traded Cookie some cash for a candy cane and a small card, probably with the address of whatever website she planned to upload the photos to.

She tucked the cash into an elaborately wrapped box with a gift tag addressed to "Donations," then hurried in my direction while the next family went to meet Theodore.

A bark of laughter wedged in my throat. "What are you doing cross-dressed as a male elf?" I asked, taking in her pointy hat and ears, curly-toed shoes, and a frighteningly authentic-looking beard.

"It's Monday," she said. "Most of the weekend tourists who were here when poor Karen died have gone home. The new folks who arrived last night for a week of holiday fun don't know I'm an accused killer." She beamed. "And today is the opening of Candy Cane Lane down by the covered bridge, so the news covered that this morning instead of the murder."

"Convenient, but you're still dressed as a man," I said.

"An elf," she corrected. "This is a disguise. So anyone wanting to cause trouble won't recognize me. It only takes one Negative Nancy to ruin things for everyone."

"The beard's a nice touch," I said. "Are you keeping it?"

"Don't be silly," she scolded. "What would Theodore think? He's the one who wears the beard in our family." She peered over one shoulder at the goat in question. "I have to go, but if you meet me here in thirty minutes, I'll take a break. We can walk Theodore so he has a chance to do his business."

I wasn't sure that was how goats worked, but who was I to argue?

I dropped the cookies off at the Holiday Mouse as planned, nodding and smiling at shoppers on my way to the counter.

Kinley, the girl running the register, caught my hand when I turned to leave. "Wait!" Kinley had been working at the Holiday Mouse since she graduated from high school last spring, and everyone loved her, myself included. She gave her customer his change, then turned bright blue eyes on me. "Holly!" She smiled. "I'm so glad to see you. Everyone loves your jewelry, and we've completely sold out." She reached below the counter, then brought up an empty display.

My hobby of melting old glass bottles into jewelry had really taken off after my return to Mistletoe. I formed the recycled glass into tiny replica holiday treats, like candy canes and gingerbread folk, then attached them to earring posts, bracelets, and necklaces as charms. These days it was a thriving business I could barely keep up with.

"Wow." I smiled back. "That's great. I'll get more pieces from the inn and bring them over. Thanks for letting me know."

She lifted a finger, indicating I should wait, then opened the register drawer and withdrew a stack of receipts. "I took a few orders," she said, passing the papers my way. "A bunch of people saw your jewelry on other shoppers in town, asked where they bought the stuff, then came to buy some."

I stared at the wad of orders. "How long have you been collecting these?"

"A couple of hours," she said. "Someone asked if she could leave an order to be shipped to her home later, and I told her I'd look into it. After that, I started offering anyone who asked about your jewelry if they wanted to leave a request. Almost everyone did. And I told them all about your website too."

"These are all from today?" I asked, mystified at the amount of unexpected work in my hand.

"Since lunchtime," Kinley said.

I blinked. It was only three o'clock. "Well, I guess I'd better get started."

She turned back to the line of waiting customers with a warm apology.

I walked outside in a slight daze. There weren't enough hours in my days to manage everything I needed to do.

Cookie waved from her position beside the giant "Meet Theodore" sign. She led me away from the crowds and didn't slow down until the nearest people were out of earshot. Theodore bleated in protest after several hundred feet, but Cookie shushed him. She craned her neck in every direction, looking a little more manic than I preferred.

"Are you okay?"

"I think so," she said. "My disguise is pretty good, but being seen alone with you will probably give me away, so we shouldn't talk long."

I narrowed my eyes. "Are you worried about someone in particular?" I asked, hoping the reporter who'd come to interview me last night wasn't lurking around again today.

"I'm not sure," Cookie said. "I think the sheriff's having me followed. I feel someone watching me all the time. Twice I thought I spotted the stalker, but I'm not sure. There are always so many people around."

"What did the stalker look like?"

"Average height," she said. "Nondescript clothing and a plain ball cap."

"What about his face? Was it definitely a man, or could it have been a woman in disguise, like you are now?"

She looked down at herself and her expression turned to surprise, as if she'd somehow forgotten about her beard and elf costume. "I don't know."

Well, that wasn't helpful. I patted her back anyway. "Don't worry. I'll find a thread and pull it, then the cops and lawyers and Karen's family will all be forced to follow the new trail and leave you alone."

Cookie turned in my direction with a snap, instantly scanning the distant crowd. "I think you'd better let Evan take the lead on this. You have some great ideas, but you also almost die a lot. Which isn't a great way to celebrate Christmas."

I gave her a hooded stare and crossed my arms.

"Tell Evan your theories, and let him send a deputy on your reconnaissance jobs. He'll do whatever you want. Just ask," she said.

I sighed and nudged her back into motion when Theodore began to nibble the hem of her coat. "I did some online digging this morning and got an insider's look at who Karen was from her social media accounts. Her friends, their profiles, her articles and commenters."

Cookie's eyes widened. "There you go! Investigate privately. From home. What'd you learn?"

"Mostly that she was indiscriminately mean to everyone. She called it being honest, and if anyone complained, she asked them if they'd prefer she lie. She was pretty manipulative in that way, and kind of a bully. She did and said whatever she wanted, which was usually whatever would get her the most attention, then scolded and belittled anyone who dared question her behavior. Usually that person became her next target."

Cookie cringed.

"She also took a lot of pictures," I said, a smile breaking over my lips. "She fancied herself a pretty good photographer and documented everything. She put a ton of images online after arriving in Mistletoe, and I'm going to use the photos to track her activities on the days before her death. Visit the places she went. See if something stands out."

Cookie looked over her shoulder again suddenly, and I tracked her gaze to a retreating form in the distance, vanishing into the crowd. "Did you see that?" she whispered. "All dressed in black? Maybe a deputy making sure I don't try to skip town?"

"Maybe," I said. "I'll ask Evan about it." I turned back to the little cross-dresser before me and grinned. "I'm going to get started on the photo tracking. Is there anything I can get you while I'm in town?"

"Fudge," she said. "And an alibi, but only if you can do the second one without getting hurt."

I kissed her cheek, then hurried away. I was already working on that second one.

Chapter Ten

I climbed down from the truck outside Wine Around, Mistletoe's favorite—and only—wine shop, featuring vintages from every era and labels from all around the world. I'd met the owner, Samantha Moss, last year under dubious circumstances, and we'd become unlikely friends. These days, I looked forward to our occasional run-ins.

I ran mentally over the pile of jewelry orders Kinley had given me as I headed for the door. I was low on glass to melt down and shape into my sweet creations, but Samantha had become an excellent resource.

Wine Around was housed in a small historical storefront with a deep purple face and hunter-green trim. The broad black window boxes spilled over with holly, and a fresh pine wreath hung below a "Welcome" sign on the door.

A group of women pushed their way inside ahead of me, loaded down with shopping bags and chatting merrily about their day's adventures as well as where to have dinner. I followed on their heels.

Samantha was at the counter, helping a man choose the perfect, and likely most expensive, bottle of cabernet. Her willowy body had been poured into a high-end black jumpsuit that she'd accented with heels, a wide red belt, and chunky gold jewelry. Small glass wine flutes dangled from her ears beneath a jagged pixie cut of jet-black hair. The earrings were a gift from me.

I got in line and waited.

She rolled her eyes when she saw me, and I grinned easily in response. Samantha was known around town for her temper and regularly unpleasant disposition. The behavior was mostly a mask, just a hard shell protecting her soft interior. Or at least that was what I told myself.

"I have at least fifty bottles for you," Samantha said as the man moved away, still considering his options. "The minute I told my Winers that you were collecting empty bottles to melt down and make into jewelry, the donations started piling up. I've got shades of blue and green I haven't seen in ages." She bent at the waist and returned with a case of empty glass bottles, then repeated the process three more times.

The Winers were members of Samantha's monthly wine-tasting club, and clearly very generous donators to my cause.

"I have more in the back," she said, a hand on one hip. "Come back for them soon, or I'll start charging you to store them."

"You will not," I said, opening my wallet. "You're my hero for this, and I know you love it." My only other local option for continuous glass acquisition was the recycle center, and a stalker dressed as Santa had put me off of that place permanently last year.

Samantha frowned. "I don't like this friendly thing we've got going. I hope you know that."

I grinned. "May I at least renew my mom's wine club membership before you kick me out or throw something at me?" Mom had loved receiving the membership as a gift last year, and she never missed a meeting. She'd acquired some pretty good bottles for the inn as a result.

"Fine." Samantha took the card from my fingertips, trying desperately not to smile. "When will I finally get you to join?"

"I don't know. If I do, can we wear matching necklaces?"

"Get out."

I laughed. If I ever joined her group, it would be for the food pairings she served with her wine. I wasn't much of a drinker, or a fan of being even the slightest bit out of control, but I really liked cheese, and according to Mom and Cookie, Samantha served a lot of it.

She returned my card with the flick of her wrist, the Visa caught between two fingertips. "I will get you to the dark side one day. Just wait and see."

"Maybe. Help me out with all these cases?" I asked.

Samantha sighed deeply but rounded the corner carrying two cases. She pressed the door open and held it with her hip. I toted the other cases into the cold, and she followed. We arranged the boxes on the front passenger side of my truck.

"How's Cookie doing?" Samantha asked, stepping back onto the sidewalk, arms crossed against the cold.

"Better than I am," I said, lifting and dropping my arms at my sides. "I hate this for her."

"I know you do." Samantha pursed her lips. She loved Cookie too. Cookie was an original Winer. "You'll figure out what really happened to that woman," she said confidently. "You're dogged, and you're a good friend. I can appreciate both, so if you think of anything I can do to help Cookie or you with whatever you're up to, let me know."

"How do you know I'm up to something?" I asked, locking the truck doors and following her back to the sidewalk.

She snorted. "You're Holly White." She spun away, vanishing back into her shop.

I laughed, then beetled toward the store next door, hoping to make it inside before my face froze and cracked in the biting wind.

I yanked on the door to Oh! Fudge, then floated across the threshold on a warm cloud of rich melted peanut butter and caramel scents. I moaned in pleasure as I drifted to the counter.

Jean and Millie stood behind an ultra-clean display case at the shop's center, broad smiles inviting me closer. "Are you here for Cookie's cherry cordial?" Millie asked. "Because we sold out hours ago. And we aren't planning to make more before Christmas. Then only one more big batch before the new year."

"What?" I bent for a look in the display case between us. Cookie loved the seasonal fudge flavor that Millie and Jean sold primarily at Christmastime for added exclusivity. Not only was it a special recipe that no one else came close to replicating, but fans could only get it between Thanksgiving and December thirty-first. I'd made a habit of purchasing a pound of it for Cookie every year. "No!" I complained, finding the tray that should've held red and white swirled fudge completely empty.

When I straightened, ready to bribe them to make more, Jean produced a deep brown box with a thick silver ribbon and smiled. "We had to hide this for you."

I rocked onto my toes and clapped silently. "Thank you!" I handed over my credit card again, then checked the area for anyone who might be listening. I lowered my voice for good measure while Jean printed my receipt. "Did Karen Moody ever come into your shop?" I asked.

"No, thank goodness," Jean said, returning my card and slip. "Why?"

"I'm just trying to figure out where she went while she was in town," I said, catching sight of a small white van outside the window. There weren't any pictures of Oh! Fudge on Karen's Instagram, but that didn't mean she hadn't stopped by. "I've got to run," I said, unwilling to lose sight of the vehicle with Christopher's construction company logo across the side. Christopher had distributed the velvet toy-collection bags and assigned a driver to make pickups. I wanted to talk to whoever that was, and now was my chance.

"Thank you for saving the fudge," I told them. "I owe you!" I collected my things and hurried outside as the van rolled around the corner, then into a parking space.

I jogged through the crowd, desperate to catch up.

The driver jumped at the sight of me outside his door when he opened it.

"Hi!" I said, not recognizing him. "I'm Holly White. My family owns Reindeer Games tree farm. Your company built our inn last year and remodeled our café's kitchen."

He climbed out and shook my hand. "Of course. I swing by the inn a few times a week with donations. I'm Thomas."

"Nice to meet you," I said. "Any chance you have a list of pickup locations for the toy drive that I can take a look at?" I asked, too excited to make small talk. "A master list of participating shops," I clarified when he screwed up his face in confusion.

"Sure." He leaned back inside and fished a clipboard from the space between front seats. "Is this what you're after?"

I swallowed the urge to fist pump, then snapped a photo of the list with my phone instead. "Have you been anywhere in the last day or two where the shop didn't have its designated donation bag?"

"No," he said, his forehead still wrinkled. "But I don't stop everywhere every day. I only go if the shop owner calls to say the bin is full. Sometimes folks take the donations up to the inn on their own, especially if they're headed your way anyhow. This time of year, most people get over to Reindeer Games regularly."

I thanked him for his time and stepped away.

Lucky for me, I was downtown with a list of locations I could check myself to see if any bags were missing.

I climbed back into my truck to get warm, then decided to drive past the participating shops and see if the bags were visible from the road. Maybe in the process I'd find a more centralized parking spot, preferably something on the other side of the square and near the coffee shop, where I could score a steamy drink.

Traffic was thick and slow on our two-lane roads lined with shops and parking spaces. Tour busses habitually double-parked to load and unload tourists, making me frequently miss the green lights as they came and went. Eventually, I made my way around the block and began to search for an open spot. A few toy donation boxes were in clear view outside shop doors. The bins were similar to mine, each shaped like an enormous gift box, though on a smaller scale than the receptacle at the inn. The velvet sacks were used like trash bag liners, folded over the box's edge, golden drawstrings hanging out.

I stopped at another red light and drummed my thumbs against the wheel.

Meg, my ex–inn guest, came into view and I gaped. She'd told me she was leaving town when she checked out. Now, not only had I seen her at Caroline's Cupcakes the day she'd claimed to leave town, but she was still here. Her canvas tote with the teddy bear images was hooked on one shoulder. The stuffed teddy I'd seen her with on the day of Karen's murder, however, was gone.

Traffic began to move, and I crawled forward, tracking Meg with my eyes.

She entered the crosswalk, and I was forced to drive on. I waited for an opportunity to pull over, then performed an illegal U-turn when the opposite lane became somewhat clear. I earned several angry honks for my effort.

"Sorry," I mouthed, waving through my window and at my rearview mirror for good measure.

Once Meg reached the opposite curb, she entered the pie shop.

Evan's cruiser was outside.

I locked my jaw, then pulled the wheel and angled my pickup into a no parking area by the dumpster along the shop's side. I had no time to wait for a free space on a busy day, and I wanted the chance to ask Meg why I'd seen her glaring at Karen on the night the critic died.

If I was quick and quiet, Evan might not even know I was there.

My racing heart and pumping adrenaline pulled me from the cab and up the walk before I had a chance to change my mind.

I stopped behind her at the end of the pie line, then feigned surprise. "Meg? Is that you?"

She turned with a smile that quickly fell. "Oh, hi," she said, turning back around after seeing me.

"I thought you were headed out of town," I pressed, increasing the pep in my tone. "I'm glad you decided to stay. I feel absolutely awful about everything that happened at the inn. It was completely unprofessional of me not to correct Cookie for her joke about another guest. And I'm truly sorry your stay was ruined."

She shot me a disbelieving look. "What are you up to? Trying to win me over so I won't say anything else to hurt your friend, the homicidal maniac?"

A pair of women in front of Meg turned to look at us, then swiveled back around, eyes wide, and immediately began whispering.

"Not at all," I said, fighting to keep my pleasant nature in place. "I'm apologizing, and I'm glad to see you found somewhere else to stay and enjoy the town." I looked her over, trying to think of a way to get her talking. "No teddy bear today." I smiled. "Did you decide to donate him? Or were you able to deliver him after all?"

Meg's jaw sank open. "Are you following me now?"

"No!" I said, on the defense once more. "I'm just making conversation." I clamped my mouth shut, unsure where I'd gone wrong.

Meg glared. "I've lost my taste for pie." She stepped out of line, then poked a finger in my direction. "Do not follow me."

"I'm not," I squeaked. *Jeez.*

I watched miserably as Meg nearly ran away from me.

"Table for one?" a waitress asked brightly, as I was up next.

When I turned to respond, Evan was standing beside his table, watching. "No. I'm with him," I said, sighing as I dragged my way to Evan's usual booth. "Hi."

"Whatcha doing, Holly?" he asked, lips pressed flat and brows arched high.

"Getting coffee?"

He shook his head as he took a seat. "Why were you badgering Ms. Mason?"

"I wasn't trying to." I slouched onto the bench across from him. "She said she was leaving town when she checked out at the inn. I was glad to see she decided to stay."

"Did you ask her about Karen Moody?"

"No." I sighed. "I was just being nice, but she wasn't having it. Clearly, not everyone appreciates a friendly face."

He looked skeptical.

"How are you doing?" I asked, changing the subject. "Any new leads on the case against Cookie? Something that doesn't point directly at her perhaps?"

"I'm working on it," he said. "You shouldn't be."

"I wasn't. I'm shopping." Which reminded me. I hadn't seen Libby yet, and I wanted to. She knew what Evan planned to surprise me with, and I needed to convince her to tell me. How else could I come up with an equal or better gift for him? If I went too big, I could scare him away. If I went too small, he might not realize how much I wanted to impress him. "Have you seen your sister? I'm hoping to run into her while we're both buying a few last-minute gifts."

"Gifts?" Evan frowned. "Libby's been done shopping since Black Friday."

I looked at the knots and clusters of people beyond the window, hustling in and out of shops. Maybe Mom had gotten the information wrong, or Libby had lied for whatever reason, or maybe Mom had misunderstood or assumed. It was another mystery, but one at the bottom of my priority list. I'd ask Libby about Evan's surprise again tomorrow when I saw her at the Hearth.

Evan stretched his long legs under the table, and they bumped into mine. "What do you think about rescheduling the wrapping party?" he asked. "We didn't get far last night. I think we need a few more hands."

He was right. There wasn't enough time between now and Christmas Eve to do the job well—maybe not enough time to finish at all. Unless shoving things into gift bags with a few sheets of tissue paper counted as wrapping. I couldn't imagine children getting excited about unbagging toys left unwrapped under the tree.

"What do you think?" he asked. "Get the gang together. Order pizza. Make popcorn."

I loved the idea. Loved knowing Evan and I shared a friend gang, that we all got together regularly for fun, and that we could count on one another for help. Like when one of us accidentally volunteered to wrap all the donations collected before Christmas, and there were about a billion of them.

"How about tomorrow night?" he suggested.

"Perfect. I'll call Cookie and Caroline. You round up your sister and Ray."

"Deal."

Evan's phone rang, and he liberated it from his inside coat pocket and looked at the screen. His expression changed, and his gaze flickered to meet mine. "I have to take this. Sorry. But tomorrow night?" he asked, already sliding free of the booth.

"Yeah." I wanted to ask what time to tell Caroline and Cookie, and if he was bringing pizza or if I should order it, but he was already through the door.

I was puzzled, watching him on the sidewalk outside. He'd never run off to take a phone call before. He spoke in acronyms and used a lot of lawman terms sometimes, but he'd never gotten up and bolted.

The strange itching at the back of my mind returned. Mom's odd inflections lately. Libby's fake shopping. Evan and his surprise.

I hopped to my feet, the proverbial lightbulb finally kicking on. Evan, Mom, Libby. These three people might be sharing a secret. And that phone call could've been about my surprise!

I darted onto the sidewalk and turned in every direction. His cruiser was unmoved, but he was nowhere to be seen.

Meg, however, stood several doors down, talking on her phone, the fingers of her free hand curled around the strap of her ever-present canvas tote. Her eyes caught mine, and she turned away from me, climbing into the driver's side of her big white pickup truck and smoothly pulling away.

I sighed. Any chance at talking to her was completely out. I stared at the disappearing pickup, thinking about the weird teddy bear image on her bag. The logo beneath the picture registered for the first time.

The tote was from some place called the Teddy Bear Inn in Great Pines, Maine.

An inn. Had Meg run into Karen on another trip? Had they argued about something? Was that why Meg had been scowling at Karen in the foyer before dinner?

I made a mental note to research the Teddy Bear Inn online, and then Evan came back into view. He was across the street and climbing into a small blue SUV with a woman behind the wheel.

Had he run off to take that phone call because it was another woman on the line? Did he flee the scene because he thought I'd be hurt or jealous about it?

I pulled the truck keys from my coat pocket and charged around the side of the pie shop. I needed to get home. I tugged the door handle, then froze, realizing I hadn't yet unlocked it. Which meant I'd forgotten to lock up when I'd run after Meg.

I swung the door open wide, then took a thorough look behind the seat and in the bed before climbing in. No boogiemen or critic killers hiding on the floorboards or cupholders.

I started the engine and cranked up the defrosters, then ran the windshield wipers to move accumulated snow out of my line of vision. Next, I had a stern talk with myself. I needed to be less impulsive. People on television always wanted their friends or significant other to be more spontaneous, but impulsivity was at the top of my personal things-to-work-on list. There might be perfectly excellent times and places for acting first and thinking later, but running off without making sure my truck doors were locked would never be one of them.

The creeping sensation of being watched returned, and I looked up quickly, checking my surroundings. A shiver rocked through me as I waited for my truck's heater to blow warm air instead of cold. When I caught a break in traffic, I edged onto the road and pointed my grill toward home. Part of me wanted to follow Evan and the long-gone SUV, maybe figure out who he'd rushed away with and why, but that was creepy, and stalking was illegal. Plus, I had other things to do.

I motored away from town, lost in thought and slowly being warmed by the truck's heater. A few miles later, a series of letters began to form on my somewhat foggy windshield.

Stop snooping, Holly White

Chapter Eleven

I pulled over, stopping in the layer of grass and snow along the roadside. A forest of evergreens reached into the bruised sky overhead. I took a picture of the message, then texted the image to Evan.

I double-checked that my doors were locked, then did it again for good measure while trying to find enough oxygen to breathe.

My mind raced as the minutes passed. Someone had been inside my truck. And they'd left me a threat. How could I be sure nothing else had been done to the pickup? What if my brake lines were cut?

I yanked the rearview mirror, swiveling it around for a better look at the pavement behind me to search for signs of leaking fluids, but only an inky ribbon of road was visible, dark and glistening, etched between two expanses of snow.

My phone buzzed and Evan's number appeared. He'd sent a text telling me he'd notified dispatch, and both he and Deputy Wesson were on their way.

I felt my constricting lungs loosen slightly. Then filled them again, deeper this time, breathing in for eight long counts and out for nine.

Before me, the fiery hues of sunset had lost their battle against twilight.

Beside me, creeping shadows drew closer, stretching from the forest in long, gnarled fingers. Only a few newly visible stars and the lights from a distant neighborhood refused to be swallowed by the rolling darkness. I'd barely seen ten cars since leaving town, and most of those had been on the immediate outskirts, their occupants probably headed to meet friends for dinner. I could only hope the next car I saw wasn't the person who'd left me the message.

A pair of headlights appeared in my rearview mirror, and my body tensed. Thankfully, a deputy's cruiser rolled to a stop several yards from my tailgate.

I powered down my window, inhaling the icy air and feeling my brain slowly begin to shed its haze. "Thank you for coming," I told the approaching deputy.

His badge said "Wesson," and I relaxed further still. This was the man Evan had sent. He appeared to be my dad's age, with a thick salt and pepper mustache and small, kind eyes. "How are you doing," he asked. "I hear you've had quite the scare."

"Yeah," I whispered, opening my door to climb out.

"Are you injured in any way?" He scanned me with his eyes and flashlight.

"Just shaken," I said, moving out of his way. "Take a look for yourself." I'd left the truck and vents running. The message was unmistakable, though the fog I'd created made it nearly impossible to see through the glass. "Nothing else was touched or taken as far as I can tell," I went on. "I had no idea anything was wrong until the windshield began to fog. Now I'm afraid whoever left that threat might've messed with the truck mechanically as well."

Wesson slid onto the seat where I'd been, then rolled the bench back to make room for his legs. "Anything feel different as you drove? Soft brakes? Response issues when pressing the gas or difficulty steering?"

"None."

A set of approaching headlights drew my attention over one shoulder, and I turned to watch another cruiser pull off the road behind the first.

Evan launched from his car in less time than it would've taken me to shift into park and unfasten my seatbelt. He came for me in long, inhuman strides, an unfathomable expression on his face. I'd seen the look twice before, and both times the situation had been far worse than a message written on glass.

"I'm okay," I said as he collided with me, strong arms going around me in a protective vise.

My hot cheek pressed hard against the cool fabric of his sheriff's coat, and I inhaled the sweet scents of gingerbread and cologne. The tears came as I hugged him back. I hadn't even realized how upset I was until he was there to be strong for me. Now I teetered on a total breakdown.

"What's the word?" Evan called, sending his voice over my head to Wesson, behind my wheel.

Wesson responded, but my mind had tuned to the beating of Evan's heart as I clung to him, my head tucked under his chin. The racing rhythm settled slowly into an only slightly frantic pattern of sweet lub dubs.

Wesson radioed for a mechanic, who graciously met us on the roadside with a spotlight and gave my truck a once-over. He didn't find any signs of mechanical tampering, deemed the vehicle safe to drive, then wished us all a Merry Christmas and handed out individually wrapped pretzel rods that had been dipped in white chocolate and rolled in blue snowflake sprinkles: a gift from his wife to anyone who needed one tonight.

Evan smiled at the pretzel, then me, and I was reminded yet again how much he loved life in Mistletoe and of the nature of the man before me.

I drove home more slowly than I'd driven to town, checking constantly for Evan's headlights behind me and wondering about the person who'd gone so boldly into my truck on a crowded day downtown. Then I remembered how deceptive a crowd can be. Hundreds of people seeing only their immediate surroundings, thinking only of their conversations, their next stops, their children in tow. Sometimes, being surrounded by people was the most dangerous place to be.

And like everyone else today, I hadn't seen anything unusual. Despite the fact someone had clearly been watching me.

Meg came quickly back to mind. She could've messed with my truck after storming out of the pie shop when I'd stayed behind to visit with Evan. Then there was the reporter who'd come to the inn, looking for a story. Maybe she'd decided to create her own material when I hadn't given her any? I liked this theory best, though it was more than a longshot, because it meant a killer hadn't been inside my truck, just a young reporter desperate to make a name for herself.

Then there were all the other people who might've wanted to hurt Karen. She'd done a lot of damage with her reviews over the years. Any business owner who blamed her for their problems could've come to Mistletoe to confront her. Maybe even a wronged friend or an ex. I was certain Karen had burned plenty of bridges without caring who was standing on them. What I didn't like about my random retribution theory was that if the killer didn't live here, why hadn't they left? Why not return home and establish an alibi? The only thing that bugged me more was the idea of another murderer in my community.

I shifted into park outside the inn, and Evan pulled the cruiser up beside me. I handed him a set of boxes when he climbed out. I took the other two.

"Planning a party?" he asked, looking pointedly at the wine cases.

"Yeah," I teased, the weight and gentle clinking of glass a dead giveaway that the bottles were empty. "I was so shaken up I drank it all on the drive home."

Evan headed for the front door instead of the back, then set his boxes aside. He removed a small knife from his duty belt and cut the line of yellow tape. "We're finished with this area," he said.

"Thanks."

The steps were covered in toy donations, and I remembered for the first time since I'd become distracted that I'd been on a duel mission in town. I was supposed to be looking for the missing velvet bag. And tracking Karen's final days via online photos. Though, to be honest, I recognized all the locations, and none were very revealing. They were typical tourist shots and a lot of scenic views.

I let us inside, relieved no new farm guests would have to see our beautiful porch as a crime scene.

Evan followed, delivering the cases of empty bottles to my office, then making repeated trips until all the toys had been brought inside as well.

He closed the front door, then my office door when he delivered the final bundle. "You want to talk about it?"

I shrugged, attempting to quickly sort and organize the new inventory. "Maybe. You have time for coffee?"

"Maybe." He smiled.

I led him to the kitchen and made two cups of coffee, then unwrapped my pretzel and took a bite. "I've barely asked any questions about what happened," I told him. "I'm being extremely careful. I'm not running around with a bullhorn or neon sign. I don't understand why I'm being threatened."

Evan sighed, holding his mug without drinking. "You've played a major role in the arrest of two killers. Two years running. Each at this time of year. People are talking, and there's an argument to be made that you aren't stirring the pot alone."

I groaned. It wasn't enough that I had to watch everything I said while trying to help Cookie. Now I had to worry about what every person in town might be saying too? "So anyone could've made the jump to assume I was getting involved, then said so unwittingly in front of the killer."

Evan tented his brows. "Maybe, but I'm sure it didn't help that you marched around town defending Cookie's name to anyone who would listen the same day Karen's death showed up in the paper. You didn't have to announce your intention to investigate. Whether you meant to or not, you were vehemently setting the stage. Now the gossip mill is running full speed, and you're the center of every story. Why do you think I spend so much time at the pie shop?"

I deflated against the countertop. "I thought you might really like pie."

"I do." He grinned. "I also like you, and I hear a lot from my favorite booth. I see a lot through the window too."

"Did you happen to see Meg or Bonnie while we were chatting today? Maybe one of them saw me talking with you and assumed we're working together."

Evan's eyes darkened. "We aren't working together. I need you to hear that."

I crossed my arms, finished with the pretzel and unhappy with where the conversation was going. "I know we aren't, but you have to promise me you won't put Cookie in jail."

"I don't have any plans to put Cookie in jail," he said.

My frown deepened. "That wasn't a promise that you won't."

Evan's eyes narrowed. "You act as if I'm not trying to figure this out. Like you don't trust me to be good at what I do. Or to do the right thing."

I glared back, unwilling to budge, but not wanting to fight, and that was the only way this discussion would end. "That's not what I'm saying."

His jaw locked and a muscle pulsed beneath the skin.

The grandfather clock began to chime, and I forced my shoulders back. "I need to set out some wine and make a char-cuterie board for my last two guests. I need to make up for the trauma they've experienced." Not that some nuts or dried fruits and meats would help, but the wine might.

Evan nodded then saw himself out with a muttered goodbye.

A little while later, I retired to my personal quarters with a French loaf, a wedge of cheese, and some apple slices, too tired to mingle and assuming the last remaining couple would enjoy having the inn to themselves.

I curled onto my window seat, filled with fancy, overstuffed pillows, and stared at the falling snow. I tallied my to-do list, relieving myself of gift-wrapping duty tonight and putting off my cleaning and paperwork until morning. I'd have help with the toys tomorrow. And once my mind was clear enough to safely use the little torch I melted the glass with, I'd work on my jewelry orders.

Until then, there was something big on my mind.

I opened an internet browser on my phone and searched for Teddy Bear Inn, Great Falls, Maine.

A dozen pages of results came back. I selected the inn's website, then flipped through the pictures. The inn was a large log cabin surrounded by pines. Not surprisingly, a bear-themed detail was present in every nook and cranny. The rooms were nice, if a little outdated, but that could be intentional given the whole cabin vibe.

Breakfast was billed as traditional but looked a little boring. And the gift shop sold a custom line of teddys and logoed paraphernalia. The bears were all identical to the one I'd seen Meg carrying.

Intuition slapped hard enough to leave a mark across my forehead, and I clicked over to the page titled "History of the Inn." An image of Meg appeared, several years younger, her expression full of hope. According to the text, she'd inherited an outdated lodge she was sure to lose, thanks to the costs of maintenance and upkeep. Brokenhearted by the thought, Meg went out on a limb, emptied her savings, and opened the Teddy Bear Inn. To honor her grandma's legacy, she'd built the theme around her grandma's pattern for homemade teddy bears.

I held my breath as I opened a new window and searched for Karen Moody's name along with reviews for Meg's property.

The top-ranked result was titled "Teddy Bear *Don't Go* Inn." Featured in last month's issue of *New England Magazine* under things to be thankful for, Karen suggested anyone who hadn't visited should indeed count their blessings. Then, she continued to destroy every aspect of Meg's ode to her grandma, from the food—"barely a step above cafeteria-quality" to the decor—"so unapologetically outdated, one might suspect they'd accidentally walked onto the set of *Twilight Zone*," to the bears—"abundant and unnervingly everywhere."

I set my phone in my lap, mind racing.

Meg had checked in on the same day as Karen.

She'd been glaring at her in the foyer before dinner.

She'd been the first to check out after the body was found.

She'd seen Cookie with the nutcracker. She knew it existed, knew where to find it and whose fingerprints would be on it.

And she'd tattled to the deputies about Cookie's harsh words at her first opportunity.

How could all that be a coincidence?

Chapter Twelve

I motored back into town the next morning after thoroughly cleaning my windshield. I'd filled all the jewelry orders I'd collected from Kinley and made excellent progress on the online orders as well. And all before ten AM. Insomnia due to anxiety over a lurking killer probably wasn't great for my physical or mental health, but it had gotten me out of bed at five o'clock and worked wonders on my productivity.

The stack of finished products teetered precariously on the seat beside me. Each had been carefully packaged, labeled, and sealed in a bubble mailer for safe travels to its new home. I smiled at the thought of tiny glass gumdrops, snowmen, and candy canes setting off on new adventures. With eight days left until Christmas, every package would reach its destination in time for the big day.

I parked outside the post office, then gathered the envelopes into my arms and got in line. Mailing packages so close to Christmas took a special kind of patience, which wasn't usually my strong suit. But when I had a goal, I could be infinitely calm.

I ran mentally over the list of toy donation drop-off locations while I waited, making a plan of attack. A figure eight around the square made the most sense with the least amount of backtracking. As a bonus, I would pass several stores I still wanted to visit for last-minute gifts.

The woman ahead of me finished up, and I shuffled forward, trying hard not to drop any packages. A man in a brown leather jacket and dark jeans pretended not to watch me perform a goofy balancing act on my way to the counter. I hadn't noticed the man come in, and he didn't have anything to mail. He shifted his attention to the flat rate postage display when he saw me looking. A moment later, he left.

I watched as he held the door for a woman on his way out. Something about him set off my internal alert system. I couldn't explain it, but I didn't like it.

When I returned to the sidewalk several minutes later, the man in the brown leather jacket was nowhere in sight. I drove to Main Street, scanning faces more carefully than usual at every red light. Then I waited for an available parking space in a conspicuous location before climbing out. No more parking illegally and just out of sight for me. I pressed the lock button twice for good measure when I walked away.

Voices of a children's choir pumped through speakers on telephone poles around the square. Kids in holiday sweaters sang "Frosty the Snowman" beside the town's massive thirty-foot spruce. A crowd applauded when the children bowed.

I circled the busiest blocks on foot, checking toy donation sites for their velvet bags. After reading Karen's awful review of Meg's inn, I wasn't convinced this task was worth the trouble, but I also wasn't convinced that it wasn't. And it seemed better to do too much work than too little, so here I was.

Store by store, every bag was in its place. None were missing. None were in an evidence locker at the sheriff's department— well, except for mine.

Clearly I was on the wrong track but I didn't know where to find the right one.

I bought a bag of warm kettle corn from a vendor to help me think.

When the bookstore came into view, I switched gears and went shopping.

A little bell above the door jingled as I stepped inside. The warm dry air welcomed me with scents of ink and paper. I admired the cases and stacks of books around us. Warm woods and high ceilings gave the limited square footage a much larger feel, and Debra had done an amazing job of turning the perfectly ordinary space into something unequivocally inviting. From strategically placed seating and throw pillows, to her artistic hometown nods: wooden fleur-de-lis bookends; water paintings of the Garden District; framed photographs of the French Quarter; and soft jazz, played on hidden speakers, instead of the typical holiday tunes.

"Hey!" Debra Jo called, popping out from behind a nearby display. "How's it going?"

"Not bad," I said. "You?"

"Very well." She smiled, absently rubbing a small charm attached to her necklace. "This is Christmas in Mistletoe. I'm not sure it gets any better."

"I can't argue with that," I said, trying not to stare at the charm pinched between her thumb and forefinger. A golden letter P, I realized, when she let it drop against her collarbone. I wasn't sure what it stood for, but I imagined making her a little gingerbread woman to go with it. She could have blue eyes and glasses like Debra Jo.

"Are you looking for anything in particular?" she asked.

"Kind of," I said. "I'd love to find a big book of photos for my friend Ray. Do you know him?"

Her smile brightened. "He takes pictures for the *Gazette*, right? And helps Cookie with her calendars."

"That's the guy." I definitely needed to find a gift that would make him smile.

"Any certain type of images in mind? Rainforests? Cityscapes?" she asked, heading toward the back of the store.

I chewed my bottom lip, following. "I'm hoping I'll know it when I see it."

"Fair enough." She stopped at a table near the checkout counter. Large photo books were arranged in half circles on a table.

"Be right back," she told me, slipping away to ring up a few customers.

I followed her briefly with my gaze, then thumbed through the photography books on display, unsure which would most please Ray. Travel photos from around the world didn't seem quite right, and sepia images of New York City in the early 1900s seemed too pretentious. Flowers and galaxies were more my things than his. And a book titled *Midwestern Collection* was mostly sunsets and cornfields. But then I saw it—a book of farm animals. I smiled as I paged through the photos of bunnies in bonnets and piglets dressed as pirates. A giggle rocked through me, and I snapped the book shut. This was everything I hadn't known I wanted and more. I tucked it under one arm, then went to select a few new releases for myself before finally making my way to the register.

Debra Jo spoke softly to a handsome blue-eyed man behind the counter. He cupped her chin in his hand as he pressed a soft kiss to her lips, and then they just looked at one another, smiling.

The exchange was tender and intimate, making me an unintentional voyeur with nowhere else to go.

I feigned interest in a rotating display of pens and bookmarks.

"Holly?" she asked. "Everything okay?"

"Yep." I grabbed a few bookmarks blindly, adding them to my pile, and deposited it all on the counter. "I think I'm all set," I said. "Thank you again for the book you brought me the other night. I'd planned to bring you some whoopie pies as a big thanks, but I walked off without them this morning."

Debra Jo waved me off. "The book was a gift. No need to reciprocate, though I feel it should be noted that I will never say no to whoopie pies."

I laughed.

She looked to the man at her side. "Holly, this is my husband, Jon."

"Nice to meet you," he said, offering me his hand for a shake across the counter, which I accepted. Jon was tall and broad, unmistakably fit, and with a distinct edge to his stare.

"You too." My gaze tracked to his hand in mine, calloused and rough, with puckered burn scars that stretched over his finger and disappeared beneath the cuff of his red flannel shirt.

He released me, then checked his watch. His smile tightened, and he placed a kiss on his wife's head. "Time for me to get going."

She nodded, her smile slipping slightly. "Be safe. See you soon."

I waited while he made his exit, then smiled at Debra Jo again. "That man is clearly smitten. How long have you been married?"

"Forever, I think." She laughed. "He's a good man. I can't imagine life without him."

The words warmed my chest, and I wondered if I'd have a husband I adored so unapologetically one day. I certainly hoped so. But it felt a little risky to dream.

"How are things going at the inn?" she asked. "It's absolutely charming, by the way. I don't think I said the words aloud while I was there, but I was thinking them all night. You've done a magnificent job."

"Thanks. That means a lot," I said, the familiar tug of pride in my chest. "Nearly all the guests have checked out, and some of the reservations are beginning to cancel, but I'm keeping my chin up." I paused to consider my words. It seemed shameful to sound positive when someone had been killed, but I wasn't sure how else to answer. "I was glad to see so many members of your book club venture out," I said, changing the subject.

Debra shot me a disbelieving look. "Are you kidding? Invite us back anytime. The experience was so perfectly Mistletoe. We all had a blast. We meant what we said about including us in your work." She winked conspiratorially.

I considered that a moment, recalling the book club's comment about seven armchair detectives. Then I checked over my shoulder for signs of eavesdroppers. "About that," I said. "Can I ask you a question?"

Her brows raised, and her chin dipped slightly in confirmation. Her fingertips returned to the charm on her necklace.

"Do you know Bonnie from the Gumdrop Shop?"

Debra Jo bunched her perfectly sculpted brows. "Of course. She's part of our book club."

"What?" I rocked back on my heels, stunned to the core. "I had no idea. I can't believe I didn't know that."

Debra Jo laughed. "I can't believe it didn't come up when we were at the inn. She's usually a hot topic."

"How so?"

"She's pretty hardcore," Debra Jo said. "She rarely misses a meeting. I was a little surprised not to see her the other night, but she's not a fan of the classics. Maybe that's why she skipped. Or I suppose she might've had a prior commitment. Holidays and all."

"Maybe," I said, still feeling off-balance from the revelation. "It's too bad she missed the meeting."

Debra Jo nodded, looking amused and a little guilty for saying so. "You'd have enjoyed her. She's our true crime buff, and she's obsessed with mysteries of any kind and reads them almost exclusively."

I tried to imagine all the things Bonnie could've learned from the pages of true crime and mystery novels. Maybe she even knew how to get away with murder.

Debra rang up and bagged my purchases as we talked. "She's smart as a whip, and to be honest, that makes her kind of a drag when we read a good whodunnit because she always spoils them

125

for us. I guess it makes her feel smart to figure it out before everyone else, but just once I'd like the chance to do that myself. No spoilers."

I grinned for camaraderie's sake, but I could've gone for a little insight on my current mystery. I'd cheerfully ask Bonnie for help if I could be certain she wasn't the killer. But I wasn't ready to discount anyone yet.

I paid for the books and told Debra about the wrapping party tonight. She and Jon were more than welcome to help if they were interested. It'd be a night of free pizza, popcorn, cookies, and guaranteed silliness with my crew. She promised to mention it to Jon, before I slipped outside.

Cookie dashed immediately past me, carrying a length of white material that fanned out behind her like a flag.

"Hey!" I called. "Cookie! Hold up." I caught her at the corner when she stopped to wait for the signal to cross. "Where are you going?" I asked.

She looked at me as if I had candy canes sprouting from my head. "Holly!"

"Hi," I said, laughing at her utter shock.

"What are you doing here?"

"Shopping." I lifted my bag into view. "Do you want to come by tonight for a wrapping party? Evan's going to ask Ray and Libby. I just mentioned it to Debra Jo at the bookstore." I peeked at my phone. Evan hadn't been thrilled with me when he'd left last night, but he wasn't one to hold a grudge when we argued, and the wrapping party had been his idea, so he'd be there. I was sure of it, even if I wasn't sure he'd be speaking to me.

"Sounds good," she said. "What time?"

"Seven?" I guessed. I hadn't decided on a time, and it didn't really matter. I was thankful for the help anytime anyone wanted to give it.

"See you then," she said, bunching the material close to her chest and stepping away.

"Hey, what is that?" I asked.

She looked at the fabric in her hands. "Nothing. Why?"

I frowned. "Is it a bed sheet?" I asked. "Are you making something with it?" Cookie was an amazingly talented seamstress, but I couldn't imagine what she was creating now. Another costume for Theodore? But why was she behaving so strangely?

She fanned the material out and I inspected the item more closely. "It's a choir robe," she said.

I frowned. It looked like something pulled out of a Brontë novel. "Why do you have a choir robe?"

"For choir."

"What choir?"

"I'm in a small production on Christmas Eve," she said proudly.

The traffic light changed, and the signal instructed pedestrians it was safe to cross.

"Gotta go," she said. "See you tonight!"

I shook my head, trying to knock the cuckoo off that encounter and failing miserably.

I swiped my phone to life and regained my bearings. I was nearly finished checking the donation bins on this block, and it was definitely time for hot chocolate and kettle corn.

The clattering of trash cans caught my attention as I headed back in the direction I'd been going before I'd stopped to chase

Cookie. I peered into the alley where the sound seemed to have originated and saw Bonnie darting across the narrow space between buildings, then around back.

A pair of men stood between us, several yards away, and both turned in the direction Bonnie had run. One ducked out of sight before I got a good look at him; the other tried to do the same, but he was too late.

The man I'd seen in the post office ran a hand through his hair, shifting his brown leather coat, and revealing the handgun and holster beneath.

Chapter Thirteen

B y seven o'clock, the inn was hopping. My only paying guests, the Hendersons, were out snowshoeing under the stars, but my friends, along with a couple hundred toys, had taken over the first floor.

Mom arrived early to set up a buffet of finger foods and sweets, the ultimate gift-wrapping fuel. I'd put on a peppy holiday playlist and a pot of coffee. The pizza was nearly gone, and the popcorn was on the counter.

Ray and Libby had brought an enormous amount of festive paper, ribbons, and bows, which was excellent because I was already running low.

Caroline arrived next, looking like an exhausted cover girl with her perfect porcelain doll face and designer clothes. She hugged each of us tightly in welcome, then kicked her boots off near the door. She tossed her coat and purse in my office. "Man, I've missed you guys," she said. "I hired two more employees to help at the shop, but business just gets busier. I feel like I haven't left the shop in a month. I'm not even sure what day it is."

"Yet here you are," I said, ready to hug her all over again. "You don't even know what day it is, but I put up the Bat Signal and you appear."

"What are friends for?" she asked. "I'm just glad you needed help wrapping gifts and not baking. I've had enough of that for today." She took a steadying breath as she examined the mountains of toys. "I see Christopher's toy drive is a success. Imagine that." She grinned.

"He's not Santa Claus," I said. "He's just a nice guy with a beard."

"Yeah, right," she rebutted. "A beard and a team of elves who help him make gifts for people at Christmas. This inn and your mom's new kitchen for starters. And he's collecting a zillion toys for children."

I smiled. "They weren't elves. Those guy were just a little shorter than average."

"They were grown men under five foot five. A whole crew of them, and they *looked* alike."

"You don't know how tall they are," I said, laughing. But she was right: they were oddly small and looked a lot alike. Did elves look alike?

"Come on," she urged. "Surely you see it. You're supposed to be the detective."

My smile fell by a fraction. I forced it back into place, but I was too late.

Caroline's eyes widened, and she took me by the elbow to steer me away from the laughter and chitchat. "What's going on?" she whispered. "Does it have anything to do with Cookie's situation?"

I checked for listening ears, then filled her in on the wiki version of my week.

"Oof," she said, blinking long and slow. "This is just like last year."

My dad bustled into view before I could respond. He was dressed like the guy on the paper towel ads. Red plaid flannel, suspenders, jeans—it was his usual everyday attire. At the moment, he also had a pitcher in one hand and a stack of plastic cups in the other. "Eggnog?" he asked. "Your mother made it, but it's Granny White's special recipe."

Caroline and I shook our heads. Granny White's eggnog rivaled Cookie's special tea for alcohol content, and a single cup would probably knock me out cold. Caroline rarely drank because she felt it wasn't good for her skin.

"Maybe later," I said, wrapping my arms around him and giving a squeeze. "Thank you for coming tonight. I know how busy you are."

"Never too busy for you," he said, pressing a kiss to the top of my head.

I stepped back with a grin, and Dad took the eggnog into the parlor.

I led Caroline to the kitchen for some hot coffee. She looked as if she could use it, and I knew I could.

When we returned to the action, steaming mugs in hands, our friends were already hard at work. They'd formed an assembly line that began with Ray, selecting toys from my office, then measuring them for paper in the parlor. From there, Mom and Dad wrapped the toys and Libby applied the ribbon and bow.

Libby saw us watching and waved us in. "Come on. We're getting backed up already."

Caroline hurried to the small pile of gifts at Libby's side. "What can I do?"

Libby pointed to the presents one by one. "Truck, train, doll, doll, puzzle."

"Got it." Caroline grabbed the master list of names Christopher had provided, along with a stack of name tags and a marker.

I went to answer the door when I heard someone stomping on the porch, presumably shedding snow from their shoes before entering. I hesitated for a moment, temporarily trapped by fear, then swept the door open with a smile. "Merry Christmas!" I called, certain I was safe with my family and friends at my side.

Samantha Moss froze, fist raised to knock. "Hi." She dropped her hand and raised one dark eyebrow. "I stink at wrapping gifts, but I brought wine."

I tugged her inside, thrilled that she'd come. "Samantha's here!"

The crowd welcomed her from their spots in the assembly line.

She performed a reluctant, hip-high wave at the crowd.

I took her wine into the kitchen.

When I returned, Samantha had been incorporated into the toy-wrapping process. She carried gifts from my office to Ray, who'd moved into the single duty of cutting paper for the selected toy.

Most of the group sang along to "Holly Jolly Christmas," which was playing through the speaker in the parlor. Samantha watched them carefully and was guarded but almost smiling. I brought her a plate of cookies and set them on my desk. "I'm glad you're here," I told her. She looked like she needed to hear it. "We all are. Thank you for coming."

She shrugged. "It's for the kids. I like some kids. And it's not like I can give them wine."

I laughed. "Definitely not."

The doorbell rang again.

Cookie stood outside, looking over her shoulder at Evan and Theodore on the inn's walkway. She had a pile of luggage at her feet. "Oh!" She started when she noticed me. "Hello. I ran into Evan in the parking lot. He's waiting with Theodore while I look for your dad."

"Dad's here," I said. "Are you okay?"

My dad was on his feet at the sound of his name. He met me at the door. "Hey, Cookie," he said, dusting crumbs from his hands. "Come on in. Do you need help with your things?" He gathered the luggage into his arms, then moved the suitcases deeper into the foyer while he waited for an answer.

"Where are you going?" I asked, swinging my attention back to her.

"Here," she said. "I was hoping I could stay with you until all this hubbub blows over. And maybe Theodore can stay in your stables with the horses. They all get along really well."

"Of course," Dad said, grabbing his coat and hat from the hooks in the hall.

Evan coughed to cover a laugh on the walkway, still holding Theodore's lead.

Dad kissed Mom's cheek, then stepped into his boots. "I'll show Theodore to his room and let the ladies show you to yours. Now, come on in here before you freeze."

Cookie hopped inside. "I'd hoped you'd say yes," she told me. "I said my goodbyes to Theodore in the truck."

I watched through the little window as Evan passed the goat's lead to Dad, then headed my way.

He kissed my head when he entered and shut the door behind him. "Sorry about yesterday."

I felt the heat rush over my cheeks, and I smiled. "Me too. I'm glad you're here."

"You need help," he said, setting a palm at the small of my back. "Where else would I be?"

I bit my bottom lip and tried not to collapse onto the floor.

"Now," Cookie said, fixing Evan with a steely gaze, "you can tell that deputy of yours to stop following me. It gives me the creeps. Maybe you can keep an eye on me instead. I like you, and we both like Holly. I'll just stick with her and make it easy for everyone."

Someone turned the volume down on my speaker, and I realized our friends had drawn closer to listen.

Evan's focus was on Cookie. He widened his stance and tucked his hands into his coat pockets. "I don't have a deputy following you."

She chewed her lip, clearly disappointed. "Are you sure? Holly saw him too, when we were taking Theodore to tinkle."

Everyone looked at me.

"I saw someone retreating in dark-colored clothing," I said. "It was busy, and the person blended into the crowd right after I took notice. I didn't see a face, and I didn't actually see anyone watching us."

"Do you think she was being followed?" Evan asked.

Caroline and Mom bookended Cookie, sliding their arms around her for comfort as the disturbing conversation unfolded.

"Maybe," I said. "I'm not sure what I saw, but if she says she's being followed, I believe her."

Evan nodded. "Then it's probably a good idea you've decided to stay here," he told Cookie. "You'll be safer on the farm with the Whites and Libby than alone in town. I'll add a security patrol up here and make sure one of my deputies is doing a loop around the farm several times a day. Our presence should be a deterrent for whoever is making you uncomfortable."

Cookie nodded, looking more vulnerable than I'd ever seen. "Thanks. I knew this was the right place for Theodore and me to be." She turned her watery gaze on me. "You're probably so used to being followed by now, it's like old hat. And if we're together, I can pretend the person is after you instead."

I gave her a sarcastic thumbs-up. She was right about me being followed, though. I had more experience in that particular area than anyone would want.

"I don't mind paying either," she said. "Since all those guests left, I'll just take one of the empty rooms."

"Heavens," Mom said, "be serious, Cookie. Your money's no good here. Come on. Let's get you settled." She and Caroline grabbed Cookie's bags from the foyer and hauled them upstairs.

The front door opened, and Evan darted toward the sound.

Dad's voice carried through the rooms, along with the stomping of several sets of feet. "Theodore is all tucked in for the night," Dad said. "Cindy Lou Who is with him, and look who I found on my way back here to wrap gifts."

I rounded the corner to greet him, unsure whom he'd run into outside, and already making plans to fish my sneaky cat out of the stables before the temperature dropped again.

Debra Jo, Becky, Brooke, Jean, and Millie were back.

"Book club!" I called, smiling widely and hurrying to welcome them.

Cookie yipped with glee at the sight of her friends as she and the others made their way back downstairs.

Mom pushed her buffet on them while Dad handed out cups of eggnog and Samantha poured wine.

When we reassembled to wrap gifts, there were enough helpers to get a second line going before the crackling fire.

I felt the perfection of the moment in my bones and made a point of memorizing the details. The music, the laughter, and the beautifully wrapped pile of toys for children on Christmas morning all filled my heart with glee.

Then the doorbell rang once more, and the impossible happed. The moment improved.

Ray's mom, Fay, and her bridesmaids arrived with a few of my mom's close friends.

It took a while to get started on the work again, but my heart soared with the realization that we had a real chance at wrapping all the gifts tonight.

Ray relinquished his position in favor of snapping photos as we worked, capturing candid and posed photos for the paper and posterity. He took a close-up of me, then moved into my personal space to show me.

"That's awful," I said.

"Wrong." He examined the photo on his camera's little screen. "You're beautiful, Holly White. Inside and out. And I can think of about twenty others who'll say the same thing." He motioned to the group around us.

"Not Samantha," I said, bumping his hip with mine.

He raised the camera again, taking more photos and smiling. "She's only here because of you."

I liked the idea I could bring people together, but I didn't love being the subject of any conversation. "Your mom looks happy," I said, nodding toward her and her bridesmaids, Ray's aunts, Kay and May, and his sisters, Shae and Renee.

"She is." He smiled warmly. "I like seeing her this way."

"Hard to believe it was only a year ago that you were determined to kick Pierce out of her life."

He slid his eyes in my direction. "I didn't think Dad had been gone long enough. But a wise friend of mine told me I had to trust Mom to make her own decisions. I'm glad I did."

"What are you two up to?" Libby asked, carrying a trio of empty wine glasses toward the kitchen.

"Just feeling thankful," he said. "You?"

"I'm on a wine run. The bridesmaids are feeling thirsty."

I laughed. "I'll help."

"Wait for me," Evan said. He joined us with four empty mugs in hand. "I've been sent for coffee."

I led them to the kitchen, then pulled Samantha's donated wine from the fridge and set it on the counter for Libby to uncork.

Evan set the mugs on the counter beside me as I prepared a new pot of coffee to brew.

"Hey," he said softly, searching me with keen, investigative eyes. "Why didn't you tell me about the person following Cookie? I just talked to you last night, but you didn't mention it. What else are you leaving out?"

I blushed furiously, feeling scolded in front of friends. "I didn't see the person's face, and I had no way to confirm her suspicions. What was I supposed to tell you?"

"Maybe that she thought I had a deputy following her?"

I scoffed. "If it was true, then you'd have already known. And either way, it was Cookie's news. Did you yell at her too? Or do you only enjoy yelling at me?"

"I'm not . . ." he let his eyes dip shut, then reopen. "I'm not yelling. I'm frustrated, and I need you to talk to me."

Ray and Libby refilled the wine glasses silently, then tiptoed away.

Samantha appeared in the doorway, stopping them. She took the glasses from their hands, then motioned them back into the kitchen. "I've got these, you all pick teams and scrap it out. I'll be back to take on the winner." She winked at me, then disappeared.

I smiled.

Evan frowned.

"Fine," I said. I dropped my hands to my sides and resolved to see his point. Even if he was being rude. I probably should've told him about Cookie's possible stalker. I just hadn't thought of it. Every time I'd spoken to him lately, I'd been in the middle of something more immediate.

I filled him in on Meg and her Teddy Bear inn, and that Karen had torn it to pieces in an awful review last month. Then

I told him about Meg's weird behavior before Karen's death and her refusal to speak to me on the subject afterward.

Evan leaned against the counter. "I already know all that. What else?"

"You know?" I asked, feeling unjustifiably betrayed. What else hadn't *he* told *me*?

He tapped the sheriff's badge on his belt as if he could read my thoughts.

I rolled my eyes. "Okay. I also got a list of the shops Christopher gave those velvet toy-collection bags to, and I've been trying to see whose is missing. I figure whoever doesn't have theirs might be the person who killed Karen." I'd told him my theory already, but I hadn't told him I'd put it in action today, and I suspected he'd want to know.

He sighed again. "That's already been done."

My jaw dropped. "How is that possible?" I snapped. "Every time I see you, you're sitting at the pie shop."

Evan's brows rose. "I'm the sheriff," he said slowly, as if I was in possession of a very low IQ. "I have an entire department of well-trained, fully capable deputies covering this case from every angle. We've already checked for the missing bag."

"Fine. How about this?" I asked, before telling him about the man I'd seen at the post office, then again in the alley. And the way Bonnie had seemed to be sneaking around him. And the fact that I was almost positive he'd seen Bonnie. I paused dramatically before adding the bit about the gun that he'd worn beneath his jacket.

Evan frowned.

"Now, it's your turn. Help me solve this mystery," I challenged. "My mom, your sister, Caroline, and Cookie are all

139

acting completely bizarre over the most inconsequential things." I flicked my gaze to Libby, then back. "Desserts for Fay's wedding reception. A choir event. Shopping."

Evan dropped his head, then slid a look in Libby's direction. I raised my brows at her. "How was the shopping yesterday?" She blanched.

Ray wrinkled his nose. "What?"

"Mom said Libby took the afternoon off to do some last-minute shopping. I was downtown, but I never saw her."

"It was busy," she said. "We probably just missed one another."

I pursed my lips and scowled.

"That reminds me," Evan said, stepping closer and changing his voice into something sweet and smooth. "I realized earlier that I never asked you to be my date to Fay and Pierce's wedding."

I looked into his green eyes and felt confusion take hold. He'd completely and abruptly changed the subject, but my addled mind didn't quite care. I'd been waiting for this invitation for weeks, and I'd almost given up on it. "I'd like that," I said, smiling from ear to ear.

His eyes crinkled at the sides and he reached for my hands, lacing his fingers with mine.

"Aww," Libby said.

Ray put his arm around her.

Evan smiled. "So," he said, before releasing me, "you get to live with Cookie. I think I speak for everyone when I say I'm mildly concerned, and also a little jealous."

We all laughed. Life with Cookie would definitely be interesting but completely worth it.

I filled the mugs with freshly brewed coffee, then helped Evan carry them back to the parlor. The stacks of beautifully wrapped gifts had doubled since we'd left a few minutes before.

I lifted my coat from a hook and stepped into waiting boots. "I'm going to run over to the stables and get Cindy," I told everyone, projecting my voice.

"I thought she was an indoor cat," Ray said, looking mildly confused.

"She was until I moved to the inn," I said. "Now she sneaks in and out every time someone opens the door."

Evan donned his coat and boots with a smile. "Determined and defiant. I can't imagine where she picked up those maddening traits."

I pointed my finger at him in warning, then turned for the door.

The Hendersons were outside, running across the lawn toward the porch steps, snowshoes in hand.

"Evening," Evan said, slipping instantly into lawman mode. "Everything all right?"

The expressions on their faces clearly answered that question.

"Fire," Mrs. Henderson said. "Just beyond those trees. It's big, and flames are shooting high. There's an awful animal sound." She paused to cover her mouth as she met us at the end of the walkway. "I think something's hurt."

"Cindy!" I leapt into a wild run, adrenaline racing, heart and feet pounding my way across the too large field between the inn and forest.

In the distance, flames licked against the onyx sky.

Chapter Fourteen

I ran until my lungs burned and my face stung from the icy air. Evan barked orders behind me, either speaking to someone on his phone or to the others who followed. I couldn't be sure, and I couldn't bring myself to look. I focused on the fiery hues of red and orange waving between the trees, beyond the stables, and I prayed Cindy Lou Who wasn't there, wasn't hurt—or worse.

My feet breached the tree line and I heard the low, guttural wail. It was undoubtedly the sound the Hendersons had heard. I'd worried the first time I'd heard it too, but that was years ago, and I now knew this was Cindy's form of verbal communication. She used the lamenting mer-ow-el when she was angry, when she begged, or when she delivered a dead mouse to my feet. Tonight she was using it as an alarm. Cindy was afraid, and with good reason.

Someone had started a fire near the stables where she'd been visiting Theodore, and now the flames reached high into the sky.

A spotlight flashed through the branches above, searching for the source of the heart-breaking sound. "There," Evan said, grabbing my shoulder and pulling me to a stop.

He passed me the flashlight, then continued on toward the fire.

A moment later, he was back. "Thank you," he said, taking the light. "The flames are in your campfire ring."

I breathed easier, then grabbed on to a limb.

Evan stilled the beam of light above us, reflecting Cindy's green eyes in the night.

On the ground, I heard the voices and footfalls of others from the inn. My dad called out orders, arranging water to stop the fire, while Evan echoed back that it wasn't an emergency.

I focused on the branches, my footing, and adjusting my balance as I moved, refusing to look down. I hated heights, and if I let my mind move away from my goal for even a moment, I'd be as stuck as Cindy.

She fidgeted above me, trying desperately to find somewhere else to go as plumes of acrid smoke blew our way. She saw me and emitted the low warbling cry once more.

"It's okay," I told her. "You're okay."

From my new position, I could see the firepit. Someone had created a large teepee of branches inside the round, brick-lined hole we used in other seasons for bonfires. But this fire was tall enough to be seen for miles, lacing its blazing hands into the night sky.

I rested my shoulder against the tree trunk, feet anchored on lower limbs, and bark biting into one palm as I tested my balance, reaching for Cindy with the other hand. She continued her cries as I hooked my fingers under her middle and dragged her toward me. She resisted, and I twisted to free my second hand as well. I levered her closer, attempting to pry her from the branches. She stretched her legs and nails trying to remain stuck where she was.

"I've got you," I promised, then cooed every sweet sentiment I could think of, willing her to trust me.

Eventually, she gave up and thrust her body against mine. For a moment, I thought we'd both tumble to the ground.

"Pass her to me." Dad's voice was nearby, no longer on the ground, and I realized he'd climbed up after me. "I've got Cindy. You get you."

Together, we managed the exchange, and Dad lowered Cindy to safety.

I retraced my steps to the lowest limb, then let myself look down.

Evan was exactly where I'd left him. Lighting my path and staring intently, as if he could protect me with his thoughts. He dropped the light onto the ground and reached for me when I made the final jump. It was only a few feet to the ground, but I stumbled under the impact, and Evan steadied me. He pulled me close and held me tight before slowly letting me go.

Dad clapped him on the shoulder, then handed me my still complaining cat.

I tucked Cindy under my coat and lowered the zipper so her head could pop out beneath mine. She protested every step I took toward the group gathered near the fire.

They turned to look at us as we approached, then parted to expose a message etched into the earth around the firepit.

Stop. Before someone else gets hurt.

* * *

The Hendersons checked out the next morning before breakfast, and I didn't blame them. While I knew the things happening around the farm were scary and unsettling, I also knew whoever was doing them had no intention of bothering my guests or anyone else. The threats were meant for me. But put in the Hendersons' position, I would've left too.

Cookie and I opted to skip the Hearth and have breakfast alone at the inn's kitchen island instead. Hot coffee paired with cinnamon rolls the size of my head was the exact comfort food we needed to start the day.

She stared at my hands while we ate. "Is it true you climbed a tree to save Cindy?"

I nodded, forcing a tight smile. "Yeah."

Cookie hadn't arrived at the fire as quickly as most. She'd come upon the aftermath when I was already turning back. Cindy had wanted to be set free from my coat, and I'd wanted her in the house, so I'd gone back to the inn with Mom and Samantha.

The wrapping party had petered out after that, and I'd gone to my room for an emotional breakdown. I'd moved Cindy's food, water, and litter box into my private quarters and kept her with me until dawn, when I'd finally come out again.

"You hate heights," Cookie said. "You were very brave. Did you put some ointment on those cuts?"

"Yeah," I said, responding to both her statement and question. I turned my hands over, my palms scratched and raw from the tree bark as I'd climbed, and the skin across the backs of my hands and fingers already scabbing over from Cindy's razor-sharp claws.

I hated heights, and for good reason after last Christmas, but I knew Cindy had been afraid, and it had made me brave for her. I would never blame her for scratching me in fear. I did, however, blame myself for letting her get outside again. She'd been an indoor cat since I'd rescued her, but I'd grown lax about keeping her indoors. I'd accepted defeat early on because it was impossible to stop guests from letting her out when they came and went all day, and Cindy seemed to enjoy her time outside. But I knew it was dangerous because anything could happen to her. And while I might never have anticipated something like this, it was still my job to look after her, and I'd failed.

Dad had offered to take Cindy home with him and Mom to the farmhouse across the property where I'd grown up. At least until I could find a way to keep the little escape artist safe. I was on the fence because they were gone as much as I was, maybe more, and selfishly, I wanted her with me more than ever.

Cookie shifted beside me, poking her half-eaten breakfast with a fork. "Who do you think was following me," she asked, "if it wasn't a deputy?"

"I'm not sure," I admitted. "Maybe a reporter? Your name was in the paper that first day, so it's possible someone's trying to get an inside scoop." I told her about the reporter who'd come to the inn. Then I thought of another possibility. "Maybe someone in Karen's family hired a private investigator to get to the bottom of things?"

"I guess," she said. "Or it might've been the real killer, keeping tabs on me."

I didn't respond because I wasn't sure I could disagree.

Cookie dropped her fork on the table, done pretending to eat. "I like your ideas better. Being tailed by reporter or a private eye sounds pretty cool. Especially the second one. Very *Magnum P.I.* I'll pretend that's what's going on and hope he has a mustache like Tom Selleck."

I wasn't surprised. She clearly had a fascination with facial hair. I tossed the rest of my cinnamon roll in the trash. My appetite was gone too, and my stomach was doing flips just thinking about being followed again.

I wondered if the man in the leather coat and gun holster could be a private investigator. It would explain why he was lurking in alleys. I told Cookie about the guy, then filled her in on everything I could remember about him.

She nodded. "Makes sense that Bonnie would be following him around. She's like that. Thinks she's a real sleuth. She hates it when I tell her you are."

I frowned. "She was pretty mad at Karen the night she died, so if you see Bonnie again before we prove she isn't the killer, try not to mention my name."

Cookie wrapped the rest of her breakfast in a paper towel. "I'm going to take this to Theodore. Then we can investigate. What's the plan for today?"

I considered lying and saying I didn't have a plan. I'd even thought of trying to ditch her, but it didn't seem right. I knew I couldn't keep Cookie out of this. She was at the center of it all, and she deserved to know everything I did. After that, she could decide how much she wanted involved. But it had to be her decision, not mine.

I set my coffee mug aside and folded my hands. "I was digging into Karen's relationship with Meg, the inn owner in Great Falls, last night when I couldn't sleep. And I found a review for something else I want to look into."

"Great," she said. "What is it?"

I bit my lip. The lead was good, but I was torn about dragging Cookie along. Even if she wanted to go. It would be my fault if she got hurt. "Karen gave a venomous review to a shop in Harpswell eighteen months ago."

"And?" Cookie asked. "That was kind of her schtick. Wasn't it?"

"Yes, but she attacked the owner personally in the article, and it cost him so much business he had to close the doors. He sued her for defamation."

Cookie's eyes widened. "Yikes."

I nodded.

"So, road trip to Harpswell?" she asked, climbing off her chair again.

"Nope. That guy reopened his shop in a new location, and it appears to be thriving. It's called Rose-Colored Glasses," I said.

Cookie froze. "We got a new glass shop last year by that name."

I nodded. "Exactly. And the owner's name is Steven *Moody*."

* * *

Cookie delivered her leftover breakfast to Theodore, then I drove us into town.

The temperature was up twelve degrees since yesterday, making it a whopping twenty-nine and rising. The sun was out, and snow fell in big postcard-worthy flakes as I snagged a prime parking space on Main Street. Narrow rivers ran along the curb where today's sunlight melted yesterday's ice.

Cookie hopped over the stream on her way to the sidewalk, then wedged her hands into her coat pockets. "What should we say to him?" she asked, eyes fixed on the shop up ahead. "He's got to be the killer, but how do we confirm it without letting him know we're onto him?"

"We don't know that he's the killer," I said.

Cookie made a dismissive little pfft sound. "It's always the husband. Don't you watch the news?"

"Well," I hedged, hoping we weren't about to talk to a cold-blooded murderer. "Steven *is* her ex, but maybe he's just another human she thoroughly burned."

She shook her head at me, disappointed in my naivete. "He moved his shop to Mistletoe last year, and then she showed up here under the guise of reviewing your inn. But we know she planned to review the whole town. She wanted to expose us all as frauds. Why else?"

I pressed my lips together. Cookie had excellent questions. And her theory certainly shed some light on Karen's desire to tear the whole town apart. She'd done her best to ruin her ex, but he'd rallied. Steven had started over in Mistletoe, and as far as I could tell, he and his shop were thriving. The creations showcased on the shop's website were magnificent, from stained glass windows to figurines, vases, and everything in between.

Cookie stopped to watch a trio of children racing through rainbows on the sidewalk. A kaleidoscope of colors danced over their fair heads of hair and pale cheeks, thrown through the window at Rose-Colored Glasses.

The little boy wore a superhero cape over his coat that reminded me of Cookie running with her robe.

"You never told me the rest of the story about where you were going yesterday when I saw you outside the bookstore," I said. "You're in a choir now?"

Cookie turned up the short walkway to the shop, pausing to admire a set of suncatchers attached to the glass door. "That's right. I'm participating in an event at the covered bridge on Christmas Eve. You should come," she said.

My heart skipped. "I love the covered bridge," I said wistfully. "And McDoogle's lights make it even more enchanting this time of year. I don't think I've ever been there on Christmas Eve."

"It's beautiful," she said. "Come with me. You'll love it."

I followed Cookie into the shop, wishing I could join her on Christmas Eve but knowing it was unlikely. "I promised Mom I'd host an open house at the inn that night."

"So?" Cookie stopped abruptly, and I nearly barreled into her. "My event starts at dusk. You can be there and still be back before your party. Trust me. I don't want to miss Christopher and his lovely beard when he comes to the inn to collect the presents."

"I'll run it past Mom," I said. "I might be able to do the prep work ahead of time, then slip out with you."

"Atta girl," she said, shooting me a thumbs-up and a wink.

"Welcome," a handsome middle-aged man in khaki slacks and a button-down shirt said. His sandy hair was streaked with gray, and he wore thin, gold-rimmed glasses. He smiled invitingly as we took him in. "Are you looking for a gift?"

"No," I said, sliding Cookie a look. "Not today."

Cookie's face was unusually blank.

I wasn't sure what she was thinking, but I was mildly surprised to see Steven looking so unaffected by his ex-wife's recent murder. Sure, he and Karen were likely still enemies in the end, but they'd loved one another once. Enough to pledge forever. "I'm Holly White," I said. "This is Cookie Cutter. My family owns Reindeer Games, and Cookie is a co-owner at Caroline's Cupcakes." I smiled, hoping that knowing we were locals would make him more willing to talk to us.

He smiled back at us. "I'm Steven Moody. I own this place, and I'm the artist behind all the glass work."

I stilled. I'd come to question him about his rocky relationship with Karen, but my gaze darted over his shoulder to his work on display. I'd always wanted to be an artist, and jewelry-making was my creative outlet of choice. Coincidentally, I, too, worked with his preferred medium. And suddenly the suncatchers, ornaments, and sculptures were speaking to me. "Your work is marvelous," I said a little breathlessly.

Steven stepped back and outstretched an arm, encouraging us to look around.

The space was set up like a greenhouse, with tall, narrow windows on every wall and a series of skylights overhead. Even the display shelves were made of glass, allowing the light, traveling in from every direction, to pierce straight through his work.

"We were sorry to hear about your ex-wife," Cookie said, turning Steven and me in her direction.

Her voice was strangely deep, with an odd sort of accent I couldn't place, and her expression was uncharacteristically flat. I tried to figure out what she was up to but couldn't.

I'd assumed I would be the one to talk to him about Karen.

"Did you have a chance to see her while she was in town?" Cookie asked.

I felt my eyes bulge.

Steven frowned. "No, thank goodness. Though, I suspect she'd have made her way over here eventually, trying to cause some sort of upheaval if she'd lived long enough. That was her way, after all. Finding nice things and ruining them. A way of life, really." The sarcasm in his tone was thick, and his voice was tight with resentment.

Cookie's expression didn't change. "I guess that explains why the marriage didn't work out," she said, the accent clearing up a bit.

With a jolt, I realized she was impersonating Evan.

Steven folded his arms in a standoff with the tiny white-haired woman. "The marriage didn't work out because she was married to her job, and I wanted someone who wanted me. If you're here to defend her, you obviously didn't know her. She was the worst. She only came to Mistletoe to provoke me. She lived to provoke me!" He fumed, absently cracking the knuckles on each hand. "She needled everyone. I told her a million times that she'd mess with the wrong person one day, and she'd pay for it."

Cookie shot me a sidelong glance as Steven began to pace, agitated. "You divorced her because she was a workaholic?" she asked.

"I divorced her because I fell in love with someone else," he said, tone softening. "Karen's been exacting revenge on the both of us ever since. She nearly ruined my career and my livelihood along with it. But I persevered. Thankfully." He wrung his hands as he slowly settled. "Karen made a business of showcasing other people's shortcomings, but she couldn't see her own. And because of that, she'd lost me years before I left." He moved to the business side of his checkout counter, putting distance between himself and the women drudging up terrible memories for him, no doubt.

Cookie stepped forward in pursuit, moving to stand opposite him at the counter. "Can you tell us where you were four nights ago at approximately nine o'clock?"

"Here. Taking inventory. Why?" A moment later, he seemed to understand. He swung his gaze to meet mine. "Is she being serious?"

"No," I said at the same moment Cookie said, "Yes."

Then Steven's eyes narrowed. "What did you say your name was?"

"Cookie," she said brightly, her terrible Boston accent slipping.

He shook an angry finger at her, his chin swinging left and right in defiance. "You're the one from the paper. You're Delores!"

Cookie stepped back. Panic swept over her fake cop face. "Nope," she said. "I'm afraid you're mistaken. Come along, Holly." Her terrible Boston accent slid into the practiced British lilt she used for calling bingo.

I gave Steven an apologetic smile, then hurried back onto the sidewalk behind her, hoping we hadn't accidentally aggravated a killer.

Chapter Fifteen

We regrouped on the sidewalk at the corner, away from the reaching rainbows and endless windows of Steven's shop.

"What do you think?" Cookie asked. "How'd I do?"

I made a crazy face. "Well, if he's the one threatening me and demanding I stop asking questions, I think you made it clear I'm not listening."

She frowned. "I asked the questions, not you. He can't fault you for that."

I quirked a brow. *Right*, I thought, *because killers are so reasonable.* "I was right there with you," I said. "We came in together. I introduced us."

She seemed to mull that over. "Well, at least you didn't ask him anything."

I slid my eyes at her, angling to keep the shop in my line of sight in case he came after us. "At least."

"Do you think he told us the truth?" she asked. "You think he really didn't see Karen before she died?"

I frowned as a fat snowflake hit my cheek and melted. "I don't know," I said, brushing the wet drop away. "It doesn't really

match up with his allegation that she'd come here to ruin him."
Though that was in line with our suspicions and easy enough to
imagine. But if that was the case, then why hadn't she made a
point of stopping in right away? Why not take the opportunity
to surprise him and make him squirm?

"So we have three suspects," Cookie said. "Steven, Bonnie,
and Meg, but I don't think Bonnie's a killer."

"It could've been an accident," I told her. "Sometimes people
lash out in anger, then it's too late to take back what's been done."

She seemed to consider that for a moment. "What's next?"
she asked, clapping her palms together. "I can see why you do
this. It's kind of a kick!"

I smiled. It kind of was.

When I wasn't being threatened or attacked, that is.

"We think about whether the people on our list could really
have done it. Do they all have means and motive? I think they
all had motive, and since the murder weapon was inside the inn,
we know Meg had access to the means. Karen knew Bonnie and
Steven, so it's possible either of them could have met up with
her when she returned alone from dinner and went inside. They
could've picked up the nutcracker, then followed Karen back out
and struck her."

"The same works for anyone," Cookie said. "All they had to
do was follow her inside, pretend they belonged there or worked
on the farm or whatever."

"Right." And just like that, our little list of three suspects
grew to literally anyone.

"Boy, we're cooking now," Cookie said, eyes bright with
hope and satisfaction.

"Evan says he's already done this, but we might as well check the last few toy donation locations for a missing velvet bag," I said. "We're already here, and of course Evan didn't tell me what the deputies came up with."

Cookie craned her neck for a look in the direction we'd come. "I forgot about that, but I don't think we have to look far."

I followed her gaze up the walk to Rose-Colored Glasses, then took several long strides in the shop's direction. The donation receptacle at the side of his door was lined in a crisp white sack, not the crimson velvet bag Christopher had delivered with the bins.

What had Evan and his deputies thought of that?

*   *   *

Evan stopped at the inn after work. He had two bags from El Guaco Taco, my favorite food truck, and a warm smile.

I hugged him on sight.

"I didn't have time to eat dinner," he said. "I saw the truck packing up for the night, and I didn't think you'd mind if I brought something to share."

"Never." I led him to the kitchen and grabbed two bottles of water from the fridge, then continued into my personal space at the back of the house.

We spread the nachos, tacos, and toppings on the coffee table, then sat together on the couch.

"This is fantastic," I told him, helping myself to a chip. "How was work?"

"Not great," he said. "I got a call from a shop owner saying two women had been in to badger and harass him about the recent murder of his ex-wife. Know anything about that?"

I froze with the nacho between my lips.

"Apparently the older woman was using an alias and some sort of accent to disguise her voice, but he recognized her from the newspaper as his ex-wife's killer. Sounding familiar yet?"

I chewed slowly, contemplating my explanation and/or a plea for leniency.

"Where is Cookie now?" he asked.

"Upstairs in her room." Watching a marathon of *Criminal Minds* for inspiration on our next moves.

"Why were you talking to Steven Moody today? I've asked you repeatedly to let this go. And you know what happens when you don't." He kicked back on the couch, twisting to face me. "I've tried to make sense of your motivations, and I can't. I don't get it. Do you have some kind of adrenaline addiction? A death wish? You enjoy worrying everyone who cares about you to the point of misery and insanity? Because I know I speak for a large group of people who would do anything to make you stop. I'd accuse you of being impossibly selfish, but I know that's not who you are. So what is it?"

I scooted away from him, twisting on the cushion to gawk. My heart pounded and I felt my fury rising. "Of course I'm not *trying* to upset people," I snapped. "That's ridiculous. And I know you've told me to stop looking for Karen's killer, but I can't and I don't want to. Every piece of evidence points to Cookie, and she plays a brave game, but I caught her hugging Theodore inside the stables tonight and crying. Hard. She's old and she's scared, and she's one of the most important people in my life. I can't sit idly by and do nothing when I could be help-ing to figure out what really happened. If I could just find some kind of evidence that proves it wasn't her so she can go back to not worrying about a life in prison, that would work too."

Evan wrenched forward, resting his forearms on his thighs. "You've got to start trusting me to do my job. I'm an excellent detective, Holly, but you're making things unnecessarily difficult for me right now."

"Have you spoken to Steven about his whereabouts at the time of Karen's death?" I asked "Because his donation bag is missing, and I feel like that's worth noting. Have you tested the bag found covering Karen to see if it was his?"

Evan let his eyes close, clearly in no mood for my theories.

I silently counted to ten before he reopened them.

"What about the guy I saw in the alley with the gun?" I asked. "Did you find him? Or at least talk to Bonnie about why she was in the alley and what she saw or heard?"

Evan pinched the bridge of his nose. "Yes." He lowered his hands, then locked me in a warning stare. "He's trained and licensed to carry a concealed weapon. And I want you to leave him alone."

"What?" I gaped.

Evan muttered something under his breath about how I never listen and why did he bother asking.

I ignored it. "Who is he? What was he doing in the alley? Why was Bonnie watching him?"

Even shook his head, his expression hardening as I spoke. "You don't need to know any of that. You need to stop this. *All* of it. *Now.*"

I raised and dropped my hands in exasperation. "You say you want me to talk to you, but when I do, you tell me not to ask questions. I'm made of questions. So what am I supposed to do?"

"Ask about something else," he suggested. "Something other than Karen Moody's murder. And not about my work."

"Fine," I said. "You left me at the pie shop the other day because you wanted to take a phone call."

His eyes flashed with an emotion that was gone before I could name it. Panic? Fear?

"A few minutes later I saw you get into a blue SUV with a blonde woman I didn't recognize. Where were you going and why?"

Evan shifted, eyes pleading. "I can't tell you that either."

"Shocker," I said sarcastically. "You wonder why I try to find my own answers? How else can I get them?"

He turned back to the food spread across the table before us, then took his time dragging a chip through the creamy green guac. When he finished, he loaded a taco with toppings.

Evan clearly had no plans to discuss the case, the blonde, or the gun toter with me, and I couldn't make him. But the night didn't have to be ruined.

"Then at least tell me what you got me for Christmas," I said with a small smile, trying to break the tension.

He rolled his eyes and smirked, willing to take the olive branch. "That's a surprise."

"See?" I said. "I ask, but you don't answer."

"Maybe you can try being patient for a change," he suggested. "For me." He took my hand, and warmth spread up my arm to my chest.

I'd learned early on in our relationship that it was impossible to argue with him properly when he touched me. My brain always grew fuzzy, and occasionally my knees went weak.

"Give me a clue, then," I said, clearing my throat and willing myself not to move closer. "Is it bigger than a breadbox? Will it fit into my stocking? How about under the tree? In case you haven't realized, there are still seven days left until Christmas, and I might literally die of anticipation before then. So, please"—I clasped my hands and smiled—"just one clue."

Evan's phone buzzed on the table, and a Boston number appeared on the screen. I didn't need to ask who was calling. I recognized the number as belonging to a detective at the Boston PD. Evan released me immediately, rising to his feet as he answered the phone.

This call was about the man hunting Libby.

My gaze jumped to the window, seeking the lights of my family's guesthouse across the field between us. The building had been the tree farm's office until it was no longer necessary, after which it was remodeled into a guesthouse for the convenience of family members coming for extended visits. It was the place I'd lived for two years after leaving Portland, and the location Libby had called home for nearly a year. A curl of smoke rose from the chimney, and the silhouette of Ray's little pickup truck was visible outside.

Libby had come to stay with Evan after a tragedy in her life pushed her into temporary hiding. She'd lost her closest friend, Heather, to drugs and the bidding of a criminal boyfriend. Libby had tried to hold him accountable, but soon discovered he was one piece of a much larger and more dangerous network. Boston police had been trying to build a case against him for a year, but, according to Evan, the process was arduous, and the guy was vapor.

Until now, maybe.

He disconnected the call, then clung to the phone a moment before returning to the couch.

I set my hand on his arm to let him know I was there. Suddenly concerns about a blonde in an SUV and my Christmas gift seemed incredibly petty and stupid. "Hey. Talk to me."

Evan grunted, staring blankly for a long beat.

Distress wrinkled the skin around his smart green eyes. "They got him."

"What?" A smile broke over my face. "Really? That's good news. Why aren't you happy?"

"Boston PD wants Libby to testify at his trial. They think he'll get off with a slap on the wrist if she doesn't. The case for a maximum sentence hinges on his connection to the death of Libby's friend, who is being portrayed as an addict and runaway. Someone who was a train wreck all by herself. The rantings in her blog are being chalked up as the nonsense of someone high on drugs, and this guy is saying he barely knew her and hadn't seen her in weeks before she died."

"She was an addict because of him, though," I argued, bristling for the mistreatment of a girl I'd never met. "And Heather didn't run away. She was moving drugs for him."

Evan nodded. Of course he knew all this. "The DA thinks Libby's word will carry weight. She can speak Heather's truth." Evan's skin looked ashen and heading for green. "Testifying will likely cement the charges. But by doing that, she'll be targeted. Not like now, where if one of these lowlifes sees her, he might hurt her. If she testifies, the guy will put a bounty on her."

I slumped, resting shoulder to shoulder with Evan, then tipping my head against him. We were silent for a long while.

"Libby will have to go back to Boston for the trial," he said. "If the DA doesn't screw this up, the guy goes to jail. Then the DEA—that's the Drug Enforcement Administration—will use him to start picking apart his network, and Libby can have her life back. That's a best-case scenario."

"Then that's what will happen. And she'll come back to Mistletoe afterward," I said, hoping it was true. "She likes it here, and I think she and Ray are getting pretty serious."

"What if he tries to stop her from reaching the witness stand?"

"Then you'll be there, right by her side, to stop him," I said.

Evan's breath seemed to shudder. "Doing the right thing is going to put my baby sister's life in danger."

"Not testifying means nothing changes," I said quietly. "She can't go back to the city she loves for fear of being spotted and hurt by one of these guys. She happy here, but it's a little like witness protection. She can't leave and no one from her past can know she's here. This big ugly thing is just hanging over her head, but if you can trust the good guys to do their jobs, it could finally be over for her."

Evan swiped his phone back to life and sent a text. A moment later, his mouth twitched into a little smile. "I told Libby I need to talk to her, and she told me to put a pin in it." He shook his head. "She's watching a movie with Ray." He turned for a look through my window. "I told her I'd be there in two hours."

I was thrilled, selfishly, at the promise of two more hours alone with Evan. "What do you want to do until then?" I asked, my cheeks burning childishly at the possibilities.

Evan laughed and all remnants of his pained expression vanished. "How are the jewelry orders coming?"

"I'll show you. Be right back." I fetched a box from my office and returned a moment later with a grin. I'd put another sleepless night to good use after the fire was extinguished and Cindy was safely home.

Together we paired the finished products with their matching receipts, then addressed and stuffed the bubble envelopes. We'd gotten the series of tasks down to a perfectly choreographed routine this summer and could pack up an unseemly amount of things in the time it took to watch any movie. Despite the weight of our news from Boston, tonight was no different.

When he left to speak with his sister, Evan took the sealed envelopes along with two bags of unwrapped toys and the necessary trimmings. He said he and Libby could each do some wrapping, and he'd stop by the post office for me in the morning.

I appreciated him more than he knew, and I hated the situation Libby was stuck in. Doing the right thing would put her in mortal danger, and part of me wondered if she should run. Get a new identity and start over somewhere warm and sunny. But I knew Libby, and she and I were the same at our cores. We were just like Evan and Ray, my parents, and Cookie. Libby would do the right thing, regardless of the cost or risk, simply because it was right.

And I'd never been so afraid for another person in my life.

Chapter Sixteen

I fell asleep with my phone in my hand and Cindy Lou Who at my side. I worried that Libby or Ray might need someone to talk to once the news from Boston had been delivered. Instead, my night was quiet after Evan left, and before midnight I fell into a deep sleep that lasted until after seven. I was thankful for the rest and the fact that I wouldn't have to wait to intrude on Libby. I was eager to check in on how she was processing her options for testifying against a criminally connected lunatic.

I dressed quickly, then headed into the chilly winter morning. Reindeer Games was the picture of serenity before the crowds arrived. The snow sparkled as sunlight caught on ice crystals, and my breath puffed out before me in tiny white clouds. Thanks to last night's snowfall, all of yesterday's footprints and sleigh tracks had been erased, leaving the field between the inn and the guesthouse pristine and unblemished. I almost hated trudging through it, but that couldn't be helped.

I knocked while I stomped, kicking snow from my boots and making my presence clearly known. Our current lack of official inn guests meant Mom was back on a temporary eleven-to-seven schedule at the Hearth, and Libby had time to visit before getting ready for her day.

The door swept open, and Libby blinked against the light. She raised an arm to shield her eyes. "Holly?"

"I brought maple bacon," I said by way of greeting, then lifted my small, insulated tote into view as proof.

She stepped back to let me in, and I headed for the kitchen to unpack the bacon before it got cold.

"It's thick and coated in maple syrup from the farm next door," I said. "You're going to love it."

The doorbell rang, and Libby turned back with a groan before she reached the kitchen.

"I guess I'm not the only one worried about you this morning," I said when Ray's smiling face appeared.

He rubbed his palms together in excitement as he reached the kitchen. "Bacon!" He snagged two slices, then passed one to Libby, who was still trying to pry her eyes open.

I smiled. "I'll make some coffee."

"How are you doing?" Ray asked her softly as I started the pot to brew.

"I'm tired," she grouched. "I'm still in my pajamas, wearing no makeup, and my hair looks like a big red haystack while two yoyos are in my kitchen eating bacon and making coffee." She handed him her slice, and he ate it.

"Didn't sleep well?" I guessed.

"Didn't sleep," she said.

"Are you going to testify?" I asked, cutting to the chase. "You know, whatever you decide to do will be the right decision. Everyone will back you on it and support you however we can."

Libby hugged her middle, looking small and unsure for the first time since I'd met her. "I'm going to testify," she said. "What choice do I have? I can't run or hide and expect to have any kind of life. I'd live in constant fear of being discovered, and what happens if I have a family to worry about one day? Their lives would be in danger too. And even if they stayed safe, how could I expect my husband to explain to our kids that Mommy was abducted by a group of drug dealers?"

I crossed the kitchen and wrapped my arms around her. After a moment, she hugged me back.

Ray joined in, curving his long arms around us both.

We discussed the Boston situation over bacon and coffee, then Libby went to get dressed for her day. She'd held herself together as we talked, but her eyes were puffy when she returned, hair done and makeup on.

"So, basically," she said, her voice noticeably scratchy, "the trial is set for three days after Christmas, and I'll be traveling into the city the day before so I can meet with the prosecutor and prepare. Evan's taking me, so you don't have to worry. I'll be fine."

I exchanged a look with Ray. Three days after Christmas was only eight days from now. And it seemed too soon. We had barely more than a week. "Can we come with you?" I asked. "Will it be a public trial?"

She frowned. "You guys should stay out of Boston during the trial. I'm not convinced these guys won't blow up the courthouse if that's what it takes to keep their business running smoothly."

Ray's skin paled.

I gave him a meaningful look and a small shake of my head. It sounded as if he and I were going on a covert, post-holiday road trip because there's no way we wouldn't be there for Libby.

His tight expression eased a fraction, and I suspected he knew what I was thinking.

"How are the wedding plans coming?" I asked, changing the subject before she sensed our unspoken intention and tried to stop us.

Ray set his joined hands on the kitchen table. "My part is nearly done, I think. Your family is taking over soon. You, with the ladies moving to the inn on the big day, and your mom, making all the ceremony and reception arrangements."

Fay and Pierce had chosen to wed in my family's barn, a massive, renovated structure on our property, used for events, most notably the annual fundraiser known as the Christmas Tree Ball. Sponsors bought and decorated trees, and Mom decked the barn to the rafters in holiday cheer and used the trees as decoration. The trees were raffled off, fully decorated, to the lucky winners. This year, the ball had been held early in the season so the barn could be prepared for Fay and Pierce's wedding. As it turned out, they wanted a winter wonderland theme, so there wasn't any need to redecorate.

Ray snapped his finger. "I almost forgot again." Ray's grin widened. "Mom wants me to ask you if you'll make matching jewelry pieces for her bridesmaids. She wants to give them each something special to commemorate the day. Preferably something they can wear again, because they're definitely never wearing those big froufrou dresses again. Unless a Bo Peep conference comes through town."

I laughed. "I would love to make the jewelry for your mom's bridesmaids. I'll work on some designs tonight. Also, who do I need to talk to about getting a Bo Peep convention in Mistletoe? Because the sheep alone would be worth the trouble."

Libby swiped her thumb along the corner of her eye. "I wouldn't have believed it a year ago, but I really like this town." She sniffed. "I mean, obviously you're all nuts, but I think you might be my kind of nuts." Her Boston accent sounded thicker as she fought back her emotions. She cleared her throat and forced a weary smile. "If I survive this trial, I'm going to find out if there is such a thing as a Bo Peep convention, and I'm going to get it here to celebrate this wonderful, silly place I love."

"You're going to be fine," I said, willing the words to be true. "You're going to safely give your testimony, and the DEA will handle the rest. Justice shall prevail, and you'll be back in Mistletoe in no time. Safe and sound forever."

"To clarify," Ray said, "will you be dressing as Bo Peep for this convention?"

Libby laughed and wiped her eyes. "It's either me or you, babe," she said.

I snorted as an image of Ray in pantaloons and a bonnet flashed into mind.

He nodded slowly. "I'll flip you for it."

"Stop," I said, choking on laughter. "You're both cuckoo. A match made by Mother Goose."

Ray's expression went soft as he looked into her eyes. "You're definitely coming back? You're not planning to resume your life in Boston after the trial?"

She bit into her lip, then shook her head. "No."

He pulled her into a hug.

"Evan's going to be elated," I said, feeling my chest tighten with emotions of my own.

Libby pulled out of the hug. "Don't tell him." She smiled. "I want to tell him on Christmas. It's my gift to him this year. He adores this weird little town, and I want to make it my town too."

Ray twined his fingers with hers.

I grinned. "It already is."

*   *   *

I walked to the Hearth for lunch a few hours later, after carrying another bag of toys into my office from the porch. At the rate donations were arriving and the speed they were being wrapped, I'd need a Christmas miracle to finish before Christopher came to collect them. I made a mental note to ask Cookie if she wanted to work on it with me tonight. She hadn't been in her room when I went to invite her to lunch.

The dining area wasn't crowded, and I was thrilled to see Ray, his mom, and her fiancé already there.

"Holly!" Fay called, greeting me with a tight hug. "Ray said you don't mind making the bridesmaid's jewelry, and I'm so excited! I've been meaning to ask you personally for months, but life has gotten away from me, and there's nothing more authentically Mistletoe than Holly White's handmade treasures."

"Thank you," I said. "That's so kind and it's no trouble. Why don't you stop by sometime, or take a look at my online store, then let me know your favorite pieces. I'll use those concepts as inspiration on something unique for your ladies. And I will pinky promise never to recreate those items for anyone other than you—custom designs for your special day."

She hugged me again, and I squeezed her back.

Libby arrived with trays of warm cookies and cocoas, then hustled away as a new set of customers arrived.

"'Scuse me, miss." A small hunchback with a fur hat and duck-head cane stopped beside us at the counter, using her free hand to clutch a ratty wool cape at her collarbone. "Might I 'ave a scrap a bread fer me tum-tum." Cookie's terrible English accent warbled from the little figure.

"What are you doing?" I asked, weirdly amused and moving out of Fay's embrace. "Who are you supposed to be now? Oliver Twist?"

Cookie snickered, then hoisted herself onto a lollipop at the counter beside Ray and Pierce. "Pretty good disguise, right?"

"Kind of," I said. "Why are you in disguise again anyway? And where have you been all day?"

Cookie leaned over the counter, waving to Ray, Fay, and Pierce, then at Libby across the dining area. "Hello," she said before turning to me with a wicked, storytelling grin. "I've been on an adventure. I'm calling it that so I don't panic. I moved to the inn so I could stick with you, and the first time I went out on my own—*BAM*!" She set her cane down and clapped her hands together. "Followed."

"You were followed?" I asked, heart rate jumping at the thought. "Where?"

"I went home to put out my trash bins. It's pickup day, and living with a goat makes a lot of mess, if you know what I mean. I can't afford to miss a week. I thought I'd stick around until the trucks came to empty them, then roll them back into the garage and call it a day. But once I got the bins to the curb, I could tell I was being watched, so there was a change of plans." She paused dramatically to be sure we were all engaged.

I wasn't sure we were all breathing.

"What then?" Pierce asked, leaning over Ray's shoulder, pulled into Cookie's tale.

"Well"—she straightened, clearly satisfied—"I abandoned the bins on the curb, and I ditched the stalker by ducking between houses and cutting across my neighborhood to the church on Frankincense Drive. I borrowed a few props from the closet of cold-weather gear left open for anyone in need, because today I was in need. And I scored all this great stuff." She wiggled her cane, then pulled the furry hat off her head, revealing a smashed version of her normally puffy white hair. "I feel like a magician in this getup."

Ray's frown deepened. "You were followed to your home?"

"I think so," she said, her confident expression wavering.

"Did you see who it was this time?" I asked.

"Nope, but that'll teach me not to go home, I guess. I just didn't want things to back up. You can't keep bins of goat mess for too long before it's a problem. So, now that's taken care of, but the home owner association is going to be on my back if I don't roll those bins back inside once the trucks empty them. I live next door to the president, and that guy's a real drag."

Ray stood. "I can go to your place and bring the bins back."

"Will you get my slippers from beside the back door?" she asked, brightening.

"Sure." Ray smiled. "Make a list of anything you want, and I'll grab it while I'm there."

Cookie pulled a pen from her purse and started writing on her napkin. "I think I saw that tattletale woman from the inn in my neighborhood when I was on my way home," she said.

"Meg?" I asked, my skin pebbling into gooseflesh. "Are you sure?" How long was she planning to stay in Mistletoe?

Cookie shrugged. "She was wearing a parka with the hood up, but I'd recognize that teddy bear bag she carries everywhere. Who else would have one of those? I'm still mad at her. Why on earth would she have repeated something she overheard, out of context, while eavesdropping? She's caused me a lot of trouble."

I wanted to argue that getting her fingerprints all over a murder weapon was the bigger problem, but she was right. Meg shouldn't have been eavesdropping.

I pulled my phone from my pocket and scrolled through my recent contacts. "I'm going to tell Evan you saw her. It could be significant."

Ray's brow furrowed, puzzling. "Is there any chance that this woman is the one who's been following you?"

Cookie's jaw dropped. "Maybe," she said. "I've never gotten a good look."

I sent the message to Evan as the pieces of a stronger Meg-centric theory began to form. Why was she still in town? And why was she in Cookie's neighborhood?

Libby reappeared to top off the drinks, then winked and rushed away.

"I'll fill her in later," Ray said.

I returned my attention to Cookie. I hated the thought of her being afraid and alone again. She'd chosen to leave the inn without telling me, but what good was I if I hadn't even known she'd left? What if something had happened to her? This was just like Cindy Lou Who all over again.

The Hearth's door opened, and I turned on instinct.

Evan walked in, expression pained and eyes on Cookie.

A deep sense of foreboding washed over me, and I went to meet him halfway.

"Hey," I said brightly, ignoring the generally bad vibes rolling off him. "What's up? Did you get my text about Meg?"

He shook his head, then slowed his steps. "I'm here to talk to Cookie."

I frowned but followed him to her.

Ray, Fay, and Pierce all suddenly looked as stressed as I felt.

Cookie looked up from her list and smiled. "What's cooking, Sheriff?"

Evan removed his hat and held it against his torso. "I'm afraid my department received a call about your trash bins."

She wrinkled her nose. "Was it the home owner association? I didn't think they'd stoop to calling the cops." She checked her watch. "I can't believe the trucks have had time to come past yet."

"I'm going to need to talk to you about this at the station," Evan said, offering a hand to help her down.

"Wait a minute." I jammed a hand between them. "What's this about, specifically? Who called? And why?"

Libby returned and dropped her order pad on the counter. She hooked a hand on one hip. "What's going on?"

Evan regarded his sister and our little circle of friends. "Someone called in an anonymous tip suggesting Cookie tried to conceal evidence in the murder of Karen Moody. The tipper said we'd find everything in her trash bins if we beat the trucks to the pickup. I assumed it was nonsense, so I sent a deputy to check it out. I was on my way here to see how Libby was feeling when my deputy called."

"And said what?" I asked softly, checking first for nearby listeners and lookie-loos.

"There were a number of printed materials hidden inside a takeout bag, most with Karen's articles or photos. All with angry sentiments scribbled over them. The images had heavy X's drawn across Karen's face and smaller ones over her eyes. Deep scratches ripped through the paper at her throat. Notations regarding the fight, indicating Karen had said something unkind about Theodore, which incited the argument that resulted in Cookie's humiliation and desire to confront her about it."

"I never argued with her," Cookie said. "I didn't even talk to her before she died."

Evan nodded slowly, understandingly, but his expression grew infinitely more grim. "Not according to the bag of papers."

Pierce stood, straightening his sweater and shrugging into his coat. "Delores, you shouldn't say another word."

"What does this mean?" Fay asked, pulling her coat on as well.

Pierce fixed Evan with an evaluating look. "You believe Ms. Cutter confronted Karen on the night of her death during the time Ms. Cutter was unaccounted for, and that encounter ended in Ms. Moody's death."

Evan looked ill. "I have to fully explore every angle. This new evidence is something I can't ignore." His green eyes found me and pleaded for understanding. "If I don't do this, it will be argued that I'm not doing my job, that I'm playing favorites or doing favors. This town has to trust me. I can't be your sheriff if I can't be trusted."

"Those papers were planted," I said stubbornly. "And if you'd read my text, you'd know that Cookie saw Meg Mason in her neighborhood when she went to put the trash out a little while ago. Meg could've easily planted that material after scaring Cookie away by pretending to follow her, then called the sheriff's department to be sure someone found it before the trash was collected."

Cookie slid off her stool as a handful of other guests began to take notice of our tense and hushed words. She moved to Pierce's side as he fished a set of car keys from his coat pocket. The heartbreak on Cookie's face stung my eyes and wedged a brick of emotion in my windpipe.

She looked to me as she passed, the sheriff on one side of her and her attorney on the other. She didn't have to say a word. She needed me, and I wouldn't fail her.

I would make sure the person determined to frame her for their own misdeeds was brought to justice.

Chapter Seventeen

I picked Caroline up at five o'clock. She left the employees in charge of her cupcake shop and joined me for an emergency road trip.

"Thanks for coming," I told her, typing the address of Meg's Teddy Bear Inn into my phone's GPS, then setting the device in my cupholder. It was already dark, thanks to the season, but Great Falls was only ninety minutes away. We'd get there in plenty of time to check out the inn and speak to the staff. Maybe even enough time to poke around the town a bit, the way Meg had been perusing Mistletoe all week. It was hard to know who might have some tea to spill on the local inn-keeper, and as much as I hated to incite gossip, I was desperate to absolve Cookie. And more than that, to have the true killer identified and arrested.

"Are you kidding?" Caroline said, dropping her designer handbag onto the floorboards near her matching leather boots. "This nonsense has gone too far. Poor Cookie! I mean, can you even imagine the things going through her head right now?" She fastened her seatbelt, then flipped her hair free. "She's the kindest person I know, and she's in police custody for murder? It's ridiculous."

I glanced her way as I headed onto the highway, rushing to match my speed with the traffic.

Caroline's voice was an indignant warble, barely keeping the emotion at bay. I could understand why. Not only was Cookie Caroline's dear friend and business partner, but it was only a year ago that Caroline had been in a similar situation.

"What is Evan thinking?" she went on. "He knows she didn't do this. He *knows* that," she repeated. "So, what's the point? How does this action help anyone or anything? Isn't it his job to protect and serve?" She raked shaky fingers through long platinum waves, eyes misting with barely tamped frustration. "Who does this help or serve?"

I considered her last question. Rhetorical as it had been, it was a good one. And it was possibly the question I needed to start asking. *Who does Cookie's incarceration serve?* Because someone was actively working to set her up.

I hit my signal and cruised into the opposite lane, taking another highway and following the ramp toward Great Falls. "As far as I know, she hasn't been arrested," I said. "They're only holding her for questioning, and they can keep her for up to seventy-two hours."

Caroline huffed out an angry breath. "Your boyfriend is at the top of my list," she said. "And it's not a gift list."

I snorted. "I'm not happy about this either, but he's just doing his job," I said, repeating his words and trying to be positive for Caroline. "He's following procedures like always. And we haven't put any official labels on our relationship."

"Please," she said, "that man is lost for you."

I did my best not to smile because we were on a serious mission. "Let's go over our Meg-is-the-killer theory."

Caroline pulled in a long breath, then let it out slowly and folded her hands on her lap. "I checked out Karen's terrible review of Meg's inn after you called to set up this little excursion. And it doesn't seem as if the inn is hurting for reservations. They hold multiple annual teddy bear conventions there, as well as birthday parties and other local events. There are a ton of good reviews. It seems to be a very community-centric business."

"I saw that too," I said. "But I can't be sure the article didn't impact her number of out-of-town guests, which would make up most of her bookings between events. Did you read Meg's comments and rebuttals to Karen's review?"

Caroline cringed. "I did, and yikes."

Based on Meg's heated online exchange, she was more concerned about the way Karen had clawed at her grandma than anything else. She specifically protested all jabs at the teddy theme, the bears themselves, and the inn decor, which had largely been passed down with the property.

"The fact that Meg was defending her family's legacy, in addition to the business, brings a whole new level of motivation. For example," I said, "I frequently run from spiders and jump at the sight of my shadow, but if a grizzly was coming for someone I love, I'd fight him barehanded to protect the other person."

Caroline sighed. "Even if it killed you," she said sadly.

"Yep."

"Me too," she said.

I turned to smile at her. "I know."

We made a loop around town when we arrived in Great Falls. The whole place had a rustic, mountain vibe. Lots of exposed beams and logs were used in the downtown setting, and a gratuitous amount of evergreens were draped in colored lights.

A pint-sized billboard on a hillside at the edge of the shopping district contained the Teddy Bear Inn's logo and a giant arrow pointing the way.

I hooked a right and headed up the mountain.

The dark ribbon of road wound upward into the night until I wondered if we would reach the moon. Eventually, the asphalt narrowed and gave way to gravel beneath my tires, and our destination appeared.

The massive log cabin was seated atop another, smaller hill at the end of a long drive. Bathed in outdoor lighting, and larger than I'd expected, the inn was surrounded by a circular patch of flat land and backdropped by infinite towering trees. The snow-covered lawn was crisscrossed in footprints, and four vehicles were lined up in the parking spaces of a small adjoining lot.

Caroline and I took a cobblestone path to the inn's front door. We were guided by a bordering row of stumpy, bear-shaped lanterns.

Caroline stopped short of the porch, where bear pendants and flags swung merrily from the rafters and handrails. "Whoa. This is a whole lot to take in."

"Yeah," I said, my gaze stuck on a gigantic red sleigh beside the inn. At least eight feet tall and anchored in place by ropes around stakes, the sleigh was filled with bears. A huge teddy sat up front, hands on reins attached to nothing. Crimson bags and open gift boxes were clustered in the backseat, each overflowing with bears of every size.

I took a picture of the sleigh, because words would never do it justice, then marched up the steps to the inn's front door and ushered Caroline inside.

The lobby was vast and scattered with people. Families in ugly Christmas sweaters played chess on table tops before a roaring fire. Children pushed oversized checkers across a burlap rug, groups worked puzzles, and individuals read in cozy nooks. It was a happy holiday scene complete with all the glassy, black-eyed teddy's looming and lurking on every flat surface.

"Merry Christmas!" a cheery voice called from behind a big log desk. The woman wore a red turtleneck topped with a green plaid vest and a headband with bear ears on top. Her name tag said "Josie." "Are you two ladies checking in?"

"Hello," I said. "We're actually here to speak with Meg Mason. Is she in?"

Josie's smile fell into a dramatic pout. "I'm afraid not, but I would be happy to help you with anything you need."

"Will she be back tonight?" I asked, ignoring the weird sing-song tone in Josie's voice.

Her bottom lip protruded. "Yes, but I have no idea when, or if she'll come here before heading home."

"She doesn't live here?" I asked.

"No." Josie smiled. "This is a business like any other. Staff covers all shifts. Every bedroom is available for guests. I can take a message, let her know you dropped by, if that will help."

I waved her off with a smile. "No, that's okay." I looked around for something to use as a segue to the topic of Karen Moody's review and the resulting impact, but came up short.

Caroline stepped forward, one arm outstretched. "I'm Caroline West," she said proudly, in the confident, media-friendly way she'd been raised. "I'd love to ask you a few questions, if you don't mind. We've been following the work of a critic for *New England Magazine* and think you may have some insight."

Josie's brows pulled together. "You're reporters?"

"Researchers," I said.

Caroline nodded. She looked Josie over carefully, then amended our claim. "We're top-tier investigative researchers," she said coyly. "And if you can help us blow the top off this cover-up, we can get your photo in the finished article, with full credit for your insider information."

"Ooh," Josie cooed, eyes widening. "What cover-up?"

"We think," Caroline said, passing off a deliberate stall as a dramatic pause, "that a certain critic gave consistently bad reviews in return for higher readership and payoffs by the various businesses' competition."

Josie lifted the receiver on her desk phone and called someone to cover her position. Then, she led us to an office near the back of the first floor. "So," she said, plopping into the chair behind a cluttered desk and motioning Caroline and me to take the seats across from her. "What can I tell you about Karen Moody?"

I blinked, then traded a cautious look with Caroline.

"Come on," Josie said. "It's no secret Karen was awful or that her reviews were unfair and intentionally mean. Or that she gave our inn a terrible review. And she was just killed. So, tell me the truth now. You're cops, right? Trying to solve her murder?" She grinned and bobbed her head conspiratorially.

"Private investigators," I fibbed, knowing better than to impersonate an officer, but not quite sure why I hadn't stuck to the researchers guise.

She leaned forward over the desk and folded her hands on the giant paper calendar, apparently enjoying this. "Karen Moody nearly destroyed this inn and Meg's family legacy along with it, so she is officially an enemy of mine. I would've lost my job if this place had gone under."

"Business has suffered then?" Caroline asked.

Josie nodded. "Locals do what they can to help. We're a close community. We host a lot of events now, and a bunch of people went online to leave positive reviews for the inn, even if they've never stayed here. Basically, the town is keeping this place afloat right now, but Karen called this place creepy and compared it to something from a second-rate horror film. Out-of-towners are steering clear."

Caroline shivered in my peripheral vision.

"How is Meg taking all this?" I asked.

"She's bonkers with frustration." Josie shook her head in apparent dismay. "She tried everything to get the review taken down or revised, but Karen wouldn't return any of Meg's e-mails or messages. Finally, she found a list of her upcoming reviews and made a reservation at the same inn where Karen would be staying. Some weird little Christmas village. She'd hoped they could talk there."

I tried not to frown at her description of my town and concentrated instead on the fact that my theory about her staying at the inn to talk to Karen was right.

Caroline scooted forward on her chair. "How did that go?"

"Terrible. Karen still wouldn't talk to her, even when they shared meals across the table from one another. It was useless. Every time Meg got close to her, Karen walked away. She called Meg the night before she was killed and threatened to get a restraining order if Meg ever tried to talk to her again. Completely insane." Josie mimed her head exploding.

Another guest, Mary Hathy, had reported hearing Karen arguing on the phone with someone. I couldn't help wondering if it was her call with Meg she'd overheard.

"Meg even took her a gift," Josie said, looking sadder now. "One of the original teddy bears made by her grandma. It was a touching and deeply meaningful offering, but Karen rejected it."

I frowned along with her, recalling the bear. "I'm really sorry to hear that." Meg had told me the bear was meant for someone else when I'd thought it was a donation.

Josie raised, then dropped her palms. "What can I say? Some people are truly awful. Her review turned Meg's inn into a meme for middle-aged insanity."

I cringed, unsure what else to do or say. I'd confirmed the idea that Meg had reasons to lash out at Karen. Not only had business been negatively affected, but her legacy had become an internet joke. "I think we have everything we need now."

Caroline popped onto her feet beside me. "Yes, thank you so much for your time." She shook Josie's hand again.

We saw ourselves out, hurrying back in the direction we'd come.

"I hope Meg is officially at the top of your suspect list," Caroline said as I shifted the truck into gear and motored down the drive.

"She's definitely not at the bottom," I said.

Karen's ex-husband had dealt with the same problem as Meg, but he'd started over and seemed to be doing a lot of business now. Of course, maintaining that business might've motivated him to confront her and ask that she not review him again, or our town. And that conversation could have escalated.

But Meg didn't have the option of relocation like Steven had. Her life and legacy were here, and significantly damaged thanks to Karen.

My thought was interrupted by a loud snap.

Caroline and I looked through the passenger window as I turned onto the road in front of the inn.

"Is that thing moving?" Caroline asked, gaze fixed on the giant sleigh filled with bears on top of the hill. "Swaying or wobbling?"

I slowed, staring and unsure what we were seeing. It didn't make sense for it to move. It had been anchored in the back on both sides.

SNAP!

The sound came again, and I realized Caroline was right.

The giant teddy bear sleigh was free of its tethers and racing over the snowy hillside in our direction.

Chapter Eighteen

I jammed my foot against the gas a moment too late, temporarily dumbfounded by the situation.

The sleigh collided with the far end of the truck's bed on Caroline's side, and my foot left the pedal, switching instinctively to the brake. A groan of metal sounded as our back end swung wide on the narrow mountain road. The weight and force of the impact had spun us backward in the direction of the sharp plummet at our left. One rear tire left the gravel road, tipping us slightly.

The sleigh was airborne, falling over the mountain's edge and into the trees at an angle. Bears flew everywhere. My truck's other back tire followed the first a moment before the rest of my vehicle lost purchase on the road completely.

Caroline and I screamed as we plunged tailgate first over the mountain. The truck thunked hard and heavy against rock and earth, tires locked as I stood on the brake pedal. I stared into the rearview mirror, eyes trained on the darkness behind us, eerily red in the brake lights.

We jolted to a sudden stop, and my forehead bounced against the steering wheel.

Dozens of bears clung to tree branches, illuminated in my headlights.

I rubbed my eyes, attempting to un-blur my vision, and failed. A sharp spear of pain sliced through my neck and head. "Caroline?"

"Yeah," she whispered. "Are we dead? I don't want to open my eyes."

"Not yet, but I don't know why we stopped moving," I said, heart racing and terror demanding my limbs to move. "I think we'd better get out before whatever stopped us gives way." I slipped the shifter carefully into park, then eased my foot off the brake and turned squinting eyes on Caroline. "Open your door slowly, then get away from the truck."

She nodded, eyes still closed, and unfastened her seatbelt with trembling hands.

I did the same.

A full and heavy breath rushed from my lungs as both of my boots hit solid, flat ground. The truck had crash-landed on a narrow plateau, its tailgate now neatly dented into a rather large outcropping of rock.

"What the *heck*!" Caroline screamed, cheeks red and eyes open. She reached up to whack a floppy bear hanging on a limb overhead. "What is it with these bears?" she growled, then smacked the nearby teddy a few more times for good measure. She made another loud grunting noise, then skulked back up the hill, sliding on her fancy-heeled boots in a path illuminated only by my headlights.

I forced my shaking legs to carry me to the edge of the plateau, then nearly collapsed at the sight of the drop beyond. A direct plummet into the waiting arms of a million trees, each ready to impale us. The sleigh's broken pieces littered the forest floor, and bears hung from the trees.

Caroline was on the phone when I reached the narrow gravel lane where our wild ride had begun. A clear pair of sleigh tracks careened over the hill from the lodge, disappearing where we stood. Where the truck had been. "First responders are on the way," she said, wiping a tear from her cheek. "I dialed the local police so I wouldn't be part of the 911 log, then I called my dad's press secretary so she can get on top of this. He's going to be livid."

I wrapped an arm around her narrow shoulders. Caroline lived in PR mode; her father, a narcissistic mayor, and her codependent mother had made sure of it. My parents would cry all the way here, terrified I was injured in any possible way. Her parents would scold her for being in a situation that held the potential for bad press. "I'm sorry."

She turned and wrapped both arms around me, thoroughly shaken and fighting it all. Another burden her parents had given her: ladies don't have outbursts. They don't get angry, because that's unbecoming. And they don't cry in front of anyone. That's a sign of weakness. Plus, it ruins makeup and makes eyes puffy. The fact she'd screamed and pummeled the innocent tree bear had told me the extent of the state she was in. Her tears made it infinitely more clear.

She stepped away a few seconds later and fished a lighted compact from her purse to fix her makeup. "Thank you."

"Anytime."

She inhaled the icy air and let out a shaky laugh. "At least this wind will fight all this puffiness."

"Silver lining," I said, already sending texts to my folks and Evan about the crash. I felt my eyes stinging with the need for tears, but I had the rest of my night for a proper breakdown. Right now, Caroline needed me to hold it together. I sent a photo of the truck's current mountainside parking spot to Evan but spared my folks the trauma. They'd likely see it soon enough.

Then I called a tow truck.

"What happened!" Josie's voice split the night air and echoed through the mountains.

We turned to see her flapping her arms on the inn porch.

"Where's the sleigh? And the bears? Why are you two just standing out here?" She moved onto the walkway and stood akimbo in the wash of porch lighting. Her jaw dropped when she caught sight of the sleigh tracks. She went back inside.

A moment later, she reemerged with a coat and trudged down the driveway in our direction. "I just got everyone settled in the theater room for a showing of Paddington, and when I came to tidy the lobby," she called, making good time down the drive, "the sleigh wasn't outside the window." Her gaze stopped at my feet, where the sleigh tracks ended, then rose to the beams of my truck's headlights shining like beacons into the sky. "No!"

"I forgot to turn them off," I said about the lights.

Josie rushed forward and peered over the edge. "What did you do?"

Caroline rolled her eyes.

Josie gasped at the silhouettes of a hundred teddies, peppered through the forest like some kind of creepy invasion. She yanked her phone from her pocket and tapped the screen.

"We're not hurt," I said, "and I've already called a tow truck."

She scoffed at me. "I'm calling the insurance company! That sleigh was an antique and one of a kind. It's irreplaceable and so are those bears!"

I bit back a retort of frustration. "Care if we wait inside?" I asked.

Josie swung an arm in the direction of the inn, and Caroline and I marched back up the drive. We made hot chocolates from instant packets at a little stand in the lobby, then watched through the window for the tow truck's arrival.

Ninety minutes later, my pickup had been towed, and Caroline and I were belted securely into the backseat of my parents' extended cab truck.

I gave the inn and surrounding property one last look as we trundled away. Something was different besides the missing sleigh, but I couldn't put my finger on it. Seconds later, the scene was gone, swallowed by the night and forest as we crept back down the mountain.

Evan was waiting at the inn when we arrived after dropping Caroline off at home.

I wasn't sure if I wanted to hug him for being there, or sock him for locking Cookie up. Since I couldn't decide, I told him I wanted to be alone, then let myself inside and locked the door behind me.

I watched from my bedroom window as he paced the front walkway for several minutes before going back to his cruiser and driving away.

And in the safety of a hot shower, I cried.

* * *

I woke to muffled sounds of laughter the next morning. My alarm had been shut off, and according to the clock on my nightstand, it was nearly nine. A full two and a half hours later than I liked to get started on my days. I scooted up in bed, wincing at the aches in my back, neck, and shoulders, pains I hadn't noticed the night before. Thankfully, I'd been spared a knot on my forehead where it hit the steering wheel, but there was a distinct black and purple crescent, a memento of the connection.

I listened for the laughter again but didn't hear it. Maybe I'd imagined it. I wished I'd only imagined asking Caroline to join me on last night's road trip.

Cindy Lou Who leaped onto the bed and bit my toes.

"Hey." I pulled my feet under the covers and patted the space beside me, eager to pet her soft calico fur.

She turned away and sat just out of reach.

I picked up my phone and texted Caroline to see how she was feeling, while I rubbed sleep from my heavy eyelids. I hated that she'd been in danger because of me.

Her response was nearly instant.

Caroline: Taking the day off to recuperate. 😌
Caroline: Feels like I was hit with a giant sleigh full of teddy bears.

I laughed, then climbed out of bed.

The soft sounds of laughter came again, and I shuffled quickly into the kitchen. Outside my rooms, the inn smelled of vanilla, chocolate, and cinnamon.

"Oh!" Mom popped into view as she rounded the corner. "Good morning, sunshine." She hurried to wrap me in a hug. "How are you feeling?" She kissed my forehead, and I winced as she looked into my eyes. "Oh, sweetie. I'm sorry." She released me with a deep frown, then turned to the kitchen island, where a crockpot of her peppermint mocha hot chocolate warmed. Trays of snickerdoodles sat next to the cocoa beside rows of iced cut-out cookies in the shape of presents. "I've got just what you need." She retrieved a bottle of aspirin from my cupboard, then handed me two pills and a small glass of water.

I took the pills while she ladled a mug of hot chocolate for me and piled cookies on a small plate.

"I hope you don't mind," she said as another round of laughter rose through the air. "I invited some of my ladies over to help with the wrapping." She hooked a candy cane into the mug, like a delicious stir stick, then floated a cone of whipped cream on top and sprinkled it with green sugar crystals. She handed me the plate, then tipped her head for me to follow her.

Six of mom's closest friends sat on the floor in the parlor, each with a personal selection from the kitchen's treats, a small pile of toys, and everything they needed to wrap them.

"Sit," Mom whispered, motioning me to the overstuffed armchair beside the fireplace. "You rest and visit while we work."

The ladies waved and welcomed me to the party, then thanked me for having them over to help out. They all seemed genuinely happy for the opportunity.

191

I curled onto the chair as instructed, and Mom set my cocoa on a small end table. I balanced the plate of cookies on my lap, then dug in.

Holiday music played softly in the background as ladies I'd known my whole life chatted about their families, shopping, and holiday plans.

My heart swelled with love and pride for my family, home, and community. Then, a fleck of guilt wiggled in, suggesting I probably should've been kinder and more hospitable to Evan when I'd found him waiting for me last night. Who knew how long he'd been there or what he wanted to say?

I hadn't wanted to think about it then, but at the moment I was pretty sure I wanted to know what was on his mind.

Then I thought of Cookie and remembered Evan was a cop first and a friend second. He was in the middle of a murder investigation, so he'd likely come by to tell me I shouldn't have been in Great Falls or following up on Meg after he'd told me to leave the case alone.

But a killer had stabbed my strawberry cupcake, had been inside my truck to leave a warning on my windshield, and had built a raging fire in the pit and scratched a threat on the ground. Last night, I believed that same person had tried to kill Caroline and me by unleashing the sleigh outside Meg's inn. And if I'd learned anything from the last two murder cases I'd been swept up into, it was that I needed to find the killer before I became the next victim.

Thinking of the runaway sleigh brought another memory to mind. The little parking lot beside the inn had been neatly lined with vehicles when we arrived.

Four vehicles.

"Everything okay?" Mom asked, her voice pulling me from my thoughts. Her smile wavered when I didn't respond immediately.

"Yes." I nodded. "Sorry, I spaced out." I shook my head in tiny motions, careful not to incite pain in my neck or temples. "Everything is delicious and wonderful, and I can't thank you enough. All of you," I amended, looking to the ladies who were listening to our conversation, "It's perfect and so appreciated."

Mom leaned in my direction, then patted my knee with one outstretched palm. "When we're done with the wrapping, we'll tidy the downstairs for you. You've been through a lot this week, and I don't want you fussing or worrying about the arrival of Fay's bridal party. I cleaned the guest rooms this morning before the ladies arrived for wrapping."

"Thank you," I said again, meaning it with everything I had. I couldn't imagine doing housework in my condition, and I'd completely forgotten the bridesmaids were coming in two days.

I rested my head against the soft corduroy material of the armchair. Time was moving too quickly, and everything was blurring together.

I finished my sugary breakfast, then went to shower and dress for the day.

I called Caroline afterward to see if she wanted to visit Cookie. She agreed enthusiastically, then volunteered to drive. I disconnected, staring at my phone and debating whether or not to give Evan a warning that we were coming to the sheriff's department later.

I froze with my thumbs above the screen as the thought I'd lost track of earlier suddenly rushed back to mind. Something had been different about the inn's parking lot as Dad had driven us away from Meg's inn, and I knew what it was. There had been five cars when we left, but only four when we'd arrived. The new addition was a big white truck, nearly camouflaged against the snowy backdrop.

A truck like the one I'd watched Meg climb into downtown.

Chapter Nineteen

I'd busied myself sketching design ideas for jewelry for Fay's bridesmaids while I waited for Caroline to arrive. She needed a few hours to deal with her dad and get ready. I wavered over whether to call or text Evan about my observation of Meg's truck, then decided to talk to him in person. I just had to be patient a little while longer.

I moved another finished sketch onto a growing pile. Once I'd started brainstorming, a theme formed. Simple silver bracelets or chains with one small colorful charm. Elegant and understated enough to work for the wedding and any day afterward. I just couldn't decide on a charm. So far, I'd conjured a gingerbread woman in a green pleated skirt, or maybe wearing a replica bridesmaid gown, and holding a red heart. A pair of striped candy canes, tipped in on one another until their hooks met to form a heart. A dove with a sprig of holly in its beak. Gumdrops in varying colors, each with the wedding date at its center. Small glass gifts with a bridesmaid's initials on the tag. Fay would have to help me choose the charm, but I was feeling confident in the concept.

My mind wandered as I set my small graphite pencil on the fresh sheet of paper. Charm ideas tried to take shape—bells, chasing lights, stockings—but memories of last night's crash kept butting in. I tried uselessly to form a picture of what had happened on the night of Karen Moody's murder, based on the pieces of information I had. And my frustration grew out of control.

I checked the time, ready for a change of pace. Caroline would be another hour, and my knees had begun to bounce with restlessness. I considered borrowing another truck from the Reindeer Games fleet, but wasn't sure I wanted to drive.

Seven minutes later, I caved and texted Evan about Meg's truck arriving at the inn while Caroline and I were inside. If it could be proven that the truck I saw was Meg's, that would have to mean something. If the inn had exterior security cameras, maybe there was footage of her releasing the sleigh. That would have to prove she was Karen's real killer. Who else would want to stop me from asking questions that badly? And why else would Meg ruin something special to her inn, something Josie claimed couldn't be repaired or replaced?

The front door opened and shut again as Mom returned from walking the last of her friends to her car. The ladies had done the impossible in under four hours. Every toy in my possession was wrapped, tagged, and restacked in my office. Mom and her crew were a force of nature.

I listened as her footfalls headed in my direction, and smiled upon her arrival. "Have I told you lately that you're my hero?"

She froze, turned, and headed in the opposite direction.

"Was that offensive?" I called. "'Cause I can't help it. It's true!"

She reappeared with a box. "Silly. I forgot to bring this to you earlier. You can take it to Evan when you see him."

I frowned. "What is it?"

"These are the rest of Ms. Moody's things," she said. Her expression grew heavy as she set the box on the counter beside my sketchpad. "The deputies came by yesterday to remove the crime scene tape and give us the green light to use the space again. I told them I'd make sure the rest of her things were delivered to the station after I cleaned. There wasn't much," she added, tipping the box in my direction. "Most of her stuff was taken into evidence, but a bit was still hanging around. I'm sure the sheriff's department will see to it that these things reach her family."

My curiosity soared, and I pulled the box onto my lap to peek inside.

"It's mostly gumdrops," Mom said. "She clearly had a sweet tooth. So, maybe we weren't as different as we thought."

I unloaded the contents onto the island. "You aren't kidding," I marveled. The contents were almost exclusively gumdrops. Assorted bags. Individually packaged flavors, some from multiple companies, including Bonnie's Gumdrop Shop. "Why would anyone have this many gumdrops?" I asked, raising my gaze to meet Mom's.

She shrugged. "Maybe she liked them, or maybe she planned to make one of those gum drop villages for a holiday party. Something like the one Bonnie puts together as a window display, but on a smaller scale?" Mom sighed. "Breaks my heart she won't get the chance to finish whatever she'd been planning."

My mind itched. What *had* she been planning?

Hopefully not to eat all these gumdrops. There were hundreds.

"Holly," Mom said, a warning tone in her normally sweet voice. "Don't."

"What?"

"Whatever you're thinking," she said, "just don't. You were nearly killed last night. You wouldn't be here today if fate hadn't put that outcropping of stones precisely where it was." Her loving eyes filled with unshed tears, and my heart ached for the pain and worry I'd caused her.

"I'm sorry," I told her, rising to wrap her in a hug. "I'll try very hard to leave this alone."

She pulled back to eyeball me a minute, then set her palms against my cheeks. "I know you worry about Cookie, but I also know you trust Evan, even if you seem to have forgotten."

I nodded, unsure how to respond.

Mom smiled and released my cheeks. "Good. Now, I'm going to get out of your hair and go find myself a hot shower and a long nap. I'm going to tell Libby we're on a cookies-and-cocoa-only menu at the Hearth today, then hunt down your father for a nice dinner at home."

"Love you," I said.

"Love you too. Call me if you need anything, and tell Cookie I'll visit her in the morning." She blew me a kiss, then headed for the door. "If you have time, pin a ribbon on your favorite Frosty. I forgot."

"Will do!" I said, turning back to the gumdrops. For kicks, I sorted them by flavor, then by brand, curiosity urging me along.

Assorted bags aside, Karen had purchased excessive amounts of eight flavors, or variations of those flavors. She'd purchased gumdrops from Bonnie's shop in all of those. And in the box she had similarly named flavors from other brands as well. I searched the unfamiliar makers on my phone. Yummy Gummy was a gourmet candy company in New Orleans, and Sophia's L.A. was an elite sweets shop in Los Angeles.

I stared at the bags. None of them had been opened. She'd been in town for three days and two nights. If she liked gumdrops so much, why hadn't she eaten any? Why so many of these eight flavors? Why these three companies? Why buy Bonnie's gumdrops if she'd brought so many of these other brands with her?

I took pictures of everything, then repacked the box. I paused with a bag from the Gumdrop Shop in hand. The label declared her products to be homemade, using only the best ingredients. The number "1921" sat beneath the logo. Bonnie didn't appear to be one hundred years old, so I could only assume her products were the result of a family recipe. But it was hard for me to understand her claim to "only the best ingredients." Were there some not-so-great gumdrop ingredients out there? What were they? And what were gumdrops even made of?

I flipped the bag over to see what exactly went into Bonnie's Cheery Cherry–flavored candies. Most of the words were foreign to me.

I pulled the Yummy Gummy package of Cherry Jubilee out of the box and flipped it over beside Bonnie's bag. The products were identical, as most of these things were. Tiny, doorless igloos made of sugar and a bunch of things I couldn't pronounce.

Gooseflesh spread over my arms, as I compared the identical ingredients lists.

I repeated the process with all eight of the most prevalent flavors. Bonnie's and their counterparts. Same thing. Every time.

My hands fell to my lap and I chewed my lip for brainpower.

Did all gumdrops have the same ingredients? Or was one of these companies stealing another company's formula? If so, that felt a lot like fraud to me. And it wasn't hard to imagine which company was likely committing the crime since Bonnie's sweets were being compared across the board to all the others.

I imagined Karen, the world's meanest critic, actually uncovering something worth complaining about, and the amount of damage she could do with that information. Then I dove head-first into a research rabbit hole.

Evan had told me he'd found reason to believe Karen had wanted to move into an investigative reporter role. The materials before me would certainly go along with that. I tapped my hand against my thigh as my theory firmed.

Allegations of fraud or intellectual theft or trademark infringement, or whatever this was, could cost the accused party everything. Their brand's reputation for sure—and a whole lot of money if the other company sued.

I opened a search engine on my phone, haunted once more by Bonnie's words the night Karen was killed. She'd said it was last year all over again. What had that meant to her? I entered her name, her shop's name, Karen's name, and the month into the browser and hit "Enter." A review came up linked to the Gumdrop Shop's website. Karen had written an article titled "Gourmet Sweets and Treats" as part of a holiday special for

New England Magazine, and the content had been her usual. She'd derided chocolatiers, caramel makers, multiple bakers— and Bonnie. Karen had called Bonnie's gumdrops inauthentic and had questioned the validity of the number 1921 on her labels, having done enough research to prove the company had only come into business a decade earlier, after Bonnie left candy- making school in pursuit of a career in edible art.

My phone buzzed with a text from Caroline.

On my way! Be there in thirty.

I pocketed my phone and donned my coat, thankful Caro- line would be here soon, and we could visit Cookie together, delivering twice the amount of encouragement and hugs. I tucked the box into a cupboard for later so I could have time to process what I'd learned before I handed it over to Evan. In the meanwhile, I'd let time get away from me, and I needed to judge the Frosties.

Build a Big Frosty was an outdoor fan favorite at Reindeer Games. Teams spent hours creating the perfect snow creation. Originally, the object had been literal. Whoever could build the biggest snowman won. The winner, or winners, got a pie. But as time passed and the players became more creative, "bigger" had ceased defining "better." Now, judging this particular Reindeer Game had become tricky.

I strode through the snow, half lost in thought, examining the amazing creations. Many of the builders were still tinker- ing with details. Others had called it a night as dinnertime had rolled around.

One snowman was inarguably the biggest, towering at least a foot above the rest. Another was a mind-bogglingly accurate representation of the character Frosty from the 1969 animation *Frosty the Snowman*. Others were typical snowmen and snow-women, complete with scarves, hats, button eyes, and carrot noses.

This year, the second tallest frosty on the field caught my eye because it made me smile. The team had used sticks to add detail to a seven-foot snowman as I'd walked the field, evaluating. They'd fashioned two small snowmen, one standing on the other's shoulders and wearing a top hat. An open trench coat had been etched around them, replicating every cartoon I'd ever loved where two kids devised a scheme to go somewhere they shouldn't, posing as one adult. "Winner!" I said, pressing the official blue ribbon into the sculpture's trench coat.

The couple stopped, stared, then burst into excited embraces. "Thank you!" they cheered.

I handed them a certificate for free cookies and cocoas or a pie of their choice, and pointed them toward the Hearth.

A sleek black sedan pulled into the nearest visitor's parking lot and honked, then flashed its lights. "Get in!" Caroline called, powering her window down long enough to wave an arm out the window.

She didn't have to ask me twice.

*   *   *

We parked outside the Mistletoe Sheriff's Department twenty minutes later, then signed in as visitors for Delores Cutter. We followed a deputy past a small set of empty cells meant for detaining criminals, and a note of panic built in my chest.

"Where is she?" I asked.

The deputy didn't stop or look back. He unlocked another door with his keycard and held it open for us to pass. "This way."

We moved through a brightly lit and bustling area with desks clustered at the center and doors lined neatly along one wall. "Sheriff," he said, stopping in the doorway of a plush conference room, complete with lighted Christmas tree and a large flat-screen television on one wall.

Evan rose from his seat, then came to greet us, and the deputy walked away.

Cookie spun in one of the fancy roller chairs at a massive table, her feet barely touching the ground. The table was engraved with the sheriff's department logo, and a steaming mug sat before her with a half-eaten deli sandwich. "Hey!" she said, waving a plastic gun in one hand. "Evan's been letting me do some simulation training. What a hoot!"

I followed her gaze to the big screen. A series of animated figures in ski masks crisscrossed a cartoon cityscape while other characters ran around screaming. It looked more like an old arcade game than any kind of official training simulation.

I cocked a questioning brow at Evan, who smiled.

"She won't shoot anyone," he told me. "She just keeps taking shots near their feet and yelling for backup."

Cookie set her gun aside. "Backup never comes, but it's a load of fun when I hit a sign and it falls over."

I grinned despite myself.

"Come on in," Evan said, a note of caution in his tone that was likely only audible to me.

Caroline and I bookended Cookie, then wrapped her in a three-woman hug.

"How are you?" Caroline asked, as I said, "I'm so sorry you're here."

Cookie patted our arms. "I'm okay. This place isn't so bad. Though I do worry about Theodore. Have either of you talked with him? Explained what's going on?"

We released her, then took seats at the table.

"Theodore is great," I promised. "Dad spoils him rotten. All the horses hate him for it."

She smiled. "Good. Did you tell him why I'm not coming to see him? He worries about me, you know. I don't want him thinking I went and kicked the bucket again. Last time I did that, I tripped on the handle and whacked my head. It was awful. We still talk about it sometimes."

I pressed my lips, unsure if that story was funny or sad. "He completely understands this isn't your fault and that you're in good hands," I told her, chest tightening with concern. There was no one kinder on earth, and she didn't deserve any of this. I shot a look in Evan's direction. "Pierce is the best attorney around, and he'll make sure your rights are protected."

Evan worked his jaw.

"You can only legally keep her here two more days," I told him. "Then you have to let her go."

"Or he can arrest me," Cookie said, looking utterly heartbroken. "I met Karen's family last night. They're pretty upset, I'm glad she had folks who loved her. She made a lot of enemies, so it's good she had people in her corner."

Caroline pulled Cookie back into a hug. "I miss you."

Evan turned to me while they spoke. "How are you feeling? Don't give me the sugar-coated version."

"Sore," I said, glad he wanted the real details, but not quite ready to talk about them. "I'm shaken but counting my lucky stars, I guess. How are you?"

"Me?" He crossed his arms, and his green eyes turned brooding. "I was scared to death for more than two hours after you texted me last night. The stress improved slightly when I saw you with my own eyes, but you blew me off. I wanted to talk about what happened. And for the record, I don't care if you're mad at me. I'm just glad you're okay."

"You mean you're not mad at me for visiting that inn?"

He pursed his lips. "I mean, I could say 'I told you so' about pushing this investigation of yours," he said finally, "but that doesn't feel helpful."

"Correct."

"Maybe we can team up," he suggested, eyes and jaw tight.

Cookie and Caroline fell silent.

"What do you mean?" Caroline asked, dipping in on our conversation.

He kept his gaze fixed on me as he answered. "Why don't we agree to openly share information related to Karen Moody's death? Then I can try to keep you safe while this mess winds down."

I cocked my head. "Will you answer all my questions? And tell me when you have new theories and why?"

"Will you do the same?" he asked.

"Yeah. What's the catch?"

He unfolded his arms. "You agree that I'm the only one who will confront possible suspects. You further agree to stand down in exchange for information."

I narrowed my eyes. "You're willing to tell me who your suspects are?" I asked, a measure of hope rising in my heart. If he had other suspects, then he was still looking for the true killer, and Cookie had a real chance of being set free.

"If it means keeping you safe," Evan said, "yes. I will tell you anything I'm not bound by law to keep confidential. And I know you won't complain about the things I can't tell you because you wouldn't want me to break the law. Also, you wouldn't want to be the reason I lose my job."

I narrowed my eyes until he blurred a little.

He grinned. "Deal?"

I mulled the offer over. There were only two days left before Cookie was released or arrested. Given the pile of evidence against her, I was almost certain she would be arrested. "Did you get my texts about the white truck?" I asked, setting up a small test.

He dipped his chin. "I did."

"And?"

"I've already asked a deputy to look into it. He's attempting to confirm the vehicle's ownership and Meg Mason's whereabouts at the time of your accident." Evan's mouth curved down on the final word.

"Do you think it's possible the sleigh situation was an accident?" I asked.

"No." His frown deepened. "I spoke to the local police and the hotel's insurance adjuster this morning. It's been confirmed that the ropes securing the sleigh were cut."

A chill slid through me. I'd been right again. Someone *had* tried to kill me last night.

And I was nearly positive Evan would soon discover the white truck belonged to Meg Mason.

Chapter Twenty

Evan excused himself so that Caroline and I could visit with Cookie alone.

We talked for nearly an hour, far longer than I imagined a standard visit would be permitted, and I appreciated it more than I could ever say. Cookie was shaken and rightly worried that the person trying to frame her for Karen's murder had done an airtight job. I promised her that Caroline and I would figure something out, and Caroline reminded her of the support team on her side. Ray, Fay, Pierce, my folks, Samantha, Cookie's book club, and dozens more. As a bonus, we still had two days to put a crack in this case against her. "A whole lot can happen in two days," I reminded her.

"Yeah," she agreed. "Just make sure some of it happens in my favor. And work quick. I want to be at Fay and Pierce's wedding." She swung her gaze to Caroline. "I'll have to go as your date. My invite specifically said no goats. Can you imagine? What a strange thing to put on a wedding RSVP. A real shame, too, because Theodore looks fantastic in a tux."

I bit back a laugh and promised to do my best to wrap things up before the wedding, or at least to set her free by then.

If my Meg theory didn't pan out, I still had the peculiar case of the gourmet gumdrops to dig into. I filled my friends in on what I'd found in the box of Karen's things and what I thought it might mean. They agreed the identical ingredients lists were reason for suspicion, but Cookie liked Bonnie too much to believe her as a murder suspect. Caroline and I weren't as sure.

"Bonnie's smart," Cookie warned. "If you go after her, you'd better play this close to the vest."

Caroline squeezed Cookie's hand on the table. "Maybe we can start smaller. Before we go pointing fingers, we can do a taste comparison. Make sure the flavors are truly the same."

Cookie's face lit at the notion. She licked her lips and dropped her gaze to my purse. "Did you bring them with you?"

"No. I left them at home," I said. "I'm sorry."

She sighed. "Maybe share a few with Theodore for me?"

"Absolutely," I agreed.

*   *   *

We climbed back inside Caroline's sedan. She checked her mirrors, then fixed me with an emotional stare. "That was the worst," she said. "I'm glad we got to see her, but ugh." She batted her eyes, fighting to keep the tears at bay. "I can't stand seeing her trapped in there. Sleeping on a cot, worrying about Theodore, and justly concerned that she might be arrested for murder when she is clearly being framed. Tell me you have a plan beyond eating candy."

"Kind of," I said. "But we should definitely try the gumdrops. I think there's something there worth exploring."

She sniffed but nodded.

We rolled away from the sheriff's department and back through town at a snail's pace. Caroline's sedan wasn't four-wheel drive, and with the gentle flux in temperatures lately, there was a slick mix of slush and ice on everything.

"I've been thinking about what happened last night," she said, stopping at a red light downtown. "If that sleigh was really irreplaceable, Meg would've needed a big reason to ruin it."

"I thought the same thing," I said.

"What did you think of Karen's ex when you went to see him?" Caroline asked.

"Talented, handsome, angry," I said, naming the characteristics as they came to mind. "He had possible means and definite motive, but only came to my attention after a lot of online research. I haven't discounted him, but he's low on my list right now."

"Okay," she said. "So, we'll focus on Meg and Bonnie. Karen's mean review could've ruined Meg's legacy, and Karen's possible gumdrop research project could've destroyed Bonnie's future."

That about summed it up.

We rode in silence to the inn, each lost in thought, and Caroline no doubt concentrating on the icy roads.

She parked in the lot outside the inn, and we went straight for the kitchen.

"Are these your new design ideas?" Caroline asked, leafing through the sketches I'd left on the counter while I unloaded the box of gumdrops hidden in my cupboard. "These are all really pretty."

"Thanks. Fay asked me to make jewelry for her bridesmaids," I said. "I was brainstorming."

"Well, I love them." She set a sketch of one bracelet against her wrist, as if trying it on. "Your creations always remind me of Bonnie's window displays, where the gumdrops seem to come to life at little candy carnivals or concerts. Yours are better, of course." She slid her eyes my way, then put the sketch down.

"As long as you don't try to eat them," I said.

Caroline's smile faded a bit as she took in the amount of candy I'd unloaded. "Holy gumdrops."

"Right?" I nodded, a bit overcome by the amount of sugar ahead of us.

She moved in close to better evaluate the scenario before her. "There are just so many. How will we keep our taste testing straight when the products all look alike?"

"Good question." I puzzled a minute before inspiration hit. "Be right back." I hurried into my office and grabbed a roll of wrapping paper with dotted gridlines on the back, then carried a piece the size of my island counter into the kitchen. "We can use this to create a chart."

"Excellent!" Caroline opened each bag carefully, then lined two of each flavor and brand in a different square on the paper. I used a pen to mark their names.

"I feel a little badly for eating a murdered woman's candy," I admitted. "I know she can't enjoy them now, but I was supposed to make sure these things went to her family."

"No," Caroline said. "I won't allow you to feel guilty. This little experiment could lead to exposing her real killer, and I'm willing to bet Karen's family would gladly pay two gumdrops per package for that information."

I smiled. Then we began to sample.

Caroline and I worked methodically through the process of testing each flavor and brand against the next. We started by weighing them on my kitchen scale and scrutinized their appearances up close. From there, we took a tiny bite of one gumdrop, then did the same with another brand, attempting to identify any differences in flavor or texture. We noted everything.

The findings were universally consistent. Gumdrops with matching ingredients lists were exactly the same. In size, shape, texture, and flavor. Bonnie's Cheery Cherry was Sophia's L.A.'s Cherry Jubilee. Bonnie's Sugar Plum were Yummy Gummy's Plum Delight. And so on.

Across the board, Bonnie's gumdrops, which were touted on the packaging as being in production since 1921, were exact duplicates of the gumdrops from two other companies, according to flavor. So the question became whether two different companies, from locations across the country but in two different directions, both stole Bonnie's gumdrop recipes.

Or had Bonnie stolen theirs?

I turned to Caroline, still examining the various labels. "Can two sweets have the same ingredients and still be different products?" I asked.

"Umm." She rubbed her forehead and slid onto a stool at the island. "That's tricky." She lined the bags, label up, in front of her. "The FDA requires every ingredient used in a product to be listed on the packaging in descending order of predominance. The primary ingredient first, then each item after that, according to their amount. These lists are matches, but the measurements aren't listed, so, for argument's sake, I guess there could be variances in how much of each ingredient is in there, as long as the items stay in order for that particular product."

"Different ratios," I said, mulling it over. "But that would change the flavor, wouldn't it?"

Caroline pulled her lips to the side. "Unless the variance is so insignificant it doesn't matter."

"What about the creation process?" I asked. "How does that change the final product? For example, can two companies follow the same recipe but handle the steps differently enough to produce two distinct products?"

"Maybe," she said, though her voice was hesitant. "Do you ever make scrambled eggs?"

I smiled, thankful she didn't use a cupcake baking analogy because I made a habit of leaving the baking up to my mom, the master. "Yes."

"Okay, so think about it like this. Two cooks are making scrambled eggs with cheese, onions, and mushrooms." She ticked the ingredients off on her fingers. "One person cracks the eggs into a pan, tosses the other ingredients on top and jabs it all with the spatula until it's mixed. The other person whips all four items together in a bowl with a whisk before adding them to the skillet. Same ingredients, different outcome."

I nodded. "The whipped eggs look different, fuller, fluffier," I said. I knew because I made eggs the first way, and Mom and Dad both went the second route.

"They taste the same," she said, "but their textures are different."

I tapped my fingers against the countertop, staring at all the exact replica gumdrops. "If Karen was looking into Bonnie's gumdrops because she'd planned to accuse her of stealing other companies' recipes and passing them off as her own, it could've cost Bonnie everything."

"Just like Karen's ugly review of Meg's inn cost her most of her business," Caroline said. "Closing the inn wouldn't just mean losing her income. She could have to sell the place and the land it sits on, which means losing her inheritance, a piece of her family history. That's devastating on a few levels."

"Agreed," I said. "Beyond that, it's a question of who would take that fatal swing with a metal nutcracker. Even in anger, most people would never lash out like that. Striking someone over the head from behind is violent and gruesome."

I imagined the murder scene playing out. Once with Meg wielding the nutcracker, then again with Bonnie in the killer's role. Unfortunately, I didn't know either woman well enough to make that kind of prediction. "Some people scream when pushed to the edge. Others throw punches. A few resort to destruction of property, but I'd like to believe very few people would ever kill."

"So, who did?" she asked.

And that was the most important question.

* * *

Evan stopped by after dinner to pick up the box of Karen's things.

I'd sent him a quick text after Caroline left, letting him know I had it, and he'd immediately promised to be here.

He paused in the foyer to toe off his boots and hang his sheriff's jacket on a hook near the door. He smiled at me a moment before his gaze went to the piles of beautifully wrapped gifts in my office. "You've been busy."

"Wasn't me," I said. "My mom and her friends did all that. Mom also cleaned the guest rooms so they'd be ready for Fay's bridesmaids. She brought the box of Karen's things down to me when she finished." I led him to the kitchen, hoping he wouldn't look inside the box when I gave it to him. I'd opened the bags carefully and resealed them with invisible tape, but it was obvious everything had been tampered with. "Coffee or cocoa?" I asked.

"Cocoa." He moved to the end of the island and gripped the counter before blowing out a long breath. "I'll take the works tonight. I've had one heck of a day."

"I look forward to hearing all about it," I said, ladling a mug of homemade hot chocolate from the small slow cooker on my counter. I sprayed a funnel of whipped topping over the steaming liquid, then doused it in mint and chocolate-flavored jimmies and crisscrossed that with chocolate syrup. I popped a candy cane into the mug, then ferried the drink to Evan, admiring the finished product.

"Did you eat Karen's gumdrops?" Evan raised an offended stare in my direction. The opened bags of sweets were piled on the island between us, tape side up.

"Technically," I hedged, setting the cocoa in front of him and hoping the sight of it would sweeten him up, "yes."

His eyelids slid shut, and he pressed two fingers to a vein that had begun to throb on his forehead. "Why?" he nearly whispered, possibly attempting to remain calm.

"You drink. I'll talk," I said.

His eyes opened and I started talking, filling him in on the details of my Bonnie theory. Then about the taste test Caroline and I had performed with Karen's gumdrops.

Evan's jaw worked between sips of hot chocolate. When the mug's contents were nearly depleted, he set the drink aside. He read bag labels, then peeled away the tape and sampled. His gaze rose to mine.

"See," I said.

He huffed out an irritated breath. "We have no way of knowing what Karen's intentions were with these gumdrops. All you have is a theory and circumstantial evidence. Also, this is not my problem. But you are, and I need you to stop finding trouble."

I guffawed. "Karen's murder is very much your problem."

"Yes," he agreed, stuffing the resealed bags back into the box. "Solving Karen's murder is my problem. Uncovering some gumdrop recipe theft scheme is not. And we just talked about you staying out of this investigation a few hours ago. What did you do? Agree to my conditions, then come straight home to do the opposite!"

I bit my lip, unwilling to tell the truth on that one. "If I'm right," I said instead, "my theory gives Bonnie serious motive for confronting Karen. An argument could have occurred then grown heated, leading to Bonnie lashing out in a way she couldn't take back. And for the record, I agreed to share all my information with you, which I am doing. All my gumdrop research was done right here at this island. No one else heard us or saw what we were doing, and I'm reporting my findings as promised."

Evan went back to his cocoa. "Fine. Anything else?"

I took a minute to think about that. "When Cookie and I visited Karen's ex-husband, Steven, at his shop, the red velvet toy-collection bag was missing. He's not at the top of my suspect list, but I haven't ruled him out yet. I wanted to ask you about it because you said you assigned a deputy to check on that."

"I did," Evan said too calmly, like the peace before a storm. "He claims not to know where the bag went or when it disappeared. Apparently the toy drop box wasn't something he kept close watch over, and he has a solid alibi for the hours surrounding Karen's death. He attends support meetings for people recovering from toxic relationships."

I blinked. "Oh."

"Believe it or not, I'm fairly competent once in a while," he said.

I smiled.

Evan shook his head and raised his hot chocolate to his lips, a smile curving behind the mug.

"All right, how about this information," I said, realizing I had more to tell. "When I was at the bookstore talking to Debra Jo, she said Bonnie was a huge murder mystery fan."

His gaze hardened. "How do you have this much free time?"

"All the inn guests left," I said. "Anyway, Bonnie and Cookie are both members of Debra Jo's book club, and they agree Bonnie is obsessed with detective novels. She reads mysteries exclusively and is really good at solving them before everyone else. You know what that means?"

"That you and Bonnie should be friends?" he guessed.

I hadn't thought about that. "Maybe." *If she isn't a killer.* "But also that someone who solves all those fictional murders probably has a good idea of how to cover a real one too."

Evan's shoulders sagged, so I brought him a stack of Mom's whoopie pies as a pick-me-up. He took one without comment, and his eyes fluttered a little as he chewed. He finished his cocoa, then tipped the mug in my direction. "Can I ask you a favor?"

"Sure." I beamed. "One refill, coming up!" I reached for the mug, but he didn't let it go.

He leveled me with the kind of no-nonsense gaze I was sure had made more than a few Boston criminals cry. "Leave this investigation alone. I know we talked about a truce and a partnership, but you're getting yourself in too deep by digging all these holes, and I have things under control. So, please stop. For me."

I stilled. What did that mean? Was I onto something? What did he know?

As I scrutinized his expression, trying to hear what he wasn't saying, the tension in his eyes and frustration on his brow began to needle me. "I'm sorry," I said without thinking. "You look exhausted, and I know I'm at least partly to blame. I don't mean to be a thorn to you. I just hate feeling helpless, and everything is going wrong. Cookie's being held at the jail. Christmas is four days away. Someone tried to kill Caroline and me last night." My traitorous voice cracked on the last sentence. I squared my shoulders, unwilling to break. "But this isn't about me. Tell me what's going on with you and how I can help."

Evan offered a small smile. "I know you mean well, but I really don't need your help. My attention is being pulled in too many directions already, and your amateur investigation doesn't have to be one of them."

I knew it was true but felt helpless to stop myself. "Have you heard anything from Boston?" I asked.

As much as I had on my plate, I often forgot that Evan's responsibilities were infinite. He was the sheriff of Mistletoe, a tourist-heavy Christmas town, and it was Christmastime. The safety and well-being of every citizen and tourist fell on his shoulders. He had deputies to manage and public relations issues to deal with, on top of Karen's murder, Cookie being framed, and his baby sister being called to testify against a career criminal complicit in the death of her best friend. My mind swam just trying to keep track of it all. And that was *without* me meddling. "I'm sorry."

Evan stroked a hand over my hair. "You don't have to keep apologizing. I know your heart is in the right place, and I'm not here to try to squash your curiosity or your spirit. But Holly." He leaned back, fixing me with a stern look. "If you could just stand down until New Year's Day. Let me wrap this up and get Libby through the trial, that would be great," he said more softly. "Meanwhile, let me do what I can to help Cookie. Being the sheriff comes with a bit of influence. Maybe I can throw my weight around. If that doesn't work, I'll turn a blind eye while you and half the town bust her out for Christmas. What do you think?"

"I think if she's still there on Christmas it's because you've arrested her." I crossed my arms, warm feelings melting.

Evan's phone rang and I turned away as he answered, trying to get my thoughts and emotions under control again.

"When?" he asked. "Where?" The urgency and concern in his tone turned my stomach. A million dark and horrible things twisted through my mind as I turned back to face him. "What happened?" I whispered. "Is it Cookie? Is she okay?"

He waved me to be quiet as he listened, pacing though the kitchen now. One hand knuckle deep in his shaggy hair, the other pressing the phone against his ear.

I stuffed my thumbnail between my teeth to keep my mouth busy while I waited.

Several heartbeats later, he pocketed the phone and fixed me with a troubled gaze. "I have to go. Thank you for the cocoa and the whoopie pies. And for agreeing to leave this investigation alone."

"I didn't agree to that," I said, rushing behind him as he headed for the foyer. "Where are you going? Is Cookie okay?"

"Cookie's fine," he said, threading his arms back into his black department-issued parka.

"Can you tell me what's happening?" I asked. "I'll see it in the news tomorrow morning anyway. If you don't, I'll just wind up worrying until the paper gets here."

He crouched down to lace his boots, then stood, expression grim. "There was an attack in town, and the victim's being rushed to the hospital. I need to meet my deputy, the medics, and victim there. I want you to stay here. I mean it. And lock the door behind me."

Panic shot adrenaline through my veins so fast I thought my feet might leave the ground. "What kind of an attack?" I begged. "A robbery? Something else? Something worse?" At least the victim had lived. Evan was on his way to the hospital, not a murder scene. I counted that as a win this week. Then the piercing fear returned. "Was it Caroline? One of Mom's friends? Or Fay's bridesmaids?" I loved every single person in my town, and the thought of any of them being attacked stung my eyes and burned my nose. "Are they going to be okay?" I asked, my quavering voice barely more than a whimper.

He opened the door and stepped into the snowy night, indecision in his eyes. I wasn't sure what he was torn between at the moment, and I forgot the question immediately when he said, "Bonnie was the victim. I'll call you when I know more."

And then he was gone.

Chapter Twenty-One

Ray called from the Hearth the next day. He'd stopped for lunch and to visit with Libby, but now he wanted to see me. He didn't ask me to come out for cocoa and cookies as usual. This time, he'd only confirmed I was home, then asked if he could stop by. The change in routine piqued my interest, and in anticipation I nearly went out to meet him on the porch.

I waited in the foyer instead, watching through the window and imagining what had prompted his visit. Hopefully he was up to something, because I was bored and could use the distraction from my own thoughts. The entire inn was spotless, thanks to Mom and her friends. All the toys were wrapped. And I was pacing ruts in the floor, not to mention infuriating Cindy Lou Who with all my nervous energy and unwanted attention.

Ray jogged up the steps, and I pulled the door open before he could knock. "Whoa. Were you just standing in there watching for me?"

"Yes. Come in." I tugged him forward, then pressed the door shut against the frigid wind.

He stopped on the wide black mat, stomping snow from his shoes and scanning the uber tidy rooms. "It's very quiet."

"Yep." My skin buzzed with excess energy and I pushed both hands into my pockets to keep from helping him out of his coat and begging him to stay a while. "All my guests are gone, and Cindy's hiding from me."

"You look a little crazy," he said, sweeping his gaze over the barrel curls I'd added to my mousy brown hair and the extreme eye makeup I'd applied while watching a few dozen online tutorials.

"I'm trying to stay busy. Keep my mind off things. But my truck's in the shop, so I'm stuck here," I said. "Alone." I'd already completed and hauled a bunch of jewelry items to the Holiday Mouse for Kinley to sell. There wasn't much left to do besides go bananas.

I'd made a bunch of phone calls after breakfast, including one to Fay to discuss the bridesmaids' jewelry she'd requested. She'd had no problem choosing from the sketch photos I'd texted, and I'd already finished those pieces too. Thanks to the recent bottle pickup from Wine Around, I'd been able to make all four charms in a couple of hours. From there, finding purpose for my time had gotten sketchy.

Ray rubbed his palms together and grinned. "Then you're about to be really glad I stopped by."

"Yeah?" I asked, a little too eagerly. "Are we going to town?"

His eyes widened and he laughed. "Yeah. Mom's wedding is tomorrow, and the bridesmaids have all flown in and taken over my house. I needed to get out, and I thought I'd make a day of it."

I smiled. "The bridesmaids will be taking over this house tomorrow and staying through the weekend. I'm looking forward to it."

He rolled his eyes. "It's too much estrogen. I like my mom and aunts. I like you and Libby. But all at once, you all can be a lot."

I laughed. Caroline had said the same thing about the bears at Meg's inn.

"I want to go see Cookie," Ray said. "I haven't gotten over there yet, and I have some things to show her." He patted his cross-body messenger bag. "I thought I'd ask you to come along."

I didn't need to be asked twice. I ran to the kitchen to grab a gift bag I'd over-embellished after I finished my makeup, then ran back. "Can we make one more stop while we're in town?"

* * *

Cookie met us in a small interrogation room. She was needle-pointing and looking a little worse for the wear.

Ray and I took the seats across the table from her, as if this was an interview for some kind of job.

"They gave me a plastic needle," she said, lifting a thin, blue thing into view. "I can't have a proper one because it's considered a weapon." She set the entire project on the table with a sigh. "And the Fire Department is having their holiday party in the big conference room, so I have to hang out in here unless I want to go back to the holding cell. I don't like the cell."

"I'm sorry," I said. "I hate that you're in here."

"Me too," she agreed in the smallest, saddest tone I'd ever heard. "I get to stay in Evan's office when he's here, but he's out.

And I'm afraid I'm going to miss your mother's wedding." She turned somber eyes on Ray.

"I'm not going to let that happen. What are you working on?" I asked, desperate to change the subject, at least until I had an idea of how I was going to back up my promise to free her.

The thin white material had a delicate floral wreath stitched on it, and the words "Maybe Wine Will Help" were outlined in the center.

"It's for Samantha," Cookie said. "She stopped by this morning with a case of Christmas Moscato for the deputies. A pretty red ribbon was tied on every bottle."

"That's nice," I said, impressed with Samantha's sweet gesture. Her temper had gotten her in a little trouble last Christmas, so the gift had likely gone a long way toward building bridges with each of those deputies.

Cookie rested her elbows on the table, then lowered her chin into waiting hands. "She told the deputies she hoped they were all being extra nice to me. Then she reminded them to be careful because wine bottles were sharp when they were broken."

I traded a look with Ray.

"Isn't that nice?" Cookie asked. "She's rough around the edges, but she looks after me."

I smiled, unsure what to say to that, but glad it made Cookie happy.

She frowned, taking her first real look at me. "Did you get a makeover? Was it one of those glow-ups all the kids are talking about these days?"

Ray chuckled.

"No, I was just trying to pass time." I tugged on a curl bobbing near my cheek, and it sprang back into place with unnecessary enthusiasm.

"The curls would work for the Bo Peep convention," Ray said, teasing, but he wasn't wrong.

"I like that shimmer eye shadow," Cookie said. "Reminds me of Vegas. When I was a cigarette girl, we used to put a little glitter on our décolletage to get bigger tips!"

"Bigger what?" Ray asked, his face going slack and cheeks pink.

I bit my lip and shoved him. "Show her why we're here."

Ray pulled himself together, then reached for his messenger bag and dragged it onto his lap. "I brought you something," he told Cookie.

He'd only managed to get the bag past security after a deputy had examined it half to death. As if we were attempting to sneak some nefarious contraband to this small white-haired woman, armed with a plastic needle.

"Samples are in," Ray said proudly. He'd told me about the surprise on our way over, and I couldn't wait to set my eyes on the prize.

He placed two calendars on the table, then pushed one in Cookie's direction.

I picked up the other.

"If you like these," he said, "I can have them printed today and ready in time for Christmas. If not, let me know what you want changed, and I'll work on that this afternoon. The article I'm writing for the paper on things to do in Mistletoe this week practically finished itself."

I flipped the sample open, eager to see what kooky props and poses I'd find Theodore in this year.

The pictures began with Theodore in a tuxedo vest and bow tie, apparently attending a lavish party thrown by the likes of Jay Gatsby. A perfect use of green screen technology that had me instantly craving more.

"I see you kicked your calendar game up a notch," I said, smiling goofily at Ray.

He shrugged. "I got some new software and thought it would be perfect for this. I wanted to give last year's buyers a new experience."

I turned back to the charming image. Green screen technology made it possible to portray anyone as being anywhere. All Ray needed was a photo of the subject and a little imagination.

"This is neat!" Cookie said, head up and spirits rising.

I could've hugged Ray. Instead, I turned the page.

February featured Theodore's neck and head poking out of a bubble bath. The clawfoot tub he bathed in was charming and surrounded by lit candles. Open boxes of chocolates sat beside a nearly empty flute and bottle of champagne on a small stand beside the tub. Red letters on white rose petals along the floor spelled "Be Goat to Yourself."

I barked a giant, insuppressible laugh, then turned the pages more quickly, loving every photo more than the last.

The calendar went on hilariously, occasionally with a traditional, non-computer-aided image of Theodore. A peek at a goat's life in Mistletoe, wearing one of his many vests, hats, and sweaters.

"He went snorkeling!" Cookie said, spotting the image of Theodore in colorful fins and a mask, swimming near the coral reef. "He's always loved adventure."

Ray sat back, resting one big foot over the opposite knee. "Do you like the Bermuda shorts in that picture, or were they too much?"

"I like 'em!" Cookie said. "And this beach photo, where he's getting a tan. He wrote my name in the sand!"

I nudged him with my elbow, thanking him for the joy he'd brought to Cookie's face. "Nicely done."

"Thanks," he said.

Cookie's smile faded as she came to the end of the calendar. She slid it off the table and hugged it to her chest. "I think this is perfect. I really miss that handsome fellow."

"He misses you too," I said. "I saw Dad at breakfast today, and he said he and Mom took Theodore for a sleigh ride last night. He loved it."

Cookie's impossibly fair skin paled further, another thought apparently coming to mind. "I heard what happened to Bonnie last night," she said. "She must've been so scared."

"According to the morning paper, she was struck from behind while leaving her store through the employee entrance in back. She was found unconscious by another shop owner and taken to the hospital by ambulance. So far, she hasn't woken up," I said. "I knew the hospital wouldn't give me any information by phone, and I'm not a family member, so I called her shop, fishing for what the employees knew. The clerk who answered the phone said her sister is a nurse on Bonnie's floor at Mistletoe General. So I offered her one of Mom's ho ho cakes and a half-dozen gingerbread men in exchange for anything she could tell me about Bonnie's condition or attack that wasn't in the paper. She said the nurse told her Bonnie was stable but still unresponsive. The doctors think she'll wake up on her own when she's ready, and they're expecting a full physical recovery."

I felt Ray's stare burning into my cheek. "What?" I asked. "I told you I was staying busy."

"If all this innkeeping and jewelry making falls through for you," he said, "you'd make one heck of a reporter."

I smiled. "Thanks."

"Bonnie's a tough nut," Cookie said. "I'm glad she's going to be okay. But I can't understand why anyone would want to hurt her. Was she robbed?"

"No," I said. "And she hasn't been awake for anyone to ask specifics."

"So, two attacks in Mistletoe in a week?" she said, her snub nose wrinkled.

That was the part that plagued me too. Two middle-aged, middle-class women had been hit over the head and left in the cold. One lived. One died. Was Bonnie meant to die but beat the odds? Was her attacker interrupted? I couldn't be sure, and none of it made any sense. If the women shared an attacker, I had to wonder if the motivation was the same in both attacks.

Or was it all a coincidence?

I supposed it was possible someone from one of the other gumdrop companies, whose products Bonnie had possibly been replicating and passing off as her own, had found out. Maybe they'd been angry and confronted her. But how would they have found out what Bonnie was up to? And if they had, why attack? Why not sue? People were all about the money, weren't they?

"I can't make any sense of it," I said finally.

Cookie grunted softly in agreement.

Ray turned to face me, resting an elbow on the table. "I have something for you too," he said, a wicked gleam in his eyes. "It's a vague but intriguing bit of hearsay regarding the Bonnie situation."

I smiled, curiosity piqued. "Go on."

"I stopped at the newspaper this morning to drop off a thumb drive with the photos I took at our wrapping party, plus some other assignments I've had this week, and I overheard a reporter say he was on scene outside Bonnie's house when the police were going through it."

"But she wasn't attacked at her home," I said. "And she's the victim. Why would they go through her home?"

Ray set a fingertip on the tip of his nose.

He dropped his hand and smiled. "The reporter was pretty upset he hadn't been able to get closer before being removed from the area by a deputy. But while he was there, he distinctly overheard the phrases 'evidence of blackmail' and 'refusal to pay.'" Ray raised his brows.

I worked to close my mouth. "He's sure that's what was said?"

"I didn't get to talk to him," Ray said. "He was on the phone when I was eavesdropping, and his editor pulled him away from the call before I had a chance to ask questions, but yes."

My shoulders slumped.

"I'll try to catch up with him later today or tomorrow and see if I can get him to open up," he said. "It won't be easy if he thinks he has the lead on a juicy story. He'll think I'm trying to steal his scoop. But I'm going to ask anyway."

"Not tomorrow," Cookie said.

Ray rubbed his forehead. "You're right. Today then. I'll see what I can do."

Fay and Pierce's wedding was tomorrow. There would be no time for sleuthing.

Cookie lifted her hands, then dropped them onto the table. "I can't believe Bonnie was being blackmailed and she didn't bring it up at book club. We talk about everything at book club. Now she's been attacked? What is happening in this town?"

"To be fair," Ray corrected, "he didn't say she was being blackmailed. He only said he overheard those two phrases. Without context. We don't know anything except that the police needed a reason to be inside Bonnie's house without her consent."

"They needed a court order," I said, chewing my lip. What made judges issue warrants? "Maybe someone knew Bonnie killed Karen and tried to blackmail her to keep quiet. Then they attacked her when she refused to pay. Or maybe Karen was blackmailing Bonnie about the gumdrops, and Bonnie killed her so she wouldn't tell. Or Bonnie knew who killed Karen and was blackmailing the killer in exchange for her silence."

"Bonnie didn't kill anyone," Cookie said, still clinging to her friend's innocence, despite the mounting evidence suggesting she was likely, at least loosely, involved with the murder.

"Well, neither did you," I said, forcefully. "And I'm not trying to find the killer today. I'm trying to find another reasonable suspect so you aren't arrested tomorrow. You come first. The rest can wait."

A tear fell from Cookie's eye, and my heart shattered.

I had twenty-four hours to cast reasonable doubt over Cookie as the killer. And convince Evan to focus his investigation on someone else so he would let Cookie go.

Chapter Twenty-Two

Ray made an extra stop for me as promised. I hopped out at the red light nearest Debra Jo's bookstore, and Ray agreed to drive around the block once or twice, then catch me again since parking was not an option. With only three days left until Christmas, the crowds were at their fullest. All the truly last-minute shoppers would be locals on Christmas Eve, when they finally got a few hours off from their own busy stores. By that time, most out-of-towners would be headed home to prepare for family events and festivities. For now, however, everyone under the sun seemed to be shopping the few square blocks of downtown Mistletoe.

I spotted Debra Jo and Jon almost immediately after entering the store. They worked shoulder to shoulder at the register, ringing up sales and bagging books. The stress of the day was evident on their brows, possibly a little more so on Debra Jo's. And I understood why. Like Cookie, Debra had a friend and fellow book club lady lying unconscious at the local hospital after a vicious attack.

I got in line and moved slowly to the front, not wanting to cut to the counter, drop the gift, and run. I hoped to tell

233

Debra Jo I was sorry to hear about what had happened to Bonnie and see what her thoughts were on the matter. After all, it was Debra Jo who'd initially told me about Bonnie's love of all things mystery, and I'd recently uncovered a gumdrop mystery directly related to Bonnie.

Holiday music played softly in the background, each tune with a smooth jazzy flair, amplifying the uniquely New Orleans vibe of the store. Framed newspaper clippings featured acts of heroism in the aftermath of Hurricane Katrina. Folklore and true stories of a famous pirate, Jean Lafitte, centered a display with greenery and twinkle lights. Children's books about pirates sat beside historical texts and related novels, drawing in readers of all ages.

As the line shuffled forward, my eyes returned to the canvas painting behind the register that I'd admired before. It was a gently muted image of a rainy brick street lined in puddles. Neon lights from nearby shops and bars reflected colorfully on the small rippling pools, and a small second line parade could be seen in the distance. Handfuls of people danced in the rain, umbrellas pumping, behind a set of men playing a saxophone, a trombone, and a drum. The street sign in the foreground bore the word "Poncet." I'd never been to New Orleans, but if I ever had the pleasure, this was a street I would be sure to visit. I imagined myself in the raging heat and smothering humidity, my brown hair swelling to twice its size as I bargained with a street vendor over a painting I'd hang in my office and treasure for a lifetime.

Someone opened the shop door, and a gust of frigid wind blew the daydream away.

The couple in front of me stepped away with their bags, and I set mine on the counter with a smile. Debra Jo and Jon exchanged a startled look, clearly thrown by the break in routine. "Merry Christmas," I said. "I promised you some of Mom's sweets, so I made a nice assortment and thought I'd drop them by while I was in town. I was just over at the sheriff's department visiting Cookie. She's looking a little worse for the wear. And so are you." I smiled and gave the bag a little wiggle. "I bet you can both use a sugar high right about now."

Jon opened the bag. "Thank you." He pushed an entire snickerdoodle into his mouth, then motioned the next customer forward.

I smiled, my gaze returning to the painting of their hometown. "Hey, have you guys ever heard of Yummy Gummy? It's a candy shop in New Orleans."

Jon's chewing slowed, and his eyes slid to meet his wife's while he worked to swallow. "Debra Jo's the candy connoisseur," he said, the words too light to match his expression.

Debra Jo tipped her head and stepped aside.

I went with her.

"I'm not sure about the candy place," she said, "but this was too kind." She motioned to my delivered sweets. "Thank you, and please thank your mother."

I nodded and smiled. "I will, and it's no problem."

Her eyes scanned my face and hair, probably trying to decide if she should mention the drastic change.

I glanced at the line of people watching our interaction, probably wishing Debra Jo would return to her register. "While I'm here, I also wanted to say I'm really sorry about what happened to Bonnie. Cookie's a mess over it, and I know you must be shaken too."

Her bottom lip quivered, and her brave facade cracked a little. "I am," she whispered. "It's awful."

"I'll figure it out," I told her. "They can't hold Cookie beyond tomorrow without arresting her, and I've got faith that won't happen. Evan makes me crazy from time to time, but he's a good sheriff, and he knows Cookie. I only wish there was something I could do to help Bonnie. I hate feeling helpless."

"I know," she said. "Me too." She glanced at the line and I knew she had to get back to work. Her brows furrowed, and she touched my arm gently. "We've just met and it's not my place to say this, but I remember the stories from last year. How frightened Cookie was when you got involved with something else like this. The papers said you were nearly killed." She whispered the last few words. "I don't think Cookie or Bonnie or anyone would want that for you again. Honestly, if I know Bonnie, I'm guessing being nosy is what got her attacked. She and I are only casual friends, but she'll go out of her way for some gossip. Maybe she finally heard something she shouldn't have." Debra Jo rubbed a heavy hand against her forehead, looking ten years older than the last time we'd spoken. "It's all just hitting too close to home, and I hate it. I don't want to hear about anyone else I know being hurt."

"Hon," Jon called, looking through the crush of shoppers. "A little help?"

"I've got to go," she said. "Be safe."

"You too." I hugged her quickly, then waved goodbye to Jon.

Ray slung his head out the truck window and whistled, drawing my attention when I didn't see him right away. He was double-parked behind two cars in handicapped spots.

I threaded my way through the crowd, then dashed between the parked cars and jumped into the truck. "What happened to driving around the block?" I asked.

He shifted immediately into gear. "It took me seventeen minutes to make the trip one time. I thought I'd better take my chances here or you might think I'd left you if I went around again."

"Thanks, I probably would have." I grinned. "I'm not sure I've ever seen it so busy."

Ray merged smoothly into traffic, then stopped at the light, six vehicles back. He hung his head in frustration. "We could literally walk faster. We were just passed by a pack of grandmas on the sidewalk with two pregnant ladies and a toddler."

I gazed out the window and laughed. He was right.

The Gumdrop Shop caught my eye on the next block, and a new idea began to form. "How do you feel about one more stop?" I asked.

Ray followed my gaze. "Why not?" he asked. "It's not as if we're getting anywhere anyway, and I can't in good conscience leave you alone when you're like this."

I shot him a droll look but thanked him anyway.

We parked in a no parking zone beside the dumpsters out back and hoped for the best. There weren't any deputy cruisers in sight, and with so many cars on the streets, it was unlikely a deputy would get here, spot the truck, and write a ticket before we finished our reconnaissance. If they did, I'd promised to pay the ticket.

237

Inside, the store was warm and crowded with shoppers. Children gathered around the viewing panel at the front window, admiring Bonnie's window display, without the icy temperatures to hurry them. Others sampled the buffet of gumdrops on toothpicks lined near the checkout counter. A sign dangling above the area encouraged folks to "Try before you buy."

Ray headed for the buffet.

I went in search of an employee who might talk about Bonnie if I prodded. The store's interior was loosely designed after the board game Candyland, complete with blocks of color painted on the floor, like a little road weaving up one aisle and down the next. Gumdrop murals were painted on cream-colored walls, and a peppy score piped through overhead speakers, a distinct break from the holiday music playing everywhere else this time of year.

I spotted a teenager in a logoed Gumdrop Shop T-shirt, crouched at the end of the row, apparently stocking shelves. I recognized her from a string of local high school football games that Evan had dragged me to in the fall. Her name was Sonali Patel, and she was a cheerleader. Her parents owned Patel Orthodontics, and her mother loved to beat mine at Bunco.

"Hey," I said with a wave as I approached.

Sonali stood and smiled. "Can I help you?"

"I hope so," I said. "I'm Holly White. My family owns Reindeer Games." I waited for my words to register. Normally if my last name didn't ring a bell, the tree farm did. And once locals identified me as one of their own, or associated me with a place they enjoyed, they became more willing to talk. "Our moms play Bunco."

Sonali frowned. Her long dark hair hung over one shoulder in thick envious waves, and I struggled not to pull my hood over my goofy Bo Peep curls. "I know you," she said.

"From the farm?" I mentally prepared a minute of farm-related small talk, something I could transition into *What have you heard about your boss's attack?*

"No." Her mouth opened in a broad smile, revealing two rows of perfectly straight, white teeth. Delight danced in her wide brown eyes. "You're the one who dates the sheriff!"

"Kind of," I said, caught off guard by the unexpected description. "You know that?"

"Everyone knows that. I saw you at the football games," she said. "Holding hands. Sharing popcorn. He's so hot. And mysterious. And his accent!" She mimed collapsing.

"True," I said, feeling absolutely ridiculous. I looked around to see if anyone was listening. I hadn't done a lot of boy-talk in high school, and at twenty-eight it seemed exceptionally strange. "I was actually hoping to talk to you about Bonnie."

Sonali stilled. "Are you a friend of hers?"

I nodded instead of lying outright. "I'm trying to make sense of what happened to her. Have you heard anything? Was she arguing with anyone earlier this week? Was someone angry with her about something? Was she upset at work lately?"

Sonali lifted her shoulders. "She's been a little irritable, but so am I. This place is a madhouse, and people don't control their children." She motioned to a pair of boys near the front. A kid about seven-years-old had his face pressed to the plexiglass barricade protecting the window display from shoppers. His tongue was out and sliding over the divider, leaving a trail of goo in its wake. His upturned and flattened nose led the way. An older boy stood behind him, laughing and eating sample gumdrops by the handfuls. Bits of half-chewed candy fell from his mouth with each bout of laughter.

"Yuck," I whispered without intent.

"Yeah," she said. "And guess who'll have to clean it up?"

As if on cue, an older woman appeared near the front check-out and waved in our direction. "Sonali. Disinfect the viewing area? Thank you!"

Sonali let her head fall back dramatically, then dropped the rest of her inventory back into a box she placed on the bottom shelf. "I'll be back," she said with a groan.

She headed toward the back of the store and through an archway, painted in rainbow colors, beneath a sign stating "Employees Only." I followed, moving quickly and with my chin up, as if Sonali was intentionally leading me somewhere. She didn't seem to notice. When she entered an open supply closet just around the corner, I kept going.

I turned the doorknob, then slipped into the office marked "Manager" at the end of the hall, thankful to find it empty. I didn't have a plan, and I wasn't sure how long I had to snoop before I was busted, so I started with the desk. Several images of Bonnie and people I didn't recognize stood in frames on each side of a big paper calendar partially covered with sloppy piles.

I thumbed through the stacks, then stopped when I came to a paperback buried beneath one mountain. *The Count of Monte Cristo* had been the monthly book club read. Why did she have the book at work if she hadn't planned to read it? And if she'd read it, why hadn't she attended the meeting?

I pulled the book from the stack, careful to mark the place where I needed to put it back. Bonnie had clearly read the story. Multiple colored flags were attached to the pages, and a number of small slips of paper with questions were tucked inside.

Gooseflesh pebbled over my skin as I skimmed the list, wondering if she'd intended the queries to enhance the group's book discussion or if the questions were meant for something else. The general theme of inquiry seemed to focus on the subject of reinvention. Keeping secrets. And people not being what they appear. All in line with the story, yet something felt off.

I pulled my phone from my pocket and snapped several photos. If the police had been at Bonnie's house this morning, they'd soon come for her office.

"All right," Sonali's voice cracked in the hallway beyond the office door. "Thank you. I'll be right there."

I returned the book to the pile, then rushed to the door and listened as hurried footfalls moved away. When I was sure the coast was clear, I made a break for it.

Back into the busy retail space, I ducked into a semi-quiet nook near the back and texted the photos of Bonnie's scribbled questions to Evan. I wasn't sure why, but they felt important. And I suspected all the strange things were connected. Bonnie's absence from book club. Her attack. The gumdrop ingredient mystery. And Karen's murder. I just wasn't quite sure how.

Bonnie had been at Reindeer Games that night. She'd come into the Hearth upset and complaining about Karen. Was it possible she'd gone to confront Karen at the inn, and she'd seen the murderer?

And now they were trying to silence her?

Chapter
Twenty-Three

I woke early the next morning, having tossed and turned all night, trying to make sense of the things I knew and those I suspected about Karen's murder. I'd let myself stew and puzzle at length while the moon was up, but vowed that once the sun rose, I would dedicate myself to Fay and her bridesmaids alone. No sleuthing on Ray's mom's big day.

I fumbled for my phone and checked the messages. Nothing new had come while I'd slept. Evan had responded to the text I'd sent with the photos taken in Bonnie's office around midnight. And after all those hours, his vague response was still a little concerning. I read it again, seeking some deeper meaning in the simple phrases.

Evan: Talk more when I'm home tomorrow. Be safe.

Talk more? We hadn't talked at all. And if he wasn't home at midnight, where was he? And why? The only thing I could think of that would pull him away in the middle of the night was the murder investigation. And the only thing that could take him away from his investigation was the case against his sister's nemesis in Boston. So why hadn't he complained that I'd been in Bonnie's office taking photos?

"No," I told myself. "I'm not doing this today. No guesses. No theories. Just. No." I stopped when Cindy growled. "Not you, sweet kitty."

I shoved off the bed and opened the door to set her free. Apparently, I could take the cat off the street, but I couldn't take the feral street urchin out of the cat.

She pawed wildly at the smooth side of her kibble-storage container in the pantry.

I scooped the food, then refreshed her water while she ate and my coffee brewed.

Two tall cups of caffeine later, I showered, dressed, and headed for the Hearth. Mom was hosting a private breakfast for Fay and her bridesmaids, and I wanted to welcome the ladies properly.

The dining area was empty, with the exception of Libby, Ray, and Mom. Tables had been covered in white cloths and trimmed in eyelet lace. Mom was setting places for the bridal party with my grandma's holiday-patterned china while Libby arranged glass sleighs carrying loads of tiny silver jingle bells as centerpieces. Ray was on a ladder. "Hey, Holly," he called, one long invisible thread of glittery white and silver snowflakes in hand. Similar chains had already been hung from half the dining-area ceiling.

"Coffee's on," Mom said, coming to greet me with a hug. "What do you think?" She opened her arms and turned in a broad circle, as if to showcase the work.

"It's a winter wonderland," I said. "Fay will love it."

I patted a pile of white batting masquerading as snow on the counter, when I went in search of coffee. I poured a mug, then took a minute to fully appreciate the café's enchanting transformation.

Mom headed for the kitchen, where scents of baking quiches and warm cinnamon rolls leaked around the swinging door. I followed.

"Is there anything I can do to help?" I asked, sipping the coffee as I watched her nearly dance around the space. She looked beautiful and so very happy. "What's wrong?" she asked, closing the oven door and setting the timer for a few more minutes.

A lump rose in my throat. She could always see right through me. "I'm okay."

"Aw, hon." Mom moved into my space, tucking a lock of hair behind my ear and cupping my chin in her palm. "What happened?"

"I promised Cookie I'd put a crack in the case," I said. I cleared my throat to stop it from cracking or warbling. "I thought I'd be able to cast enough doubt on her as the guilty party that Evan would have to let her go. Instead, I've let her down."

"Nonsense," Mom said, brushing the hair from my shoulders and looking at me as if I could do no wrong. "Cookie hasn't been arrested. You can't go around taking on the responsibilities of the world or beating yourself up for things that haven't gone wrong yet."

"She's in jail," I deadpanned. "I'd say that is definitely wrong."

"She's there for questioning," Mom reminded me. "They're holding her while they work the case. That's all. What am I always telling you?"

I pulled my lips to one side. "Lots of things."

She crossed her arms with a smile. "Which one do you think I'm reminding you of now?"

"Don't jump to conclusions?" I guessed.

"That's the one," she said. "And it's not over till it's over."

"I don't even know what that one means." I stole a grape from a bowl. "Where's the bride and her party?"

"I'm not sure," Mom said, a measure of concern presenting on her brow. "Probably just running a few minutes behind. Fay hasn't seen her daughters in a while, and you know how that can be."

I did and I hated it. I knew, logically, that going away had caused me to grow and become the person I was now, but if I had life to do over, I wasn't sure I would've left Mistletoe.

"Have you decided what you're wearing to the wedding?" Mom asked.

"I bought a dress." My cheeks warmed nonsensically at the words. It was a modest but slinky sheath that did wonders to accent my best assets while making me feel like a queen. I'd spent nearly a year in search of it. I even planned to wear heels. It wasn't often a girl living on a tree farm had an occasion to dress up. In fact, the last remotely fancy event I'd attended was our Christmas Tree Ball, and that was in costume. "I can't wait for you to see it."

"That makes two of us," she said. "And Evan's picking you up?"

I smiled. "I hope so." I said. If he didn't show up as promised, at least the wedding was in my parents' barn. I couldn't ask for a destination more convenient than that.

My phone buzzed and I pulled it from my pocket. Cookie's face appeared.

"Hello?"

"I'm free!" she sang. "Pierce and Fay and a whole gaggle of women stopped down here this morning to bust me out, and the sheriff didn't even argue. He just nodded and let me go!"

"You saw Evan?" I asked, my heart soaring for Cookie, and my mind jumping seamlessly to the next most important bit of information.

"Yep. He told me he'd see me tonight! I've got to go. We're almost there."

I disconnected with a smile. "She said . . ."

"I heard!" Mom clapped her hands and bounced on her toes. "I think she spoke loudly enough for Libby and Ray to hear."

I grabbed the ready trays of fruits, dips, and cheeses. Together, Mom and I headed into the dining room.

*   *   *

My afternoon was a flurry of activity, beginning with a quick trip through our trees to hide a few pickles. Today's game would be handled by the farm staff, so Mom and Dad were free to prepare for the evening's wedding. The game was an easy, fun-for-everyone adaptation of something my dad had grown up doing as a kid. His mom had always hidden a green pickle-shaped ornament on the tree for her kids to seek. The one who spotted it first got a special treat. We'd lost Grandma while I was in college, but the tradition lived on, both in my parents' house and on the farm. Guests finding a pickle before closing time would get a cookie. I made sure to put a couple low enough for little eyes to see.

Afterward, I arranged fresh flowers in each of the guest rooms, then delivered the baskets of local goods Pierce had asked me to put together as gifts from him. He'd given me a stack of cash and carte blanche on the items to include. The only request was that I choose things ladies would enjoy and that the items be a collection of Mistletoe's best products. I'd had no problems fulfilling that request. I'd started with plush terrycloth robes and matching slippers. Then peppermint hand creams and foot scrubs. Chocolates from Oh! Fudge. Wine from Wine Around. Maple syrup from the farm next door and an assortment of cookies from Reindeer Games. I'd assembled the baskets last night so the cookies would be freshly baked, then tied them with excessive amounts of white satin ribbon and set the small jewelry boxes containing silver chains and handmade charms on top.

Snow fell in big puffy flakes all afternoon as the ladies prepared for the ceremony. They drank champagne cocktails and noshed on finger foods, chatting merrily as makeup artists and hair stylists did their best work. The outdoor accumulation amounted to several inches before sunset, and it was sure to create a magical backdrop for Fay's photos.

For Dad and the farm hands, however, an afternoon of fresh snowfall meant a lot of extra work keeping the roads and parking areas clear and treated against ice.

"It's time!" my mother called from the foyer, dressed in an elegant black pant suit and wool coat. She winked at me as the women hurried to grab their things.

Fay and her bridal party would be transported to our event barn by a team of horse-drawn sleighs.

The photographer, who'd been taking candid photos of the group for an hour, hurried outside for pictures of the horses and sleighs. Pierce had brought someone in to prep the team with silver reigns and bridles, braided manes and tails. The horse pulling the bride's sleigh had a beautiful silver brow band with white feathers.

The women burst into motion, racing around for their clutches, shoes, and wraps. Each bridesmaid wore an over-the-top silver gown, the wide bell skirts stuffed with miles of crinoline. The matching elbow-length gloves and white fur shawls added to a look that was undeniably fairytale-esque. They'd worn their hair up to showcase the gown's beautiful neckline and the simple silver chain with a custom glass charm made by me. Fay had chosen small red and white candy canes, twisted into the shape of each lady's first initial.

I helped Mom escort the bridal party to their waiting sleighs, then waved them off for pre-wedding photos.

Mom hurried toward her waiting red pickup parked several yards away. "See you soon!" she called over her shoulder, fishing the keys from her coat pocket. "You look beautiful!"

"Thank you!" I said, returning the sentiments, though I still needed to get dressed. I checked the time, then bolted gracelessly to my room.

Fay had given the women handling her bridesmaids' makeup, hair, and nails instructions to do mine as well. She called it a gift to me, and the results were stunning. Once I'd stopped unintentionally crying and fully intentionally thanking her for the kind words and generous gesture, my reflection in the beautician's mirror was practically unrecognizable. Lip gloss and mascara were the extent of my makeup routine on a good day. What the professionals had done to me was mind-blowing. Nothing

248

about the look was heavy, but the way they'd applied everything had somehow made me glow. They'd used things like highlighters and bronzer, and applied a dusting of something shimmery across my cheeks.

I shooed Cindy and her sneaky claws away from my closet, then freed the long golden dress from its garment bag. I admired its flow as it hung there, light dancing over its soft sheen, and looking impossibly perfect. I lowered the zipper with care, then stepped into the most luxurious satin I had ever touched. The fabric crisscrossed loosely over my chest and cinched below my bra line, then flowed in generous waves to my toes. The view from the back was much the same, an elegant, plunging V of butter-soft material.

I tucked my cell phone and necessities into a black satin clutch, donned my black velvet heels and stared in awe at the woman before me.

I nearly collapsed when the doorbell rang.

Cindy Lou Who did her best to trip me on my way to the foyer, trying constantly to redirect me to her food bowls.

"Stop," I whispered, steadying myself before unlocking the door and sweeping it open to greet my date. "Hi."

Evan stepped inside and closed the door behind him, a sharp wolf whistle blowing through his perfect lips. "Wow."

An instant wave of heat and pleasure spread across my cheeks, then down my neck to my chest. "Thank you," I said as casually as possible, though I was sure he saw my ridiculous blush. "You look nice too."

Lies. He didn't look nice. He looked like someone had ripped him off a billboard in his black suit. He was tall and lean and a little dangerous looking. Like the anti–James Bond. And I felt my toes curl inside my heels.

Evan took my hand, kissed my knuckles, then spun me slowly. "You're breathtaking," he whispered.

I fought a smile, enjoying the attention too much and immeasurably pleased he liked the look on me. "Are you ready to go?"

He shook his head slightly. "I have a couple questions first," he said, his voice low and a little gravelly. "Any chance we can be a few minutes late to this thing?" He slid his free arm around the small of my back, hauling me closer.

My head tipped back as our torsos aligned. "Maybe," I laughed, already lost in his mischievous, happy eyes. "I love this mood on you. Does it mean good things were happening while you were incognito last night and earlier today?"

He nodded slowly, a mischievous grin blooming.

"You let Cookie go," I said, placing my palms against his chest. "That must mean you have your eye on the real killer and enough evidence to let your previous suspect go."

"I know who did it," he whispered. "I put in a request for a warrant. My men are waiting for it now, and I'm gonna get him."

"Who?" I asked instantly, a thrill spreading over me.

Evan chuckled, and his breath washed over my face, lightening my head. "What if, for now, we just dance? Tonight we can pretend to be two normal adults who aren't investigating a murder."

I wanted that too. My knees weakened as I inhaled the intoxicating scent of his familiar shampoo, cologne, and that uniquely Evan smell. "Okay," I agreed, stepping close and tipping my chin to look up at him with a smile. "But you did it."

"Almost," he said. "Now it's only a matter of time." He leaned over me, his broad shoulders curving in as he held me tight.

My cheeks heated wildly from his touch, and I struggled to control my goofy smile. "You had another question?" I asked.

"If I kiss you, will I ruin your lipstick? And do you mind if I try?"

"Do your best," I whispered.

*　*　*

The ceremony was beautiful. Fay wore a simple silver gown that complimented her bridesmaids'. Her hair was down, and her eyes rarely left Pierce's. My parents sat across the aisle from Evan and me, making goo-goo eyes at one another the entire time. Halfway through, I was certain I saw them silently mouthing the wedding vows to one another as the minister recited them for the bride and groom.

"That's nice," Evan whispered, his breath tickling my neck and ear. He raised our joined hands and pointed at my parents.

"Yeah," I whispered back, feeling my heart swell with the hope I'd one day have that too. When I turned to look at him, I found deep emotion smoldering in his eyes, and I struggled to pull in a breath.

The crowd erupted and everyone stood, breaking our private spell.

We followed the wedding party toward the music, already pumping through dozens of overhead speakers. The lights dimmed and mirror balls began to spin above the recently delivered dance floor, transitioning us instantly from wedding to reception.

Guests broke into bunches at the barn's center, with some heading to the bar and others to a dinner buffet that had been quietly erected behind a divider during the ceremony. Many had gone straight for the dance floor, including Cookie and Caroline, Libby and Ray.

"Care to dance?" Evan asked, sliding an arm around my waist and squeezing my side gently with strong fingers.

A thrill cruised through me, and I quickly agreed. "I'm not sure I've ever seen you so at ease," I said. "You look so . . ." I struggled for the word. "Satisfied."

"Things finally went right last night," he said. "I knew I could cut Cookie loose this morning, knew you'd be happy, and I had a date tonight with the most beautiful woman I've ever known. If things keep going my way, I'll get that warrant before midnight. If the warrant fails, I still have Bonnie. The doctors are confident she'll come around soon, and I'm banking on her ability to shed the light I need on this case."

We reached the dance floor, and he turned me in his arms. "But for a little while, let's just enjoy this," he said.

"Deal," I said, promising myself there would be time later to ask him anything I wanted. Like whom the warrant was for. What he thought Bonnie knew and how he'd figured things out.

The heat of his palm warmed me though the satin of my gown, and there was suddenly nothing more important than our dance.

We swayed easily together. My arms looped over his shoulders, and his arms were protectively around my waist.

He lowered his forehead to mine, and everything else fell away.

"It's been a good year," he said softly. "Recent threats aside."

My mind flashed over the memories we'd made. Movies. Dinners. Hikes. Ballgames. Pumpkin patches and corn mazes. Barbecues and parades. "It has," I agreed. He'd even endured my obsession with the movie adaptation of Jane Austen's *Emma*. I'd thought the work was pure brilliance, and he'd thought the namesake character was a lot like me—always ready to get involved in other people's troubles. Though, Evan admitted to wishing I meddled in matchmaking, like Emma, instead of his investigations.

"Ever wonder where we might be next year?" he asked.

My fluttering heart took off at a sprint. Did he plan for us to be together another year from now? I hadn't been brave enough to let myself look that far ahead, terrified of jinxing all the great things we had. A strong friendship. Fierce camaraderie and respect. And chemistry that could start a forest fire.

I looked into the depths of his green eyes as I pulled his lips closer to mine.

His phone rang before we made contact.

I gasped softly at the hard shove back to reality.

A single look at the message had him stepping away. "I have to go." He scanned the barn carefully, gaze jumping across the knots and clusters of happy faces. "Stay with our friends. I will be back."

"Where are you going?" I asked, snaking a hand out to catch his arm as he tried to turn away. "Did you get the warrant?"

His lips twitched into a smug, satisfied smile. "Bonnie's awake."

Chapter Twenty-Four

I forced a tight smile and turned back to the party. *I will not sleuth today,* I reminded myself forcefully. *Today is about Fay and Pierce.*

"Hey there!" Cookie said, bundled like an Everest climber and carrying a plate stacked high with food. "Can you believe I'm here? I've never felt so free!" Her gaze darted wildly, as if trying to take everything in at once.

"I'm glad you made it," I said. "Your being here makes the night perfect."

"I think so too. This party turned out great. Your mom really knows how to decorate a barn!"

I laughed and squashed the urge to hug her for fear of ruining both our dresses.

The barn doors opened, and a line of people trickled in. The ceremony had been small and intimate, but Fay and Pierce had invited hundreds to the reception, and it seemed they were all beginning to arrive.

Cookie shielded her food from the swirl of cold air. "I'd better get moving," she said. "I promised Theodore I'd have dinner with him, but I don't want to miss the bride throwing her bouquet!"

"Okay, hurry, but be careful out there," I warned. "It's cold and slick."

She pulled a "get serious" face. "Good thing I borrowed one of the farm's snowmobiles!"

I laughed again, relieved she didn't plan to hike across the farm to the barn in the fast-falling snow. "Well, then I'll see you soon."

"You betcha!" Cookie hurried away, and I went to see about a drink.

A pair of Cookie's book club ladies, Brooke and Becky, were in line at the bar. Both looked absolutely stunning.

"Hey!" I said, embracing one woman, then the other. "It's so nice to see you!" I bit my tongue against the urge to tell them Bonnie was awake. I was sure they'd want to know, but I'd gotten the distinct impression from Evan that fact might be a secret for now.

Brooke swigged from a water bottle, cheeks flushed from a few rounds on the dance floor. "This is the best party I've attended in years. I haven't been out dancing in so long I'd forgotten how much fun it can be."

Becky retrieved a flute of champagne from the bartender and tapped it to Brooke's water bottle. "Cheers!"

"Cheers," Brooke echoed.

"Designated driver?" I asked, nodding to Brooke's bottle of water.

She smiled wide and proud. "Nursing. I left the little one at home, but honestly, I already miss her."

"I bet! Did you ever get your sedan unburied the other night?" I asked, remembering her comment during book club.

"Yes!" Brooke laughed. "Jon really did bring his tractor over and shovel me out. He drove us all tonight when he heard there might be whiteout conditions later."

Becky nodded. "He's the sweetest."

The music changed and Brooke began to bob and shimmy. "This is my song."

"They're all your songs," Becky laughed, already leading the way to the dance floor.

I stepped forward, and a woman about my age smiled from her position behind the bar. She wore traditional livery, and her black tie had a fleur-de-lis pin at its center. Her name tag read "Hailey."

"Beautiful dress," she said with a distinct Southern drawl. "I think it's the best one here. And there are a lot of excellent dresses here."

"Thanks," I said, standing a little taller. "I like your pin."

She looked down, confused as if she'd forgotten it was there. "Ah. I like to take a little piece of home with me wherever I go. I'm getting my master's degree in business law at the university, but I'm originally from New Orleans. I bartend on weekends for the cash, but also to meet people outside school. I met Mr. Lakemore at one of his company's events, and he hired me on the spot for tonight. If only finding a job practicing law would be that easy."

I smiled. "Pierce is a great guy. Stay in touch with him," I advised.

Another burst of wind blew through the space as more guests continued to arrive. I shivered in response. "I might be getting tired of the cold," I confessed. "If only a trip somewhere south was in my future."

She laughed. "If you want hot, try New Orleans. It's beautiful, but it is *hot*." She emphasized the last word, working her entire face into the pronunciation, then smiled. "But seriously, if you ever get there, look my sisters up. They run a walking tour company that specializes in French Quarter history. It's pretty interesting. A whole other world compared to here."

"I'll do that," I said. "I'd really like to visit Yummy Gummy," I mused. "If there's even a shop in town." Debra Jo and Jon hadn't heard of it, but there must have been a corporate headquarters at least. Either way, I had some unanswered questions I wanted to unload.

"Yummy Gummy?" Hailey laughed. "There are about a half dozen of those shops in the Quarter alone. I swear every time you round the corner, a new one's popped up. People love that stuff."

A couple moved into line behind me, and Hailey nodded politely to them. "I'll be right with you. What can I get you?" she asked me. "The groom insisted I bring everything, so your options are nearly limitless."

"Something cool and fruity without alcohol," I said, slightly distracted by her previous statements. Why had Debra Jo and Jon said they hadn't heard of a candy company Hailey had described as being so popular? Maybe the couple had left town before Yummy Gummy had gotten so big?

"No alcohol, huh?" she tapped her fingernails against the bar, evaluating options.

"I'm unofficially in charge of the bridal party's overall happiness, so I need to keep my head straight," I explained.

She snorted, already pulling a tall glass from beneath the counter. "You're going to have your hands full."

I followed her gaze to a ring of silver gowns where Fay's sisters and daughters danced around the bride and her groom, nowhere near the dance floor.

Hailey stuck a spring of something green into the glass of pale purple liquid, ice, and bubbles. "Here you are." She pushed the drink in my direction. "Blackberry faux-jito. A mocktail of juice, spritzer, and a bit of mint."

"Thank you," I said, stepping aside to stuff a tip into her jar.

I took my drink to a table and enjoyed the cool sweetness while basking in the perfection of the moment, the happiness on all my friends' and loved ones' faces. I said a silent prayer for Libby as I watched her dip and twirl in Ray's arms on the dance-floor. There was danger ahead of her in Boston, and I hoped she'd make it through unscathed. I sent up wishes of hope for Evan and Ray as well. I couldn't imagine how either man would handle themselves if anything happened to Libby, and I wasn't sure how I would either.

"Holly," Fay called, hurrying in my direction with one arm outstretched. "Help."

I stood immediately, scanning her for signs of injury or trouble.

She unfurled her fingers, revealing a small candy cane charm in the shape of an R. Her daughter's charm. "Renee and I were hugging, and her necklace hooked on mine." She patted the heavy diamond and sapphire work of art lying across her collarbone and dripping expensively into her neckline. The carat

258

weight alone guaranteed a win in every battle against my little charms and clasps.

"No problem," I said, popping open my satin clutch. "I brought my jewelry pliers just in case." If anything was going to go wrong on Fay's special day, it wasn't going to be a problem with my jewelry.

Fay sighed heavily in relief. "Thank goodness! We want to take some posed photos with the girls, the cake, and bouquets, but Renee needs her necklace."

I fished the pliers from my purse, and Fay passed the charm gently into my hand.

Renee inched into view looking painfully guilty. She handed me the necklace. "I had to really tug to separate us, I hope I didn't ruin it."

"I'm sure it's fine," I told her. "Worst-case scenario, I can make you a new one and get it to you within a few days. Your photographer can probably superimpose the charm onto any shots where it's missing if he has to, but I don't think it's going to come to that." I used the flashlight app on my phone for a good look at the charm. "The glass is in great shape. All you're missing is the jump ring."

"What?" Fay asked.

"It's a little silver ring," I said, digging back into my clutch. "Kind of like the ones on a keychain, but tiny. I used them to connect the charms to the chains." I unloaded my clutch onto the table when I didn't see any jump rings. I closed my eyes to think, then groaned. "I set them on the counter when Mom came to get you guys. I must not have picked them back up when I went inside."

"Mrs. Lakemore," Pierce said, strolling into view and reaching for his bride. "Are you ready for our first dance?"

Fay and Renee looked desperately in my direction.

"Go," I said with a smile. "You dance. I'll run to the inn for the jump ring. It'll take ten seconds to get the charm back onto the necklace, and I'll be back here in time for your cake and bouquet photos."

The women hugged me, then headed for the dance floor.

I grabbed my coat and dashed out the door.

A blast of icy wind nearly froze my face in shock, and my heels slid slightly on the frozen walkway. I changed direction immediately and hopped into Dad's pickup truck instead.

One tug on the visor released his keys, and I was on my way, making a two-minute drive home through blinding snow. My grip on the wheel turned painful as a rush of memories crashed over me. The last time I'd been behind the wheel of one of the farm's trucks, it hadn't ended well. I fought off the fear, concentrating instead on the job at hand. I visualized myself repairing the necklace and returning it to a happy bridesmaid. A moment later, I was home.

I ducked inside and fixed the problem in under a minute, as promised, then headed back outside on a cloud of victory.

Music from the barn drifted through the night air, paired with laughter and muffled words through a microphone as I hurried down the walk to the little lot where I'd left Dad's truck.

Parked vehicles filled every visible parking space from the Hearth to the barn, and many had formed a line along the road's edge between the two.

A large white pickup had appeared beside mine while I'd been inside.

My heart clenched with memories of the crash outside Meg's inn. A white truck had been there when we left, but not when we arrived. A truck I was sure belonged to Meg.

And Meg had no reason to be here now.

I moved in a broad arc around the vehicle, seeking the tell-tale Great Falls bumper sticker I'd noticed when she'd driven away from me downtown.

The bumper was clear.

I sagged in relief, blinking against the incessant snow, and a nervous laugh bubbled out.

I hurried on, finishing the loop around the truck, careful not to slide on my heels. I peeked into the passenger window when I reached the driver-side door of my truck.

A navy-blue travel mug in the cupholder was emblazoned with a fleur-de-lis. The letters NOLA underscored the image.

I wondered idly if this was the big ole truck Debra Jo had said her husband had bought when they'd moved to Mistletoe.

Funny they had a truck like Meg's.

Like the one I'd seen at her inn after the accident.

I stared a moment longer, snow flying around me. There were lots of white trucks in the Maine, so why was this one bothering me so much? Maybe because it kept turning up. Because I'd seen a man with a gun in an alley near Debra Jo's bookstore. Because Debra Jo knew Bonnie and chatted on about what a good sleuth she was.

Had Debra Jo known Karen as well?

Did it matter? I shook the questions away and turned for my truck before I became an ice sculpture.

I grasped the door handle, then screamed at the reflection of a man in my sideview mirror.

Jon Burnette stood silently behind me.

Chapter Twenty-Five

I spun to face him, adrenaline shooting through my veins. "Hi, Jon." I lifted one hand in an uncertain wave. "What are you doing out here?"

He was dressed in black from his boots to his ballcap, and not for a wedding reception like Evan. No, he was dressed for the outdoors. His expression was remorseful and grim. "You weren't supposed to turn around," he said.

My heart skittered and my breath caught. "Why?" My voice hiked an octave and shook as the word wiggled from my throat.

He took a step forward and I took a step back.

My foot slid as my heel landed on a frozen patch of parking lot. I gripped the hood of dad's pickup to steady myself. I took a mental inventory of what I had to work with, if this encounter was what I thought it might be—a forthcoming attack on my life.

"Don't go," he said softly.

"I have to," I said, voice cracking with undisguisable fear. "The bride is waiting for me. I came here to grab something for her." I lifted my clutch as proof, as if he cared. The resolve on his face said otherwise.

He'd made up his mind to do whatever he came to do.

I couldn't let him succeed.

Dressed in a slinky gown and heels, now separated from my vehicle, running would be a last resort, but what else could I do? Call for help? My phone was inside my clutch. He'd surely stop me if I attempted to make a call or even retrieve the device. Fight? Jon had at least sixty pounds on me, and from the looks of him, it was all muscle. My only available weapon was a beaded handbag that didn't weigh enough to hurt anyone.

A hearty gust of wind began, burning my lungs and cutting straight through the thin material of my dress. The small wrap I'd trusted to warm my torso had long ago stopped working, and my toes had officially gone numb.

The music and laughter floating from the barn seemed a world away.

Not a single other soul was in sight.

My gaze dropped to his hands as he pulled them from behind his back, where I'd presumed they were clasped. The large stone in one gloved palm left no room for misinterpretation.

"Why?" I asked, my scrambled mind beginning to lose its grip. "Because of Karen? Bonnie?"

"Because of you," he said. His voice was cold and his features hard. "You just wouldn't stop snooping. You're just like Karen, and I can't let you put my wife in danger. I took a vow to love, honor, and protect her."

"Cherish," I croaked. "You only have to love, honor, and cherish her. You don't have to murder for her." Was that what was happening? Had Debra Jo played a role in Karen's death? And when I began to put things together, Jon had gotten scared and had stepped in to silence me and prevent her from going to jail? "You don't have to protect her from me. I would never hurt Debra Jo. I'd never hurt anyone!"

He took another step, and I stretched my arms out between us. "I really wish you would've left things alone," he said. "But you had to keep coming at us."

"I never came at you, I don't know what you're talking about. You have the wrong person. I've only looked into what happened to Karen Moody, the critic from *New England Magazine*," I explained, bumbling three clumsy baby steps backward for every one of his confident strides.

"I know who she is, and I know you saw the man I was talking to in the alley. You told the sheriff."

My next backward step took me off the pavement, and my foot sank into the icy snow. My arms pinwheeled as I struggled for balance in the nearly two-foot drift, leaving my dress wet to the knee. "That wasn't me," I said. "I didn't see you in any alley." But I had seen someone else. Someone with a holster and sidearm. "Do you mean the man with the gun?" I asked, the memory springing to mind. "*You* were talking with him? Is that why you hurt Bonnie?" I asked, the pieces slowly coming together, though the picture was still unclear.

"Bonnie," he groaned, shaking his head as he scanned the dark, empty night.

Probably checking for witnesses.

"Who was that guy?" I asked, stalling as I formulated a plan.

There was a landline in the stables. Could I make it there before him? Or at least put enough space between us to use my phone before he stopped me? Even in a gown and heels?

"He's the US Marshal assigned to protect us," Jon said.

It took a minute for me to remember what I'd asked. "Protect you from what?"

"People like you. Like Karen Moody and Bonnie. People who stick their noses where they don't belong and put our lives in danger. All to improve their careers or satisfy their curiosities," he muttered. "If the wrong people found out we were here . . ." Jon's gaze snapped back to me. "Debra Jo was brave to testify about what she saw in New Orleans, but the man she put away will never stop looking for her. And it's my job to keep her safe."

"I don't know what you're talking about," I said. Then something else hit me. "You're in witness protection?" My limbs burned with cold and possible frostbite as I worked over the new information. Suddenly the move across the country, when she so clearly missed New Orleans, made a lot more sense. They'd moved because they had to, not because they'd wanted to.

Jon's silence told me I was right.

"So, you killed Karen because she was going to expose you," I said as understandingly as possible.

"Exposing us would've gotten Debra Jo killed," he said, deep sadness in his eyes.

Maybe he understood the irony.

Karen had wanted to be an investigative reporter. She'd come here to uncover dirt on my town, then stumbled onto Debra Jo and Jon's secret. "She was looking into the Yummy Gummy company in New Orleans," I said. And another piece of the puzzle fell in place.

He growled, low in his throat. "She confronted us when her research led her to the stories of a local office worker who single-handedly caused the fall of a criminal empire. I begged her to let it go, but she wanted the store. Whatever the cost. It could've been over then," he said, through clenched teeth. "It should've ended with her."

"Then Bonnie started digging?" I guessed. "Trying to prove Cookie's innocence too?"

He scoffed. "Bonnie was trying to blackmail me," he snapped. "She overheard Karen when she cornered me. She'd wanted to talk to Karen about the case she'd been building on her stupid gumdrops. Instead, she saw an opportunity to leverage money from me to deal with the lawsuits. I couldn't deal with both of them. So I silenced one. That should've been enough to scare Bonnie away, but she couldn't put two and two together, and I couldn't exactly tell her I'd killed Karen. Then you showed up asking about the candies." His eyes bulged, and I feared he might explode.

A pair of headlights flashed over us from the distance, a driver on the main road, or maybe, hopefully, someone headed up the gravel lane in our direction. As I turned to see for myself, Jon lunged.

I screamed and toppled backward, falling onto my backside in the snow.

He grabbed the hem of my dress and hauled me toward him with one hand. "Perfect. You slipped on those heels and cracked your head." He raised the rock in his opposite palm, satisfied with the narrative that would be told. "I'm sorry, Holly. There just isn't another way."

I brought my knee up between us then snapped my leg out, connecting the sole of my shoe with his face.

The rock fell from his hand. Blood poured from his nose as curses flew from his lips.

There was always another way.

I ran. "Help!" I screamed. "Help!" My wobbly, frozen legs carried me toward the barn at an awkward sprint. Every frantic breath of air raked my throat and burned my lungs. "Help!"

His fingers caught the back of my small wrap and jerked me to a halt. My legs flipped out from beneath me, and I fell with a heavy thud.

"Help!" I screamed, louder, longer, more desperately as I tried to get up and run once more.

But Jon's arms were a vise as he dragged me upward and cemented my back against his chest, one powerful forearm crushing the space beneath my ribs. A heavy glove clamped over my mouth, effectively stopping the screams. In the next heart-beat, we were moving toward the woods.

I swung my feet and elbows toward him, in an attempt to loosen his grip. To inflict pain. To do anything that would stop him from taking me further away from potential rescue.

All around us, century-old pines reached into the air, their evergreen branches forming a dense canopy that made the world instantly darker. No moon. No stars. Only me, a killer, and the forest.

"You couldn't just leave us alone," Jon complained, as if killing me was really putting him out tonight. "You had to keep digging. Keep pushing. Asking questions all over town. I heard you in the cupcake shop, and I saw you in the pie shop. Always talking to shoppers and employees and the sheriff. Telling every-one Cookie didn't do it, all while you kept trying to find out who did. You wouldn't listen to my warnings. You had to know who killed Karen, but I can't let you tell this story." He scrubbed a hand over his face. "I can't let my name or Debra Jo's wind up in the news again. That's what I was trying to stop from happening when I confronted Karen at your inn. I begged her to let it go, but she cared more about the glory of a breaking story than our safety." He made an unintelligible sound. "We came here to start over. Not to be hunted by a bunch of malicious, selfish women. Some days I think we were better off in New Orleans hiding from the crime cartel."

"What?" I nearly screamed the question, and my dire situation became suddenly impossibly worse. Jon had killed Karen to protect his wife from a crime cartel? Afraid her story would announce his and Debra Jo's location if it came out. He'd attacked Bonnie in an attempt to stop her blackmail on the same subject. And now, because he thought I posed the same threat, he had to kill me too. Lest a New Orleans crime cartel come for him and his wife.

My hopes for survival sank perilously, and tears blurred my vision as I stared into the endless expanse of trees. I'd just saved Cindy Lou Who from this place, and now I was the one who needed saving.

Except no one knew I was out here. They'd find my truck at the inn.

Though Jon's path across the field would be easy to find with a little light, if someone came looking.

Would someone come looking?

I imagined Cindy's terrified face as I'd tried to collect her from the tree, the way she never appreciated anything I did for her, and how much I would miss that when I was gone. Then I got an idea.

I stopped flailing and went limp in Jon's grasp.

"What the . . ." He tried to adjust his hold after the sudden change, but I slid. "What are you doing?" he snapped. "Stop it."

I worked my legs between his as he walked, hooking my toes behind his calves and generally making it impossible for him to move comfortably, the same way Cindy loved to do to me.

And he tripped.

"Oof," I grunted as the air pressed from my lungs, caught temporarily between the frozen forest floor and a big, muscly killer.

Jon swore as he pressed up onto his hands, and rolled me over. I brought a fallen limb with me and cracked him on the head.

I launched myself forward again, stumbling and gasping for air as he got his wits back. I couldn't catch my breath in the cold, and my chest ached from landing on a cluster of little rocks and twigs. I couldn't run. Couldn't see clearly through the spots formed in my vision. My dress ripped as I stepped on the hem, which fell over my right foot now that I'd lost a shoe in the fall.

Unsure what else to do, I grabbed the nearest tree branch and started to climb.

A large, gloved hand latched onto my calf as I pulled myself up.

I kicked his chest, shoulders, and head with my remaining high heel.

He ripped the shoe off, and I used the momentary break to grab the next limb.

Tears blurred my vision as I climbed. I hated heights. Hated being chased. Hated being alone and afraid. I grasped blindly at the rough, biting limbs and felt the skin on my fingers and palms tearing each time my grip slid.

The precious sound of sirens rose in the distance, and I cried in earnest relief.

"Go," I told him, hysterics taking over. "Leave me alone. You're going to be caught when they get here!" I hoped with all my heart that was true as I balanced on a branch too far off the ground to be safe in my condition.

I thought of Evan's sudden departure and realized Bonnie might've been able to identify Jon as her attacker. "Bonnie's awake," I told him. "Evan left the reception to see her, and she probably told him everything. Now they're coming for you!"

I dared a look over my shoulder, down the dark tree to the place where Jon stood on the ground, about eight feet below. I waited, heart in throat, for him to turn and run.

Instead, he grabbed onto the tree with a snarl and began to climb. "I'm not leaving without you."

A horror movie–worthy scream ripped through me at the sight of him climbing. I moved faster, taking myself higher with every second, trampling and tearing my gown as I went.

"Killing me won't stop this now," I cried. "You're only making everything worse."

"Silencing a witness never makes things worse," he seethed, fumbling to make progress behind me.

My toe caught in my gown again and I slipped, barely catching myself with my arms, my chin connecting hard with the branch I clung to. My legs dangled a moment as I worked to find purchase for my bare toes. If falling directly to my death didn't finish me, then falling into Jon's reach surely would.

"Help!" I screamed, thanking the heavens for the emergency vehicles now arriving.

Red and blue lights carouseled through the trees, and dogs barked nearby.

The beams of a hundred flashlights lit the forest floor within seconds, and I realized the lights belonged to the wedding reception guests.

"Holly!" Voices rang out below, echoing through the trees and the night, all calling my name.

I twisted my body for a look at the answer to my desperate prayers. Men and women in uniforms searched beside men in tuxedos and women in ballgowns.

They'd come for me. And they'd come in droves.

My sobs turned ugly as catastrophic fear mixed with unparalleled relief. "Here!" I called, forcing the word painfully past the lump in my throat. "I'm here!"

Jon turned back, beating a hasty retreat down the far side of the tree, his boots scraping loudly over the bark.

"Jon Poncet," Evan called. "Mistletoe Sheriff's Department. You are under arrest." His deep voice rang with authority in the night, and I lost my remaining composure.

The beams of every flashlight seemed to fix uniformly on my face as I sobbed.

"Holly!" Mom shrieked. "Baby!"

Dad appeared in Jon's absence, already moving swiftly up the tree, as I backed slowly down into the protection of his arms.

Chapter
Twenty-Six

I curled on the couch in my personal suite several hours later, nerves still ringing from the night's events. I'd given my official statement, then showered and changed into flannel jammies and fuzzy slippers. Mom was with Cookie and the bridesmaids in the parlor, but I'd needed to get away and decompress. Everyone had graciously understood.

Cookie said she and Theodore would go home tomorrow, but I wasn't in any hurry to see them leave.

"How are you feeling?" Evan asked for the tenth time in an hour. "Can I get you anything else?" Evan had walked me to my suite, then waited while I'd cleaned up and changed.

I'd asked him to stay with me a while.

He'd been waiting on me hand and foot ever since. In the past hour alone, he'd wrapped me in a soft blanket, insisted I put my feet up, and brought me sweets—a cup of my favorite cinnamon tea and slices of warm apple pie leftover from the reception I'd ruined.

"I'm okay," I said. "I wasn't hurt."

His gaze flicked to my skinned palms, then trailed over the blanket covering countless cuts and bruises on my feet and legs. "I shouldn't have left you."

"You had to leave me," I said. "Bonnie was awake. You had to talk to her."

"I thought you'd be safe at the reception."

"I would have been, if I hadn't left," I said, reaching for his hand. "How did you know Jon was the killer?" I asked. Evan had known when he'd arrived to pick me up for the wedding. He hadn't wanted to talk about it then, but now that the cat was out of the bag, I wanted details. "What did I miss?"

Evan covered my hand with his and tipped his head slightly. "Remember how I told you there was evidence in Karen's room to suggest she'd wanted to make a move from magazine critic to investigative reporter? That was based on the files I found in her room, detailing the lives of Debra Jo and Jon, along with their pasts in New Orleans. Somehow she'd acquired copies of court records that included testimony Debra Jo had given under oath about the murder of her boss, and his links to a robust crime circuit in the city."

My mouth opened to ask questions, but I lifted my mug to my lips instead, determined not to interrupt any information Evan was willing to divulge.

"Debra Jo was an administrative assistant for a successful real estate developer until she discovered her boss had ties to the criminal organization. She was in the file room one evening, working late at the request of her boss, when she heard a man arguing with him. She was on her way to see if he needed her to call security when she recognized the other man as Little

Romeo, a well-known figure in the city's organized crime circuit. Romeo had a gun, so she hid, called the police, then recorded the exchange with her phone. When Romeo heard the sirens, he pulled the trigger and captured the footage of her boss's murder. It didn't take long for Romeo's men to figure out who else had been on site that night, and the threats on her life began."

I tried to imagine sweet Debra Jo in her hometown, afraid but determined to do the right thing. First taking the video. Then testifying. Much like Libby would soon do in Boston. "She must've been so scared," I said, relating deeply to that particular emotion. "Jon told me he just wanted to keep her safe, but Karen found out and wanted to write about it. Then Bonnie overheard. He assumed I knew the truth too, but I didn't have a clue," I admitted.

Evan shifted on the cushion beside me, stretching his long legs and crossing socked feet on the floor. "I knew you were on the wrong trail, and I hoped you would stay that way a while longer. I've been keeping loose tabs on him for days. I couldn't get the case facts and tangible evidence to line up with my gut. He told Debra he was plowing driveways the night I believe he trailed you and Caroline to Meg's inn, but I'm sure the GPS in his truck will confirm otherwise. I've got a warrant for that information now."

"I knew I saw his truck there." My stomach rolled at the horror of it all. "I feel a little guilty for thinking it was Meg."

"She made it easy," he said. "She was angry and standoffish. Rightfully so. Karen's review cost her a lot. She came here to make amends, then this happened."

"Now she'll never be able to get Karen to change the negative review," I said, sighing a little in disappointment for Meg.

Though it seemed she had a supportive town behind her, ready to help while she recovered from the critic's harsh words and now the loss of her family's signature sleigh.

"What will happen to Debra Jo?" I asked. She'd already been run out of her hometown. Would she be forced to leave Mistletoe too?

"That will be up to her," Evan said. "We don't have any reason to think she knew what was going on."

I sipped the heavenly tea, savoring the flavor and letting it warm me from the inside out. "Jon knew Bonnie saw him in the alley with the marshal. He knew I'd seen the marshal too, and he knew I told you."

"That wasn't you," Evan said. "Not the way he thinks. When I saw Karen's notes on the Burnettes, I contacted their former local PD and was patched through to that guy. I assumed when we spoke that he was the detective on some related case until he flew up here and sat down with me. He filled me in on what he could. I told him about you before you ever saw him in the alley."

I rolled my eyes. "Would've been nice if you'd told me any of this earlier."

"I was trying to keep you out of it."

"How'd that work for ya?" I asked.

Evan smiled. He tried to fight it but lost. "The marshal took Jon back into custody tonight. Given his overall situation, I don't think you'll have to worry about seeing him again."

I stifled a shiver, deeply thankful for that news. Another memory shook loose as I sipped my tea. "Ray told me a reporter saw deputies going through Bonnie's house while she was in the hospital, and one of them used the word 'blackmail.'" It was a solid clue. I just hadn't known what to do with it. "I thought someone was blackmailing her, but she was blackmailing Jon."

Evan made a low groan. "Bonnie is being sued for buying gourmet gumdrops in bulk at an extremely discounted price, then repackaging them as her own. Three major brands have lawsuits against her right now. Bonnie thought she could black-mail Jon out of enough money to tackle her legal costs. She had no idea he'd killed Karen."

I nearly bounced a hand off my forehead. "She's so lucky to be alive."

"Truly," Evan said. "And she's not the only one." His expression fell and his eyes went distant and brooding.

"You saved me," I reminded him, setting my hand on his.

He turned his palm to mine, lacing our fingers while frowning.

"Tell me something I don't know," I said. "Awe me."

"Okay. How about this? The person Cookie thought was following her was the marshal. I didn't know that until after you told me and I looked into it. He was doing his own due diligence, following a hunch that Jon was involved in Karen's murder after the details began to come out. It didn't take him long to real-ize Cookie wasn't a viable suspect, or to witness Jon in Cookie's neighborhood on the day those photos and articles about Karen were found in Cookie's trash. Once Jon realized we'd set our sights on him instead of Steven, he apparently decided to help us build a case against her."

I considered that a minute. "Cookie saw Meg in her neighbor-hood around that same time," I said. "Was that a coincidence?"

"Sort of. Meg was on her way to see a friend about a mile from Cookie's place, and got turned around trying to find it. We confirmed with the friend."

"So many moving parts," I said.

He nodded, an amused look in his eyes. "That's usually how it goes."

"Why didn't finding Steven's donation bag at the crime scene implicate him in the murder?" I asked. He'd told me earlier that his deputy knew Steven was the only one missing the bag.

"Alibi." Evan wrinkled his nose. "Steven attends weekly support meetings at the church for people recovering from toxic relationships. We have him on video coming and going, and a group of people who saw him there."

I rested my head against the couch. "Sad." I couldn't begin to imagine being married to someone so rotten I still needed therapy to heal the damage he'd done years later, even after remarrying. "What will happen to Bonnie?" I asked. "Cookie counts her as a friend and was genuinely worried about her after her attack."

"Bonnie's got some big punishments coming," Evan said. "Blackmailing is illegal. Not to mention the financial trouble and lawsuits that predate any of this mess."

I leaned against his strong shoulder. "You are my hero, Evan Gray."

"Thanks, but I think the real hero tonight was Cookie." He laughed. "She heard you yelling and used the phone in the stables to call 911. The operator said she was having dinner with her goat."

I wrenched upright, a peal of laughter escaping me too. "She was! I saw her on her way out of Fay and Pierce's reception. She was supposed to hurry back so she wouldn't miss the tossing of the bouquet."

Evan laughed again. "You know she would've caught those flowers."

"Definitely," I agreed, setting the cup aside as my eyelids grew heavy. "One more question." I yawned. "How did Jon get his hands on my nutcracker?"

"He followed Karen inside after dinner. They argued, and when she tried to walk out again, he grabbed it off your desk."

Which is visible through the open French doors in the foyer, I realized.

What a mess.

I snuggled against Evan, sorry my near murder had left a black mark on Fay and Pierce's wedding day, but I was immeasurably grateful for the way their guests had come pouring out for my rescue.

"I should probably get home," Evan said, resting his cheek against the top of my head. "It's after midnight. Officially Christmas Eve. And I have a surprise for you tonight," he added with a whisper.

Chapter Twenty-Seven

Reindeer Games was officially closed for Christmas Eve, but my parents' arms and doors were always open, especially to our community, and the good folks of Mistletoe knew it. This year, thanks to Mom's newly remodeled café kitchen, she'd opened the Hearth for everyone dropping by on their way to the annual Snowball Roll, and her hot chocolates were flowing. Even Fay and Pierce had stopped for a cup before heading to the airport, where they'd catch a plane to Paris.

Dad was flipping hotcakes by the dozen, serving to anyone in the mood for a bite.

I was working my way through a tall stack, and wishing I could bathe in the heavenly maple syrup, bottled next door.

"So," Libby said, raising one perfect brow, along with a cup of hot cider. "What's this business about a snowball roll?" she asked. "Apparently I missed it while I was staying at Evan's last year, and it's some kind of big deal?"

Ray's easy smile turned to faux shock. "The Snowball Roll is a very big deal. It's a tradition."

She shot him a droll expression. "I assumed that much. There's nothing this town loves more than its traditions."

That was true. People in historic towns loved to be a part of history, and locals had been chasing their balls down our hill since the early twentieth century.

"I'm going to sit it out this year," I said. "But you guys should do it. I'll cheer you on."

Evan shot me a curious look, then trailed his gaze over my body, probably looking for signs of hidden injuries. "You're not racing?"

Thanks to the season, all evidence of my week's dangers had been carefully covered either with clothes or makeup. I'd learned the trick from the woman who'd prepped me for the wedding, and I'd used it to cover the healing bruise on my forehead. My turtleneck, jeans, and boots did the rest.

"Not this time," I told him. "Today I have plans to sample fares from as many food trucks and vendors as possible while I watch others partake in the fun. Are you rolling?" I asked him.

He worked his jaw, a glint of humor in his eye. "Not today. I've got a lot of work to do this afternoon, and I can't risk breaking my neck."

Libby furrowed her brow. "You guys still haven't told me what it is. Maybe I want to do it."

Evan grinned. "Maybe you can race your boyfriend. Ray can show you the ropes, then you can whoop him."

"That's how it went for Evan and me the year we met," I said, nudging him with my elbow.

"I'm always up for a whooping," Ray said with a wink.

Evan pointed at him. "No."

Libby laughed, then kissed Ray's cheek. "It's on! What do I have to do? Just roll a snowball?"

The three of them looked to me for a proper explanation. I had probably explained the event about a thousand times more than either of them, and that was just this season.

My great-grandfather had held the first event nearly seven decades back, when Reindeer Games was still a small and floundering tree farm. The enthusiasm present today was a direct result of his dedication to local outreach all those years ago. Grandpa White grew the business to a thriving success when it was bequeathed to him years later, but it was his father who'd made Reindeer Games a real part of our community.

"The Snowball Roll is always the final Reindeer Game of the year." It happened on Christmas Eve morning, shortly after breakfast, so folks had plenty of time to attend or participate without having to miss any of their personal or family festivities happening later that day. "It's more of a town party than a game," I said. "And everyone gets involved. Some compete, others cheer on the players. Vendors bring their food trucks. There's music. It's a pretty big deal. I'm sorry you missed it last year."

"I slept in," she said. "Evan told me about it after it was over."

He shrugged. "We had a lot going on last year."

I shivered at the reminder. "Have you been to Spruce Knob?" I asked Libby, redirecting the subject.

The tree-barren hillside at the edge of our property was significantly bigger than any ski resort bunny hill, but not quite a black diamond ride. I'd learned to ski there as a kid, and I still raced my dad to the bottom every year on round plastic sleds.

"I don't think so," Libby said. "Is that where everyone's going?"

I followed her gaze through the emptying dining area, then out the window as folks trudged past with rosy cheeks and pop-up chairs.

"Looks like it," I said, my smile widening. "When you get there, you have to register to play and sign a waiver in case you get hurt. Mom's friends always work the table. They'll give you a number and assign you a lane."

Libby nodded. "I need a waiver to roll a snowball down a lane?"

Ray laughed. "You roll the snowball down a giant hill. As fast as you can. About fifty feet from the starting line, the lanes go out the window, and it's a massive, out-of-control, free-for-all of balls and people."

"What?" she returned on a bark of laughter.

"You make a snowball," he told her, miming the action with his hands. "However big you can hold. When the whistle sounds, you put it on the ground and start rolling it over the hill. The first person to the finish line with their snowball wins."

"You have to have your snowball," I reiterated. "If you get there without it, you lose."

Ray nodded. "And if more than one person arrives at the same time, the one with the biggest snowball wins."

Libby's smile faded. "A downhill race through all this snow? How do you keep track of a snowball in this?"

"Well," I said, "If you're doing it right, the snowball should be getting bigger all the time. We got all that snow last night, and it's the good, sticky stuff, so we should see some pretty big balls on the field today."

Libby slapped a palm on the table. "I'm in."

Ray gave her a high five.

Evan and I laughed.

Mom waved to me as she hustled to my side, then motioned Evan and me to scoot. We inched closer to the wall, and she made herself comfortable on the edge of our bench. "How are you feeling, baby girl? Can I get you anything? More hotcakes? More coffee?"

I looked sheepishly at the plate I'd nearly licked clean before me. "I think I'm good," I said. "I'm saving room for a funnel cake."

She smiled knowingly. "That's smart. How about you, Evan? How's everything going?"

He straightened a bit. "I have a little paperwork left over from last night, but I plan to be at Cookie's event later." He turned bright eyes on me and smiled. "I was hoping you'd be my date, if you don't have other plans."

I beamed. "I'd love that."

"Perfect," Mom said, swinging her attention across the table. "How about the two of you? Will you be there?"

Ray looked lost, but Libby nodded enthusiastically. "I can't wait. It's all I've been hearing about for a month."

I frowned. "Cookie only told me about it last week." And only after I'd caught her running down Main Street like her pants were on fire.

Mom kissed my head, then scooted back out of the booth and started to clean up. The last of our guests had already gone.

"Let us help," Libby said, snapping into waitress mode and dragging Ray behind her. "You two go on ahead," she instructed, smiling at us as we sipped the last of our coffees.

Evan grinned. "What do you say? Ready to go watch some friends and neighbors fall down a hill?"

Did he even have to ask?

* * *

Evan picked me up at five sharp. I felt a little guilty leaving Mom to handle the preparations for the open house, but they'd vehemently insisted. And I hadn't pushed back for long, eager for an evening out with Evan.

* * *

"You look beautiful tonight," he said, helping me into my nice wool coat.

"Thanks." I'd blown out my hair and applied a little makeup, but my cream-color beanie had instantly mashed my hair back down. I'd chosen my favorite tunic sweater, also in cream, and my softest skinny jeans for our date, and selected black zippered boots that climbed up my calves. "I'll change for the party when we get back, but I didn't want to freeze outside. Cookie says this thing is at the covered bridge?"

"It is," he said, leading me to his waiting truck and opening the door for me. It was truly a special occasion when he wasn't traveling in the cruiser. "And I'll do my best to help you stay warm."

My face heated nonsensically, and I bit the insides of my cheeks. "You look great too," I said, scanning him again as he climbed behind the steering wheel. "Are those dress pants, Sheriff?" I asked. His legs and feet were all I could see clearly beneath his long dress coat, scarf, and hat.

"They are." He gave me a warm smile, then pointed the truck away from the farm and turned holiday music on quietly in the background while we talked. "The inn is really shaping up for the open house," he said.

"Mom and her ladies have been at it most of the day. She insisted I rest after the events of last night, but I am absolutely fine. Dad's coming to help once he treats the roads for ice again."

Evan looked me over. "You're sure you're fine?"

"I'm better than that," I said. "At the moment, I'm very close to perfect."

"I'd have to agree with that," he said, a boyish grin on his sweet face.

"How's Libby doing?" I asked. "She said you're taking her to Boston in three days to meet with the district attorney. Do you want to talk about it?"

He dipped his chin in a quick nod, worry crowding his brow. "I've made arrangements to stay outside the city, and called some trusted friends and connections to help keep her safe while she does what she needs to do."

"Will it be a public trial?" I asked, bracing myself for his response. "Ray and I are coming either way. We can wait outside if we have to, but we're going to be there for her. And for you."

Evan's eyes flashed back to mine, then back to the road, his mouth set into a firm line. "I'll find out," he said. "And I'll let you know."

I smiled, shocked half-silly. "You mean you aren't going to tell me to stay away from the city?" I asked. "That going anywhere near the trial is too dangerous, and I shouldn't reveal my association with you or your sister. Etcetera."

His lips kicked in a goofy half smile. "Would it matter if I did?"

"No, but you could at least try to protect me. Jeez." I said, my smile growing with each word.

He shook his head, then laughed. "Honestly, having two friendly faces in the courtroom or in the hallway will mean a lot to both of us."

I sat taller, happy with the conversation's outcome. "I wonder where all the cars are," I said, baffled by the empty road before us. Normally the lineup for a look at McDoogle's lights was long but well worth the wait.

"Speaking of vehicles," he said, "your truck was outside the inn. When did that happen?"

"Dad brought it to me after lunch." I wasn't in any hurry to drive it further than absolutely necessary, but it was fully repaired and that was important. "He and his buddy made a trip to the Great Pines body shop after the Snowball Roll and surprised me this afternoon."

"I still can't believe how close I came to losing you," Evan said softly, his eyes going tight and his gaze distant.

"That reminds me," I said. "I was thinking about how easily you answered all my questions last night, and I have one more."

"Go for it," he said. "If I can tell you, I will."

"Who was the woman in the blue SUV?" I asked. "The one who picked you up when you left the pie shop?"

Evan's expression softened. "Someone who helped me with your surprise."

"Really?" I asked, a jolt of excitement coursing through me. "Who was she? How did she help? Surely you can tell me something by now. It's Christmas Eve night. I might explode from anticipation before morning. If you let that happen, all your secrecy will be for nothing."

He smiled. "She was meeting me at the pie shop, and she called to let me know she'd made it to town. You showed up, so I needed a change of plans." He took my hand on the seat between us. "Now, be patient and try not to explode."

We rounded the bend where McDoogle's lights began, and two of his deputies appeared in the road beside a small wooden barricade. They swept it away as we arrived, tipping their hats as we passed.

"What was that about?" I asked, twisting at the waist, watching as the men disappeared in the distance.

When I turned back, the world around us was alight and twinkling.

Thousands of white lights hung in swoops over the picket fences lining both sides of the road. Larger, bistro-style bulbs hung in sweeps and boughs overhead, laced through the reaching limbs and branches.

Chasing lights ran around star-shaped frames, performed loop-de-loops and cruised straight up arching poles like fireworks.

I pulled in a breath of wonder and amazement, loving every single moment, as always.

Evan released my hand to turn down the radio. A moment later, he lowered his window as well.

Cold air whipped inside as we rolled along the lighted lane, bringing the sounds of a choir along with it.

"Did you do this?" I asked, several minutes too late, still playing mental catch-up with the string of perfect moments. "Did you close the road to everyone else? Is this a private showing? Just for us?"

Could he do that? Didn't people get mad?

"For you," he corrected. "And only for a little while. I wouldn't want to cause a riot, keeping citizens from their traditions."

I smiled, then turned to seek the choir, growing louder as we continued down the beautifully illuminated lane.

A pack of flickering candles came into view outside the covered bridge, also heavily adorned in twinkle lights.

Evan parked in the designated area near the bridge, then climbed out and circled the hood to my side. There were a few other vehicles already there, likely belonging to the carolers.

I took his hand and let him lead me up a gravel path to the choir.

Cookie and a dozen or so others held music books in one hand, white taper candles in the other. All were bundled in period clothes like a cluster of nineteenth-century carolers.

"This is Cookie's event?" I asked.

"And aren't they great?" Evan asked as we listened to the merry holiday tunes.

When the carolers began to sing, "O Holy Night," Evan led me on to the bridge.

Heavy plastic sheeting had been hung in strips to cover the open ends and sides. He held a sheet back for me to cross inside.

Several tall patio heaters stood at the edges of the space. A sea of battery-operated candles flickered on the floor and railings. A small table for two was dressed in scarlet at the center of it all. On the table stood a small silver box tied with a silver ribbon.

"Evan," I whispered, completely at a loss.

He pulled out my chair and I sat.

The carolers grew quieter behind us as they made their way down the gravel path to the parking lot.

A silver tray sat on each side of a short glass vase with white roses. One tray had a set of round cookies, like the ones Mom had asked me to try. A silver silhouette of a woman's head and shoulders centered the blue and the white icing on each. The cupcakes filling the second tray were undoubtedly Caroline's.

"It's an *Emma* theme," I said, recognizing the silhouettes as perfect matches for the one on my copy of the book. My eyes and nose stung with intense and barely tamped emotion as I thought of all the people Evan had enlisted to do this for me. "I can't believe you did all this."

Even crouched beside me, pulling the gift box from the table and presenting it to me formally. "I wanted to show you that I care and that I pay attention. Even if I don't always know how to say it."

I leaned forward to kiss his cheek before taking the box from his hands. My heart and curiosity soared as I held the rectangular gift.

Evan smiled. "Open it."

I tugged the satin ribbon away, then set it on the table before removing the lid. Inside was a beautifully engraved silver frame.

My favorite quote from *Emma*, delivered by Mr. Knightley, was scripted neatly, along with the date, across the bottom.

"If I loved you less, I might be able to talk about it more."

"I thought we could put a photo from tonight inside," he said, his voice going low and gravelly.

I raised my eyes to meet Evan's. The look of fear and expectation I found there simultaneously broke my heart and made me want to cheer. "We?"

In the distance, the choir's voices sang sweetly. Their candles flickered against the night.

Before me, Evan reached into his coat pocket and produced another, smaller box, then opened the lid. "Holly," he said, raising the perfect diamond solitaire to me, then shifting gracefully onto one knee. "You're usually the one with the questions, but I'm hoping I can ask you one tonight."

I sucked in a shuddered breath as the realization of the details of this night hit me. He'd done all of this. Organized all of this. For me. My world blurred with unshed tears. "Evan."

He looked over my head, and I turned to see a small crowd making their way onto the bridge with us. Their arms were linked. Their smiles wide. My mom and dad. Cookie and Caroline. Ray and Libby.

They'd all known.

Behind them, others had joined the carolers, filling up the space between the parking area and bridge. Our friends. Evan's deputies. Even Samantha and the ladies from Oh, Fudge!

The town had come out to witness his proposal. And my heart soared anew.

Evan took my hand in his, and I turned back to face him. "I never dreamed, when I moved to this special little town, that I would one day fall in love so completely, or so irrevocably. You make my life brighter and me merrier. You are my very best friend. My partner and my heart."

"Yes," I said, reaching for his cheeks as tears rolled over mine.

The little crowd chuckled softly, and my dad hugged my mom.

"I haven't asked you anything yet," Evan whispered.

"Oh." I put my hands back in my lap and bit my lip against another premature acceptance. "Sorry."

He grinned. "The woman you saw me with was a jeweler from Boston who helped me to reset my great-grandma's engagement ring. The stone has been in my family for three generations." He removed the perfect ring from its box, and pinched the golden band between his shaking fingers. "Holly White, I love you more than I will ever know how to accurately express, but if you will do me the honor of becoming my wife, I will work hard, every day, to make sure you never doubt or forget."

I stared into his sincere and pleading eyes, glossy with unshed emotion. "Yes," I repeated, slow and fervent. "Absolutely. Unequivocally. Yes."

The little crowd on the bridge erupted into cheers, which spread like wildfire down the path to the parking lot. Cars honked and headlights flashed on the road, and the choir began to sing once more.

Evan pulled me to my feet, then slid the ring onto my finger. "Merry Christmas," he said.

And I kissed him.

Acknowledgments

T hank you, lovely reader, for joining Holly and her crew on another holiday journey. It wouldn't have happened without you. Knowing you requested and petitioned for this book to happen warms my heart more than you will ever know. Readers are powerful. Don't ever underestimate that. You make my dream possible. I'd also like to extend a special thanks to the lineup of cozy mystery readers, reviewers and friends whose names I've borrowed for use in this book. Debra Jo, Karen, Meg, Becky and Brooke, thank you for giving cozy readers a place to hang out and share their love of this amazing little genre online. As always, thank you to my critique partners, Danielle and Jennifer, to my agent, Jill Marsal, and to the power house team at Crooked Lane Books. Also to my family whose endless support and silliness never fails to keep me in material.

Read an excerpt from

STALKING AROUND THE CHRISTMAS TREE

the next

CHRISTMAS TREE FARM MYSTERY

by JACQUELINE FROST

available soon in hardcover from
Crooked Lane Books

CROOKED
LANE

NEW YORK

Chapter One

"Hold that pose, Mrs. White," my best friend, Caroline, called. She rose onto her tiptoes, phone poised before her, sizing up my mother for another photo. Caroline's long blond hair hung over her shoulders in loose waves, and her pale brows furrowed over bright blue eyes as she snapped the dozenth picture since her arrival.

Mom paused, frosting bag frozen above a tray of cutout reindeer cookies, where she'd been piping patterns onto the little blankets over the reindeers' backs. "Cheers," she said, beaming for the camera.

"Got it!" Caroline lowered her phone, and Mom's bright smile fell into a more natural one.

"I still can't believe you asked me to be on your show this week." She set the frosting aside and rubbed her hands into the folds of her apron. "I hope you won't regret it."

"I won't," Caroline assured.

"You'll be there, right Holly?" Mom asked me.

"Try to stop me," I said, stealing a cookie from her tray. "You'll knock them dead for sure."

Mom tucked a swath of thick brown hair behind one ear and grinned. I looked like my mom. She was twenty years older than me, a few inches shorter, and a couple dozen pounds heavier, but that didn't diminish the effect. Our dark hair and eyes, fair skin, and pointy noses left no room for mistaking our relationship. I imagined looking at her was a lot like looking into a mirror that showed my future, and I was okay with what I saw. Mom was beautiful, happy, and kind. As in love with Dad as the day she'd married him, and over the moon about her life in historic Mistletoe, Maine.

I hoped all that joy and contentment came with the looks, because our personalities were quite different. I'd inherited Dad's big mouth, for example, and much to Mom's eternal dismay. I'd also recently come to realize I was a bit of a busybody. I suspected I should work on the latter, but that particular personality trait often helped me get things done. I usually knew who to ask for what, and where to quickly find anyone or thing I needed. With little more than a week left before Christmas in a holiday-themed town, and my wedding scheduled for Christmas Eve night, I needed all the help I could get.

I sipped my cinnamon-flavored coffee, then slipped another stick of ammo into my hot glue gun. The morning was getting away, and Caroline would soon have to leave and open her cupcake shop on Main Street. Then Mom would flip the sign on the large wooden doors behind us, opening the Hearth, our family's tree farm café.

Reindeer Games was the only tree farm in Mistletoe, which made it, by default, the most frequented. My family and I made it the most fun by intent. Mom was the baker. Dad was the lumberjack. I was the innkeeper. Collectively, we were living our best lives.

The Hearth was Mom's domain, essentially a life-sized gingerbread house where she baked and sold her cookies and cakes, along with a variety of hot drinks and occasionally soups, to guests. Red and white candy-striped booths lined the dining area under gumdrop-shaped chandeliers. Eyelet curtains adorned the windows, and hand-carved chocolate-bar tables with licorice-legged chairs sprinkled the floor. The furniture had all been made from trees grown on our property. Scents of warm vanilla and spun sugar had long ago permeated everything in sight. It would've been the perfect venue for Caroline's feature on Mom, but this was the busiest week for Reindeer Games, and Caroline had likely sold more seats than the fire code would permit inside our little café.

"I still can't believe I'm going to be on television," Mom said, setting a hand against her throat, mystified.

"It's not television," Caroline said, returning to her lollipop-shaped stool at the counter. "It's a web show on my YouTube channel."

I grinned as Mom frowned, trying to make sense of the answer.

Caroline had opened her shop a couple of years back with a little help from our friend Cookie, and Caroline's Cupcakes had become an instant hit. They rarely made it to closing time without selling out, even at five bucks a pop! Earlier this year, she'd started a weekly livestream, called *Merry in Mistletoe*, as a favor to her father, the mayor. He'd hoped to generate positive press for our little holiday hamlet following a string of annual Christmas murders. Three in as many years, to be exact.

The most recent murder had earned us some negative national attention, and a lot of locals had feared tourism would suffer this season as a result. So Caroline had been doing her part to showcase the merrier aspects of Mistletoe by featuring locals and their lives. This month had been all about the shops, trades, and destinations. Mom was the featured baker, ready to talk about a day in the life at Reindeer Games and more specifically, the Hearth Café. Like most things Caroline touched, *Merry in Mistletoe* had grown into yet another wonderful success.

"I don't understand," Mom said, wide brow furrowed. "It's a show on your channel."

"Right, and folks can watch live or replay it later. We'll also have a studio audience for the recording."

"But your channel isn't on television," Mom said.

"Correct."

I went back to hot-gluing twisty metal spirals into the tops of pine cones with flat bases. I didn't have the vocabulary or wherewithal to help Mom make sense of livestreams or online channels. Honestly, I had no idea how it all worked. I was just glad it did.

Mom looked to me for help, then caught sight of my craft. "What are you working on, hon?"

I lifted a finished product for her inspection. "Do you like it?"

"Adorable," Mom cooed, ever supportive.

"What is it?" Caroline asked.

"I thought we could set these on the reception tables. If we slip a place card into the spiral, the pine cone becomes a seating marker."

The results would double as a cute nod to our location. Not to mention, Evan and I were on a budget, and there were few things more abundant on a tree farm than pine cones.

Caroline took the finished product from my hand. "I love it. We can spray them with faux snow and a little silver glitter. They'll sparkle under the twinkle lights and mirror ball."

Mom gave a dramatic sigh. "My little girl's getting married."

Her little girl was twenty-nine, but I was, in fact, getting married. A smile spread over my face.

I'd met my fiancé, Sheriff Evan Gray three years ago, after finding a dead body on the farm. Evan had thought my dad was a reasonable suspect, and I'd worked hard to help the new sheriff see my father for what he really was, a six-foot teddy bear in a lumberjack's clothing.

Time was a funny thing, because our first meeting felt both as if it had happened yesterday and as if it had occurred a millennium ago. And though we'd been planning for a year, it was hard to believe the big day was only a week away. We'd be married on Christmas Eve in the big barn on our property. Mom and her ladies had decorated the cavernous space for the annual Christmas Tree Ball last weekend, and it was still decked out in twinkle lights and set up for a party. What better, prettier, more perfect place for our ceremony and reception?

Pulling together a wedding at this time of year hadn't been easy, but it'd been a group effort, with Caroline at the helm. After months of to-do lists, endless choices, decisions and dress fittings, Evan and I were in the home stretch.

"One week to go," Caroline said with a dreamy sigh. "Are you ready?"

Physically? Emotionally? "One hundred percent."

Did I understand how a zillion last-minute things were going to get done while we all simultaneously performed our full-time jobs in Mistletoe the week of Christmas? Not at all.

Mom stroked the backs of her fingertips across my cheek, sentimentality carving lines around her eyes and mouth.

I pressed her hand to my face, then kissed it before setting her free.

Caroline set the pine cone down. "Your big day will be perfect. I'm making sure of it. Just like your mom's internet debut. Your dad has your ticket for the live recording, by the way. We sold out for this one, which is doubly great because all the proceeds from ticket sales will go directly to the Mistletoe foodbank."

Mom looked ready to burst with pride. "That's wonderful news."

"I only wish we could've held the show here," Caroline said. "You'd have been able to actually bake a batch of your whoopie pies, instead of just talking us through the steps and recipe. And look at this place." She waved an arm around her in explanation. "Nothing says Merry in Mistletoe like this café."

I added another finished pine cone to the basket and evaluated the number of place markers remaining. Then I performed some mental gymnastics in an attempt to determine if there was enough time to finish the entire project this morning. I hoped the correct answer was yes, if I worked fast enough.

Caroline sipped her cooling cocoa and sighed with contentment. "Thanks for being so patient while I got enough shots. I'll add this morning's pictures to the collage I'm using as promotional material on the website and social media."

Mom waved her off and pulled a chocolate cake from the refrigerator. "I'm right here doing this every morning. Today I was just lucky enough to visit with you ladies while I worked. Tell me what you think of this," she said, sliding the cake onto the counter. "The icing is a ganache with peppermint chips."

Caroline widened her eyes, then swiped a fork from across the counter. "That sounds amazing."

Mom grabbed a knife and a plate, then glanced at me. "Holly?"

"No, thank you," I said, distracted by my craft.

"You're making great time on those," Mom said. "How's Evan doing with his list?"

"He's nearly finished."

I tried not to sound as jealous as I felt. I was too easily distracted. Evan, on the other hand, was single-minded where anything of importance was concerned.

He'd been involved with the wedding planning since the day he'd asked for my hand. Some grooms might not care about the details, but I hadn't gotten one of these. Evan considered things like registering for gifts, tasting cakes, and selecting caterers fun little adventures and new life experiences. Not to mention excellent opportunities for two busy people to have a few extra dates. He held my hand, listened to my opinions, and made me laugh when I wanted to scream. He kept me grounded when I couldn't decide between two nearly identical shades of white for tablecloths, and he insisted every DJ we interviewed play our song so we could dance. He'd also assigned himself a set of things to accomplish this week so I wouldn't have to. He knew I had my hands full with tasks only I could perform, like a final gown fitting, a bridal luncheon, and an inn full of VIP guests for the next few days.

"He's a good one," Mom said. "A partner."

I nodded. It was true.

Caroline grabbed a metal spiral from my stack and took the pine cone from my hands, assembling the product after I'd administered the dollop of glue.

"Thanks."

She smiled, set the cone aside, and opened her hand for the next. "How's it going at the inn?"

Caroline's dad had spent a large portion of the town's annual tourism budget on bringing the state conservatory of ballet to Mistletoe. The group would perform *The Nutcracker*, a holiday staple and emblem of Christmas since 1892, for several nights before returning to the capital for a final Christmas Eve performance. Mayor West and the local business owners thought the added ballet would secure this year's seasonal success.

The mayor had made special arrangements for the choreographer and several key dancers to stay at the inn. The dancers weren't my typical guests, but if it helped Mistletoe, and they cleared out on Christmas Eve morning, I was happy to help.

"It's been good so far," I said. "They arrived after dinner last night and went to their rooms pretty quickly." The bulk of my communication had been with their choreographer, George, and most of our exchanges were in the form of emails before their arrival. His messages mainly were lists of demands: specific foods and drinks to have on hand; the necessary number of blenders for post-workout protein shakes; and a transport vehicle large enough to accommodate the guests and their equipment to and from the theater.

Thankfully, he hadn't requested a driver, because that would've been me, and I was already buried under an avalanche of tasks.

"I saw them this morning," Mom said. "Not long before you both got here."

"You did?" Caroline and I asked in near unison.

I'd taken a long shower after waking and setting out the fruit and blenders. Then I'd headed to the Hearth before the dancers got up. Or so I'd thought.

"Sure did," Mom said. "They rolled in here just after six, looking so cute in their pink silk coats."

"They were here at six AM?" I asked, still processing.

The inn had been still when I'd tiptoed around setting up the blenders. I'd assumed they were all asleep.

"Yep." Mom covered the cake and slipped it back into the fridge. "They filed in here; collected their coffees, yogurts, granola, and fruit to go; then loaded up in the transport van and headed out. The coach said that will be the daily routine."

Inn guests received complimentary breakfast and dinner at the Hearth. I kept a hearty assortment of drinks and snacks on hand for the moments in between.

"Ballet master," Caroline said, leaning in Mom's direction. "The one who teaches the dancers the choreography is the *master*, not a coach."

Mom nodded. "That's interesting, and . . ."

"Pretentious?" I guessed.

Mom pressed her lips together, fighting a smile.

"It's what they're called," Caroline said on a dreamy sigh. "I love the ballet."

I tented my brows. "Yeah?"

"Oh, yeah. Since I was small," she said. "My parents took me to see *The Nutcracker* every Christmas, then to other shows as I got older. I always wanted to be a dancer."

"Really." I let the unexpected announcement settle, and I could see it. Not only did Caroline have the grace and work ethic for something as grueling as professional dance, but she also had an abundance of artistic flair.

Mom refreshed her hot chocolate. "He said they'll practice at the theater every day, before and after the show begins."

"Rehearse," Caroline said. "Sorry." She cringed.

"Rehearse," Mom corrected. "Apparently they'll be gone until after dinner every night. I asked about their preferences for tea and meal service, but they're going to eat elsewhere, so I don't have to worry about those, I guess." She deflated a bit. "I was looking forward to feeding ballerinas."

Caroline tucked a bite of cake into her mouth and let her eyelids flutter. "This is killer. Please tell me I can have the recipe."

Mom produced a note card from her apron pocket and passed it to Caroline with a grin. "I hoped you'd say that."

"Ah! Bless." Caroline took it reverently, then checked her watch. "Are you guys going to the parade this morning?"

Mom shook her head. "I can't. I have too much to do before I open. But I wish I could. I'd love to see the dancers perform."

Caroline sucked chocolate ganache off her thumb. "It's only the lead ballerina in the parade. We set her up in a snow globe with some promo. Dad gave me his ticket for opening night. And extras for my friends, if you're interested."

Mom waved her off. "I'll be here from opening to closing all week, aside from taping your show."

"Well, count me in," I said. I loved outings with Caroline, and seeing her so excited about this particular show only made me look forward to it more. "But don't envy the dancers too much," I said. "From what I saw last night, they're treated like children. One woman had to sneak out to ice skate. The choreographer shut her down, saying she could get hurt, and he couldn't allow that. And they had a time for 'lights out.'" I formed air quotes around the final two words.

Caroline didn't seem offended enough, so I continued.

"They had a bedtime," I clarified, hoping to make the words register. "Can you imagine that? Or being told you couldn't do something you loved, like skating? Another dancer snuck out for a walk at midnight just to get a few minutes alone. I saw her leaving, and she reacted as if she'd been caught committing murder."

Caroline finally frowned. "Do you think they're all friends? Spending so much time together must make them close. Maybe there's a deep camaraderie that overshadows all the rules. I follow the conservatory on social media, and I've always wondered about the interpersonal dynamics outside training and performing."

Mom gave a humorless chuckle. "If their usual schedule is anything like the one they're maintaining here, I can't imagine they get much time outside training and performing."

Caroline rested her chin in waiting hands, elbows planted on the countertop. "What do they talk about?"

I added dollops of hot glue to two more pine cones and passed one to Caroline, continuing our speedy little assembly line. We each pressed a wire spiral into place. "In the few minutes I saw them, they seemed fixated on the big Christmas Eve performance at the capitol after they leave here. Apparently there's a one-night-only, sold-out event at the State Theater on Christmas Eve, and some scouts will be there. All the dancers want to be chosen for something bigger. They talked about possibly heading out after the matinee performance the day before, but they aren't scheduled to leave until the next morning."

"There are ballet scouts?" Mom asked, checking the time. "Like the ones who recruit for sports?"

I shrugged and followed her lead with a peek at the clock.

The Hearth and tree farm would open soon, and the twelve days of reindeer games were in full swing, so tour buses were likely already en route. Tourists who weren't starting their days with my family were probably looking for a good spot to watch the parade along Main Street.

"Apparently an offer from a larger ballet company would come with lots of press and pressure, but they all want both," I said, summarizing what I'd heard the dancers say. "Honestly, their performances here seem a little like obstacles in the way of the big show."

"Costly obstacles," Caroline mused. "But at least people are excited about *The Nutcracker*. I'm interviewing the lead ballerina at the start of this week's show. Dad thought it would be another good way to keep the enthusiasm going. And great cross promotion. Hopefully, fans of the ballet will tune in for the interview, and viewers of my show will buy tickets for the ballet."

I tried to picture the dancers I'd checked in last night. "Which one is the lead?"

"Tiffany Krieg. She plays Clara."

I squinted my eyes, still unsure.

Caroline tried again. "She has all that great thick hair like Libby."

Mom looked up, and the three of us stilled.

Libby was Evan's little sister and a waitress at the Hearth. She lived in the on-site guesthouse where I'd stayed before moving to the inn. More importantly, she was our friend. Recently, she'd become withdrawn, but so far no one was talking about it.

Mom sighed. "Something's going on with her. I don't mean to pry, and I know it's none of my business. If she wanted me to know, she would've told me. But I'm officially concerned. Do either of you have any idea what's wrong?"

Caroline and I shook our heads.

"No," I said.

Libby had pulled away unexpectedly several weeks back, talking less and less at first, then only coming out in public for her shifts. Most recently, she'd begun to dramatically change her hair and makeup. It would've been evident from outer space that there was a problem, but so far, she hadn't opened up to anyone. Not us and not Evan. Not even her boyfriend, Ray.

I slid off my stool and set the final finished pine cone into a basket with the others, then moved the hot-glue gun to the business side of the counter, to cool. "I'll be back for these," I said. "Since the inn is empty, I'm going to meet Evan at the pie shop. Maybe we can watch the parade together."

I probably should've spent the day addressing the stack of Christmas cards on my desk or wrapping toy donations for the holiday gift drive, but I really enjoyed a parade, and any excuse to see Evan was a good one.

"That sounds lovely," Mom said. "Do you need any help wrapping gifts later?"

"Not yet," I said, knowing she had enough of her own chores to worry about. I'd do my best, then ask for help if I truly needed it.

"Well, let me know if you run low on paper." Mom tipped her head to a row of gift wrap tubes leaned against the wall near the café's tree. "Christopher dropped more off this morning. I must've missed him, because one minute the paper wasn't there, and the next minute it was. He left a card to say he has more if you need it."

Christopher was a family friend who'd begun as a contractor building the inn. He was heading up the annual toy drive for the second year in a row and apparently providing the wrapping paper.

Caroline made a deep humming sound. She turned her palms up when I looked at her.

I fought a smile. "Christopher isn't Santa Claus."

"He looks a lot like him," she said. "White hair and a beard, rosy-red cheeks, and twinkling eyes."

I shook my head.

"Holly, he heads the annual toy drive, knows everyone by name, and comes and goes without being seen. I'm just saying. It all checks out."

Christopher certainly had some Santa-esque qualities, but that didn't make him St. Nick.

I redirected my thoughts downtown and put on my coat.

Caroline followed suit, stretching black leather gloves over her elegant hands, and threading thin arms into a designer wool swing coat. "I'd better go too. It's time to open my shop if I want to get all the extra pre-parade sales. Cookie took the morning off to watch from the sidewalk. I'll take the pine cones and get them sprayed with faux snow and glitter."

We said our goodbyes to Mom, then split up in the parking lot.

Caroline got into her smart black sedan, and I headed for my truck, a big red pickup with a red nose tied to the grill, all-weather antlers protruding from the windows, and a "Reindeer Games" logo painted along both sides.

I did a double take as I noticed Libby's SUV rolling down the drive, away from the farm, the transport vehicle used by the ballerinas following closely on its bumper.